EMBEDDED

A DAKOTA JUDD NOVEL

JOHN LANSING

WHITE STREET PRESS

First White Street Press trade paperback edition, June 2025

ISBN (Print): 979-8-9885166-5-1

ISBN (Digital): 979-8-9885166-4-4

Cover design by Karen Phillips

ALSO BY JOHN LANSING

The Jack Bertolino Series:

The Devil's Necktie

Blond Cargo

Dead is Dead

The Fourth Gunman

25 to Life

Mia - the prequel

———

Good Cop Bad Money (with Glenn Morisano)

The Test

To my heart, my soul,
my Vida

CHAPTER 1

Dakota Judd wasn't a man who questioned decisions once made. He'd had more than enough time to dissect every moment of the incursion. He could've turned a blind eye; after all, it was war. But reliving the raid, in fractured dreams that continued to insinuate themselves into his waking moments, was a burden he'd carry for life.

His action sure as shit created an unexpected detour. But with disciplined daily pushups, chin-ups, and laps, his body was still intimidating. He lived by the Ranger credo, "Further, Faster, Harder." That much he could control. Life behind bars, he took one day at a time. Rangers were trained to expect the unexpected, but nothing could prepare him for what was in store from the woman who sat across the metal table from Dakota.

Jean Steele was an African American FBI Agent with high cheekbones, chestnut skin, shoulder-length brown hair, who wore a professional navy pantsuit. She was an attractive woman, something not lost on Dakota.

They were in the Greeley Federal Penitentiary's visiting room designated for cops and lawyers. No cameras or recorders allowed.

Steele removed her sunglasses before starting the interview, revealing sharp, intelligent, brown eyes that locked on Dakota's.

"So, Mister Judd...you've served six years of a seven-year sentence," she said, glancing up from her notes.

Dakota picked up the light scent of J'adore. The perfume his ex-fiance wore.

"And three months before your early discharge, having been granted early release for exemplary compliance with institutional regulations, you blow it all by stabbing a Black inmate in the thigh, severing his deep femoral vein, leaving him to bleed out in the weight-room, almost killing him. Dakota...you don't look like a foolish man."

"Is that a question, or an answer?" Dakota's eyes creased into an easy smile. He hadn't had a conversation with a good-looking woman for a very long time, and was intrigued by her visit and up to the challenge.

"In this case, it was kill or be killed," he said matter-of-factly. "The man was out of his league, and I had no choice."

"They didn't find a weapon on the victim."

"I left it in his leg. I'm sure it's all in your report."

"The Federal paperwork is in process to rescind your early release."

Dakota was aware they weren't only going to rescind, they were going to add two years to his original sentence, bringing the life-killing number to nine.

"Why are you here, Agent Steele?" Dakota asked, cutting to the chase. "What did I do to deserve a visit from the Feds?"

Steele held his gaze. "The government needs your help."

"Why the interest?"

"You've had no gang affiliations since your arrest and conviction. That couldn't have been an easy ride."

Dakota leaned back in the metal chair and let her talk.

"The OC Wolf Pack are an anti-government white supremacist militia operating out of Orange County. We've been picking up chatter on the dark web and social media. The Wolf Pack may have a link to California Senator Jack Bradley, who's up for re-election.

"Bradley's constituency leans heavily to the extreme right. He hides their bias like a momma bear protects her cubs. The Wolf Pack are crude. And even though they share similar philosophies with the senator they are to be seen and not heard. That's where Blackfox Elite Protection fits in. We think Blackfox is providing the money used to fund Bradley's re-election and a growing list of homegrown militias."

"What's their MO?"

"Blackfox recruits ex-military, retired cops, FBI, and guns for hire. It's an elite private security force that has no compunction employing known felons. They're supported by a group of wealthy right-wing patriots...their description. Blackfox is getting fat on government contracts, assisted in part by the CEO's tight relationship with the senator who's the Chairman of the House Armed Services Committee, to the tune of forty-five million in the last quarter."

Agent Steele had definitely piqued his interest. "Aren't you gonna ask where I stand?"

"If I thought you stood with them, I wouldn't be sitting here. Neither would you."

Dakota didn't argue the point. "Where do I fit in?"

"We need someone outside local law enforcement."

"And outside of the FBI," Dakota intuited.

Steele nodded. "A few of our retired agents still have friends in high places. We're aware of leaks. We need to shore them up. You've got the bona fides. Your skill set, your attack on a commanding officer while serving in Afghanistan. Your exemplary record before the assault charges, your silver medal. That, and now, stabbing a Black inmate three months before your release, should make you a rock star with the skinheads in quadrant-D.

"We need someone to cozy up to the supremacists who have ties to the Wolf Pack in Orange County and a probable link to Blackfox, our main target. Best-case scenario, you infiltrate Blackfox upon your release, and deliver their plans."

"Why?"

"The Alt-right's first armed insurrection on the U.S. Capital failed, but shook the world. We want to shut these militia groups down before there's a second attempt that succeeds."

"Why would I sign on?"

"That's up to you. The Army is about to rescind your pardon and add time to your release date for attempted manslaughter. When you get out…you'll be handed over to the United States Probation Office, where they'll dog you with years of probation and a host of rules that if not followed, will stack on more prison time. You'll be living in purgatory."

"I don't respond to threats," he said without attitude.

"We're offering you a lifeline."

"I'm sure you'll understand, Agent Steele. I've got trust issues with the government."

"I understand, and Blackfox will understand. I'll be your handler. You won't have to deal with the suits."

"You're wearing a suit."

"I'll have your back. Infiltrate Blackfox. Become our eyes and ears, and you walk away a free man. Your conviction, expunged. Pension reinstated. You can work, vote, get married, have kids. A normal life."

Steele pulled a contract out of her attaché case and slid it across the table.

"How do I explain you?"

"I work at your law firm." Steele hands him a contact card. It read, Jean Clarkson. Associate at Peluso, Costa, and Litto, Attorneys at Law. "It passes the sniff test."

Not the way Dakota thought his day was going to unfold.

"Take some time," she continued. "Read the fine print. I already had a conversation with your representative, Joseph Peluso, and sent him a copy of the contract. It guarantees your future for services rendered."

"What did he say?"

"He was inclined to accept, but wouldn't give me a definitive answer until we spoke. Said it was your call."

"Sounds like Peluso." Dakota Judd lifted the paperwork, maintaining eye contact, trying to get a read on this federal agent before diving into the contract that might just be the answer to his prayers. He held the life-changing document in his hands, but his mind drifted on the scent of J'adore.

The contract was fifteen pages of legalese that protected the government from any liability in the execution of said agreement.

Shorthand for: If Dakota signed the contract, he was agreeing to risk his life in service to the government. If successful in the mission, he'd have his life back. He'd be a free man with no one looking over his shoulder. If he failed, well, he'd be back in the slammer, or he'd be dead. Dakota straightened the pages, looked deep into Steele's eyes, and nodded his assent.

Steele handed him a pen.

Dakota signed on the dotted line.

"Good," Agent Steele said. She slid the contract into her attaché case and pushed away from the table. "I'll be in touch." Steele started toward the door and then turned on her heel.

"And Dakota…try and stay alive for the next eight weeks."

CHAPTER 2

The sound in the prison cafeteria was mind-numbing. Banging trays, trash-talking, forks spearing meat, and feet tapping a mile a minute from a bad dose of crank. Hyped up men turned the long wooden tables into percussive instruments. Three long lines of men snaked toward the trusties who doled out a lunch of high-carb, low-interest food. Dakota balanced the dented metal tray as he made his way to the rear of the room, where he could sit with his back to the wall. He knew the recent attempt on his life wouldn't be the last.

Dakota passed a table filled with white supremacists, who flashed the "okay" sign, designating their affiliation and allegiance to hate. Dakota returned the hand signal, and saw a few head-bobs at the table in appreciation of his not taking any shit from a Black man.

Dakota cleaned the bone on his sinewy chicken leg like he was taught by his father, and felt a charge in the air before he caught the glare of three Black inmates who bypassed their regular table, gaining speed, striding in his direction.

Dakota was ready for them. He pulled out a shiv he fashioned from a cafeteria fork and held it under the table.

The men were about to pass the Aryan table, when a bald inmate with a red swastika tattooed on his neck stuck out a leg the size of a tree trunk, tripping the lead man. Food, tray, and inmate went flying.

Moving as one military unit, the Aryan table cleared. Trays, fists, feet smashed the three men to the ground, preventing their attack before it began.

Bleeding and swollen, one of the men threatened death to the perpetrators, hefted up his downed comrades, who limped back to their table, wondering what the hell had just occurred, but not wanting to linger and get thrown into lockup.

Dakota flashed the "okay" sign for a second time in his life to the Aryan Brotherhood, knowing their favor would have to be repaid. Either with affiliation, or retribution to a prisoner of their choice.

The only retribution Dakota was interested in was with the man calling the shots. The man who wanted him dead.

It had been one hell of a day, and Dakota fell onto his bunk and passed out, oblivious to the constant din of prison noise. A nightmare from the past infiltrated his dream state.

Dakota sprinted through a splintered doorway and took out a sniper on a nearby rooftop with a short pulse from his M4, clearing the way for his men to exit the building, return incoming fire, and make their way toward the gates at the edge of town.

Dakota laid suppressing fire as two Rangers leapfrogged past him. He hugged the wall, moving slowly, and heard panicked screams emanating from a squalid mud-brick house. And then primal wails.

Leading with his gun, Dakota kicked in the door. He heard Captain Mullrooney's shouted slurs and knew there'd be hell to pay as he entered the structure. The main room was barely lit with a single amber bulb hanging from a wooden beam. What looked like blood spatter dripped down the wooden-planked far wall. A woman lay on the ground, her head tilted at an unnatural angle. Her face a death mask. Her neck and dressing gown, a mass of red.

As Dakota stepped into the room, the captain shouted. "Haji motherfuck-er!" It wasn't clear who Mullrooney was interrogating until he moved to the side, slashing with his combat knife, drawing blood, and revealing the victim's face.

The captain had an unarmed teenager, dressed in nightclothes, by the throat. Blood leaked from multiple wounds as the captain screamed, red faced, "You little goat fucker!" and sliced the kid's arm again. "Ibrahim al-Assiri? Where is he?"

The boy was going into shock. The cuts, the loss of blood, and bearing witness to his mother's slaughter.

"Let's go, Captain. He doesn't know shit," Dakota said, trying to diffuse the captain's rampage.

"Stand down, soldier," Mullrooney ordered.

The kid keened.

"Let the boy go!" Dakota shouted, having witnessed similar violent acts in the past.

Captain Mullrooney's face twisted into a tight grin. The damn man was enjoying himself.

"You want me to let him go?" the captain taunted over the sound of automatic gunfire bleeding in from the battle being waged in the street. He slammed the boy against the mattress. "You dumb fuckin' Haj," he hissed. "Open your fucking eyes or I'll cut your dick off."

Another explosion rocked the structure. Dust rained down from the ancient rafters.

The boy's eyes snapped open, looking past Mullrooney. He locked eyes with Dakota, who took a menacing step forward.

The captain cocked his head as if giving thought to Dakota's request, and plunged the blade into the boy's chest, killing him instantly. The teenager's hot blood streamed onto the dirt floor.

"He was trying to escape," Mullrooney said for the record, as he wiped the bloody serrated edge on his pant leg, and spun to leave.

Dakota smashed the butt of his M4 into the captain's forearm, breaking bone. The knife fell out of the stunned officer's hand. He cracked his superior's upper arm before the knife hit the ground and then nailed the captain's elbow, shattering bone. The captain howled in pain. "You're a dead man," he said, grabbing his useless right arm.

Dakota startled awake in the middle of the night with a blazing headache. He sat up until his breathing returned to normal and fell back onto his bunk, keeping one eye open, just in case.

————

Dakota was seated on the first row of the splintered wooden bleachers known to be White-Aryan-Brotherhood turf. A move not lost on any of the hundred fifty men who milled around the open field in the center of the prison's yard.

Turly, the Aryan who interceded on behalf of Dakota in the cafeteria, wiped the sweat off his bald pate like he had a full head of hair. The man was fireplug stout, crazy blue eyes, arms like hams covered in ink extolling the virtues of an Aryan Brotherhood, and an all-white America.

"Why didn't you kill the prick?" Turly asked as if that should've been the natural course of action.

"Ya see, some people really need killing," Dakota said. "I never had issues following orders. Killing a man in the heat of battle. But I let Captain Mullrooney off with his life…he got off easy, you see. But I took away his skill set…his ability to kill another kid for the fun of it. Cause he could. He had the power. I may be sitting here, but Captain Mullrooney's career is stalled, and he thinks of me every time he wipes his ass."

"Good work with the spook. He's a contract killer." He pointed to a neat piece of cartilage missing from his upper ear. "That motherfucker pulled a Tyson on me before my men could beat him down."

Dakota was next up on the chin bar, slid off the bench and stretched. He turned to Turly and lowered his voice. "Don't bet against me," and he winked.

Turly said, "60?"

Dakota's face creased into a hard grin.

"70?"

Dakota flipped his thumb toward the blue sky.

"Don't fuck me up here," Turly warned, and meant it.

Dakota nodded, jumped up, and grabbed hold. He started humping out pull-ups. His arms, brick hard. The inked hilt of a sword was exposed on the skin of his upper arm. As he reached chin-high on the bar, his t-shirt stretched tight, exposing the rest of his Ranger tattoo that decorated his entire flexed shoulder. The sword impaled an ornate, black devil's skull wearing a jaunty, maroon beret. The skull seemed to come alive and grin, taunting with the smooth rhythm of Dakota's physical exertion.

Nothing special…not yet…until he hit number forty. The White, Black, Hispanic, and Asian gangs started moving their lips, heads bobbing, keeping count of the pull-ups at forty-five. At fifty…money started changing hands. At sixty, some men lost their cigarette money and voices started to rise. At seventy, more bets were laid down, dollar bills changed hands, crowds pushed closer, surrounding the high-bar. Eighty…money was flowing like water and the energy increased. This was better than Vegas. The guards in the tower leaned forward to watch the action. At number eighty-five, heads started shaking in disbelief. The losers spit on the trampled grass. Dakota saw Turly collect a wad of cash, and jumped down when he hit ninety reps. The echo of the losers' "motherfucker" filled the air.

Turly tightened his bankroll and stashed it in his front pocket. "You didn't need our help," he said as Dakota sat back down on the scarred wooden bleacher.

"No, but if you're ever in trouble, I have your back. Your move was greatly appreciated. I've got forty-nine days until I see the back side of that chain link fence. Someone's paying to guarantee I don't make it."

"How'd you get past the gorilla?"

"His DNA was all over the tape on the shiv. My lawyer finally got off his ass, and made an appearance. There was nothing they could do. And hell, I deserved some good fuckin' luck for time in."

"No shit." Turly's eyes narrowed, and he looked like he was rolling something around in his lizard brain. "I'm still staring down five."

"One foot in front of the other."

"No shit… What's your lawyer's name? I might reach out."

"Joseph Peluso. At Peluso, Costa, and Litto." Dakota knew the big man would Google the name on his burner phone as soon as he hit his cell. "Fucker sent a coon with attitude to deliver the paperwork. We'll have words when I get out," he said in case Turly had one of the guards who escorted Agent Steele to their meeting in his hip pocket.

"Lawyers."

"Eh…Peluso did the heavy lifting."

That seemed reasonable. "What are you lookin at on the outside?"

"An empty house. I lost everything else when I fucked up Captain Mullrooney. Feds stole my life, my savings, and my future. I ain't a fucking fan of the government or the Jews on the jury who convicted me."

"Fuckin' Hebes. Well…we may have some things. Who knows?"

CHAPTER 3

A few weeks passed without incident. Dakota had a full tray of food, and as he passed the Aryan table, he could see a space next to Turly had been purposefully left empty. A good sign. A few of the men glanced up without attitude, so he set himself down and dug in.

"Where are your people from?" Turly asked, not aggressive, more probing.

"Texas," Dakota said. "Moved to California and settled south of LA in Redondo Beach back in the '90s. There was more work."

"There still is," Turly said, leaving it at that.

The sound in the room grew in volume as the end of lunch neared. He polished off his cold black coffee and noticed Turly slide a piece of paper under his tray as he grabbed up his own and headed down the aisle.

Dakota leaned forward, grabbed the note with his tray, and slid the torn piece of paper into his side pocket.

———

Five a.m. and the prison was already up and running. The laundry was situated next door to the kitchen where Diego Beltran worked. His next executioner, Turly's note had read. His penmanship was almost illegible, but the price on Dakota's head read loud and clear. Fifteen grand. The going rate was five. Beltran was tied to the Mexican Mafia. A stone-cold killer. Three tears were tattooed under his eye, but the number was light.

Calendar pages were flipping toward Dakota's release date, so he knew it was only a matter of time. He was folding hot sheets fresh out of the large wall of dryers, stacking them on a long metal table. The hot, circular dryer windows reflected the door to the laundry room. Dakota had a strong feeling if today was the day, the attack had to occur in the next ten minutes before the room filled and a "hit" became too complicated.

The sound of spinning dryers muffled the door opening. In one swift motion Beltran darted across the concrete floor, leading with his shiv.

Dakota waited until the last second, and as Beltran thrust the knife toward his back, he spun and the knife impaled a hot sheet. Dakota's leg pistoned out and slammed into Beltran's kneecap, causing ligaments to snap and Beltran to lurch forward. Dakota stopped him in place squeezing his knife hand and muscling it back, until the weapon clattered to the floor. The man's knee gave out and he dropped hard. Dakota went to work.

"Who sent you?"

"Blow me."

"Wrong answer." Dakota hovered over the man, one knee on his chest. "Who ordered the hit?"

"Fuck you, Pendejo," he said, beads of sweat breaking out on his face that contorted in pain. Dakota grabbed the blade and held it against the man's throat.

"One more time. You can walk out of here alive. Your call."

Beltran wasn't ready to die that morning. "It came from outside," he said, panting from the pain. "No names. Just the payoff."

Dakota lifted the man off the floor. "If I see you again, or anybody in your clique, you're dead meat. If we pass in the cafeteria or the common, turn and walk in the other direction. Now get the fuck out of here."

Diego Beltran turned and tried for some semblance of machismo as he dragged his bad leg and banged out the door.

Dakota was a blur of motion. He wiped his prints off the jailhouse shank and slid the evidence behind the bank of dryers. He shoved the torn sheet into one of the washing machines in mid-cycle as two inmates pushed through the door, walked to their stations, no one the wiser.

———

Dakota was cleaning out his cell, packing a few novels in a brown paper sack. He heard footsteps echoing on the concrete walkway and knew who owned the swagger before he saw his face.

"What are you doing in my neck of the woods?" Dakota asked before looking up into Turly's narrowed eyes.

"Favors owed."

Dakota stood and walked closer to his cell bars, lowering his voice. "I owe you big-time, Turly."

Turly passed a folded piece of paper through the bars. "Roadhouse in your area. Don't look like much, but good people. I opened the door. If all goes well, there might be some work for you. Your call. You owe me nothing."

"But my life."

"Don't forget your friends," Turly said, and continued down the cellblock.

———

The sun broke above the ridge of trees. Dakota stood outside the prison, head tilted back, raised toward the heavens as he witnessed his first sunrise as a free man. Lost in the moment, he didn't hear the sound of metal doors clanging shut behind him. The sky morphed from salmon-pink to blue as the sun started its march across the sky. He took in a deep breath of chilled air, checked his Timex, and glanced past the dark shadows of trees so tall they blocked the sun from the empty road that fronted the penitentiary.

He wasn't entirely free. He had a mission that if accomplished, and if he came out alive, a lot of ifs, then, and only then, would he genuinely be free. But right now, in this moment, he felt lighter. A sense of peace and optimism washed over him. He was up for the challenge and would find a way to excel and succeed. Not sure how, but again, a Ranger was trained to expect the unexpected.

The light breeze running through the woods carried a scent laced with pine needles and heather. He hadn't realized how beautiful it smelled when he was in the workout field. He'd learned how to shut down parts of his brain to exist. But he did leave lockup with his primal instincts fine-tuned.

Billie Judd's blue 2000 Corvette convertible pulled to a stop. Aunt Billie jumped out and gave her nephew a bear hug. "Here, lemme take your luggage," she said, dry, getting a laugh out of Dakota, and tossing the paper bag into the car's modest trunk. The bag held a few paperbacks, articles of clothing he'd worn upon arrival, a dried-out wallet, keys that probably didn't fit the lock on his front door anymore, and some pocket change. He'd arrived with seventy dollars. The cash disappeared before the steel door had slammed shut. He left with fifty greenbacks he'd worked for folding sheets and the pocket change.

The Corvette was low-slung, and Dakota loved the smell of the black leather seats, aged with spider cracks from the sun. His aunt had been his favorite member of the extended family, taking Dakota on fishing outings as a kid.

Billie burnt a long, shrieking, strip of rubber as the classic car fishtailed, leaving behind an obstinate cloud of white smoke.

"Engine sounds strong," Dakota said, grinning, enjoying the moment.

"Just replaced the gaskets, the rubber, and had Trixie tuned up. Still a good ride."

Dakota nodded in agreement. "Thanks for the lift."

"Wouldn't have missed it for the life of me. Congratulations."

Dakota's dark hair buffeted in the wind. He closed his brown eyes and let the sound of the 350V8 lull him into his new reality. Conversation would come later. It always did with Billie.

"You hungry?" she asked.

"I could eat."

"I passed a diner on the way up. Let's get some chow and then hit the road."

"Sounds like a damn perfect plan."

CHAPTER 4

REDONDO BEACH, CALIFORNIA

The Judd family house was a modest bungalow in the hills of Redondo Beach. It had been a derelict teardown that his father brought back to its original glory in the early nineties. After Billie handed off the new set of keys, they made plans to get together when Dakota came up for air.

"It's all about you for the next few days," Billie said, heartfelt. "Whatever you need, alone time, talk time, whatever." And the wise woman let it go at that, jumped into her car. "Oh, your father's gun is in the nightstand beside the bed. Probably better if it stays there, but you can never be too safe." She started the engine, but sat idling. She looked over at her nephew and asked, "Does Sarah know you're back in town?"

"Don't know how that could've happened, unless you let it slip."

Billie feigned hurt. "You know me better than that."

Dakota grinned. "I haven't talked to Sarah since they dragged me out of the courthouse. It was the right thing to do at the time. And now…mixed emotions." And then he added, "No good could come of it. My guess, she's married, with kids. I'd just muddy the waters. And oh, by the way, I've got a target on my back."

"There is that," Billie agreed.

"I'd have to lie about my contract with the FBI. If things went south, I'd be putting her life in jeopardy. It's all a non-starter."

"You know best, Dakota. Had to ask the question. And you're right. You're radioactive."

That assessment put a smile on Dakota's face. "I love you, Aunt."

"Back at you," Billie said, grinning as she threw the Vette in gear, waved over her shoulder, and drove down the hill.

Billie Judd was Dakota's aunt, friend, and mentor. An Army MP who served in the Iraq War. A retired detective who never lost her respect for the force. OCPD blue still ran through her veins, but she understood there were gray areas in life. Billie was there supporting Dakota when his father, Billie's brother, turned his stubborn back on his own son in his time of need.

Growing up, she was the one person Dakota felt comfortable sharing feelings with when life got confusing. Aunt Billie could spin ideas like a Rubik's Cube master and helped Dakota discover new solutions to youthful problems, and another important skill set, how to tie off a hook and rig a fishing pole.

Billie's the gift that keeps on giving.

A large wicker basket, wrapped in cellophane, sat next to the faded, red metal rocker on the porch next to the front door. It held a bottle of Macallan 18, two boxes of DeCecco spaghetti, a hunk of Pecorino Romano cheese, Genoa salami, a bottle of Rao's marinara sauce, and Italian crackers. A gift from his lawyer, Joseph Peluso. The card read, "Welcome home, my friend. I'm here if you need me. Call when you settle."

Dakota keyed the door, placed the basket on the glass coffee table, tossed his paper bag on the family couch, and stared at the indentation on the sofa cushion where his father sat every night when he returned from the precinct. Dakota took his father's seat next to the knotty-pine side table that held his father's television remote, and his beer-bottle stains.

It felt wrong.

Dakota got up and did a slow, thoughtful walk through the house. The furniture was the same. Billie told him his dad wasn't much for change after his mother passed. Her death still took Dakota's breath away.

I think he wanted to reach out, Billie had shared. But time got the best of him and God had other plans.

The place was frozen in time. Photos of his father and mother adorned the wooden mantel over the green tile fireplace. Weddings, vacations, and road trips. Big smiles, better times. The only face conspicuously missing was Dakota's.

Billie warned him his room, well, he wouldn't recognize it. It was an understatement. All of his things were gone, along with any reminder that he had ever lived in the house, or that he'd ever existed. His bed, clothes, posters, toothbrushes, papers, letters from old girl-friends. Diplomas. All gone. The walls were painted green. His father knew it wasn't his color of choice when given the option to choose, back in the day. Dakota couldn't say it didn't sting.

His aunt had gone above and beyond getting the place ready. Surfaces dusted. Sheets changed in his parents' room. A new flat screen in the living room. A phone, laptop, cable, internet, the whole nine yards. She figured Dakota had some catching up to do. As always, Billie was right.

The house had been paid off years ago. Over breakfast, they worked out a schedule to pay the back taxes Billie had sprung for after his father passed. Dakota insisted. Billie relented.

After the first walkthrough, when emotions he wasn't ready to deal with surfaced, he poured himself a stiff glass of scotch – silently thanking Peluso for the gift – grabbed a seat on his front porch, and let out a deep, ragged sigh.

It was answered by a purr.

A neighbor's tabby cagily approached the red, metal rocker, and when he realized all was safe, bumped his head against Dakota's ankle until the scruff of the overfed cat got rubbed.

Only home an hour and already made a friend. More than he

expected. He took a sip of the aged single malt. A taste he hadn't experienced in years. He tamped down the emotion that was threatening to overwhelm, and savored the moment.

It was radical. Surreal. Sitting on the porch of his home, and not in a jail cell. The quiet was deafening. He wasn't sure he'd be able to sleep. And then a mockingbird's song echoed in the night. "Not bad, huh?" he said to the cat who answered by banging his head against Dakota's ankle again. It made him smile as he complied.

His town had changed in his time away. This was a middle-class neighborhood in his youth. Filled with kids, backyard barbeques, and barking dogs. Now it was littered with overblown McMansions.

Still, he loved the place. The postage-sized front lawn sported a modest view of the Pacific. Seagulls soared along with every other Southern California bird in the books, and on cloudy days and nights, when the marine layer hung low, he could smell thick salty air.

Dakota decided to take a few days to acclimate to normal society, and then phone his lawyer and set up a meeting with his new boss. Agent Jean Steele.

He walked through the house, poured another glass of scotch, and headed through the kitchen to the backyard. The shrubs were overgrown and the hedges reached seven feet tall. They needed trimming but provided privacy from his neighbors.

He keyed the side door to the detached garage, snapped on the light, and felt something dislodge in his chest as he came face-to-face with his parents' cars. He pulled the dusty car cover back, and there it was. His mother's silver, 2003 BMW 330 convertible. Her pride and joy. It was the first new car she'd ever owned and she loved to drive it fast. Dakota offered to buy her a new car when he started making money. It kind of pissed off his father. But Shirley loved her car, and she loved her son, and appreciated his thoughtful gesture.

The Beemer was cherry, and Dakota was caught by surprise when a few wet drops fell onto the hood as he reminisced. Damn, if it wasn't his tears. He hadn't cried since the day she died.

He was in his second deployment. At least his mother was spared the embarrassment of the trial. Having to witness her son being dragged through the mud. Or her husband disowning his own flesh and blood.

Dakota didn't shed a tear when his father turned his back on him.

Captain Mullrooney had been a fine actor on the witness stand and made a compelling victim. Dakota never denied the assault. For his honesty he was pilloried by the Army. It would have broken his mother's heart.

His father never recovered from her death. The bottle was his attempt at self-medication. He was an angry man, and his career as a detective at the Orange Police Department stalled. He took an early retirement and was dead two years later.

The last time Dakota had seen his father's face was on sentencing day. Retired Detective Ted Judd, cold and tight as a winter's night, withheld eye contact, turned his back on his son, and strode out of the courtroom.

His father's ride was an army green 2011 Ford Bronco. It had four-wheel drive, eight cylinders under the hood, and sixty-five-thousand-miles on the speedometer. He liked a simple life, and his car reflected his personality. Just the facts ma'am. The red mud splatter that was crusted on the side panels probably came from his bi-annual hunting trips to the high Sierras.

His father's workbench told his personal story. Every tool, oiled, sharpened, hanging in a designated place. There was some rust now, but order still. There was hell to pay if you borrowed a tool and misplaced it. Dad's way or the highway, always. Whenever he heard his father working in the garage, yelling "Shirley" across the yard, he knew his mother had probably taken one of his tools and had no idea where she left it. Mother and son were thick as thieves and shared conspiratorial smiles.

Dakota knew the man was jealous of the easy relationship he had with his mother and had to admit, he enjoyed his discomfort. Maybe it was an Oedipal deal and he was a shitty son. Who the hell knew?

Dakota wiped his eyes with his sleeve and grinned, knowing his father's car would be a perfect fit when he showed up at the RockPile, the bar he'd visit in the next few days. It was the white supremacist hangout that Turly opened the door to, and the first stop on his mission statement as a free man.

Dakota knocked back the scotch, switched off the light, and walked toward the house with a heavy heart. He knew he had to tamp down the emotion or he'd never make it out of his new assignment alive.

CHAPTER 5

Dakota stared into FBI Agent Jean Steele's intense, brown eyes and leaned back from the burnished wooden table that filled much of the comfortably appointed suite located at the rear of Peluso, Costa, and Litto, Attorneys at Law, offices. It had a private entrance from the parking structure in the five-story building in downtown Laguna Beach.

Parking on the fifth floor was restricted and could only be accessed with a personal key card. Joseph Peluso understood the need for discretion, or the entire enterprise could self-destruct. He wasn't going to let that happen on his watch.

Steele was dressed in civilian clothes and got straight down to business.

"Just so we're clear," she began. "We," she said, wagging her forefinger between them. "Me and you, are attached at the hip until this case is concluded."

First thing that crossed his mind was the picture of being attached at the hip with the FBI agent, but he let her continue.

She brought him up to speed on the players who hung out at the RockPile. Steele showed him bios, long-distance photos, headshots of the militia regulars, and a few men who worked at Blackfox.

"How much do you know about your friend Turly?"

"Not much, he was more interested in my story. I didn't push. He's a smart man. Can't tell from the photo, didn't look like it from a distance, but you could read it in his eyes."

"He was a radical, hard-right sociology professor who attracted a small group of true believers. He expounded the philosophy of Jim Mason. A neo-Nazi who wanted to overthrow the government, burn it to the ground, and rebuild a perfect social order on the ashes. That perfection was pure white. Turly was the group's spiritual leader."

"That's a church I'd steer clear of."

"That's a church we hired you to join, and become a true believer. Learn how to hate. Hate to the bone. There can be no question of your allegiance, or you'll come out of this in a pine box. And I'm responsible for keeping that from happening."

"You look concerned," Dakota said.

Steele rubbed the crease between her eyes, knew it was a tell, and chose to ignore his attempt to reach out. There was a clear chain of command at play here, and Steele was going to remain in control. This case was her creation, and her career would rise or fall with the success of the mission.

"I don't have to tell you," Steele started, thought better of it, and switched gears. "I'll share all intel that crosses my desk involving you. But, the attempts on your life are an ongoing concern."

"You being my caretaker does increase the chances of my meeting the grim reaper."

"How so?"

"You're Black."

"Wow...you're good. Should've been a cop," she said dry as a bone.

"Hah!" he barked, enjoying the moment. "I knew the risk when I signed the papers. Let's keep rolling."

Steele slid a phone across the table and an envelope. The bulge screamed cash. "The phone's a burner. We'll exchange numbers. Only to be used to call me, and..."

"Vice versa," he answered.

"Right. There's two grand in twenties and tens. I'm sure you have to buy some clothes and personal items."

Dakota wondered if Steele and the FBI had checked out his house, to see if there were any surprises before proffering the offer. How else would she know he'd returned to a barren house? Billie would never have shared his personal information with anybody. He made a mental note to change his locks again and install security cameras around his house.

"We've got another three ready to deposit into your checking account. Set it up, get the info to Peluso, and we'll wire the money. Don't get flashy. Your friends in prison vetted you before you were released. They know as much about you as we do. Well, not as much as the FBI but you get the point."

"I do."

A hint of a smile appeared, and Jean Steele stood and picked up the photos and her files. "Take it slow, but not too slow. We'll talk."

"I'll need a few days to get settled, and then I'll make an appearance at the bar. You'll be the first call I make," Dakota said.

Steele liked the answer. She turned and walked out of the office and down the hallway toward the back elevator, knowing Dakota was sizing her up.

The woman definitely worked out, Dakota thought. Not zero body fat, but damn close. Interesting, he thought and texted Joseph Peluso, "all done."

Five seconds later, Joseph appeared in the doorway, two long neck Dos Equis in hand. He passed one to his friend. They clinked bottles and took deep drinks of the beer. "Waited a long time for this, my friend. How're you holding up?"

"Pretty fucking good." And then he added, "In all honesty, Joe, not bad at all." Dakota knew his friend was concerned, but wasn't about to share anymore of his emotional morass for a while. He'd keep it loose. "And thanks for the housewarming. Scotch went down real smooth."

Joseph blamed himself for losing the case and took the defeat personally.

Dakota let his friend off the hook as best he could. Right now, it was all about getting some semblance of normalcy back into his new life. Then he'd crash the RockPile and get the show on the road. Just the thought made his blood pressure tick up a beat.

CHAPTER 6

Dakota pulled the Ford Bronco onto the gravel lot that butted up against the RockPile. The large neon signage blinked harsh yellow in case you forgot where you were headed. The cinderblock structure reminded him of the houses he saw in Afghanistan. Simple, and sturdy. Two windows on either side of the black enameled door were filled with buzzing, colorful, neon beer signs that dated back to the early sixties.

He pulled to a stop next to three Harleys, and his ride looked right at home. These were hard-core bikes with well-worn seats and rubber that spoke of high mileage. No weekend warriors in the group. A few high-end SUVs with dark-tinted windows and 19-inch wheels, and an assortment of trucks. Classic Rock 'n' Roll bled into the parking lot through the concrete block walls as Dakota turned off the car and dismounted.

He was wearing a new pair of jeans that looked worn, a black t-shirt, and a light blue chambray work shirt. Nothing flashy. He'd taken Steele's advice. He walked through the thick-scarred door and grabbed a stool at the bar without making eye contact with the well-oiled patrons. Conspicuously missing were any women except for the bartender. She was blonde and as weathered as the front door. She tossed a coaster onto the bar, gave Dakota the once over, not unhappy at what she saw as he slid onto the stool, said, "Hey," and ordered a shot of Bulleit Bourbon, water back.

The joint was filled with two classes of degenerates. The men who drove the SUVs and were employed at Blackfox, and the locals who arrived on the Harleys he saw in the lot. It was relaxed enough, but he'd felt all eyes follow him to his seat at the bar.

The music was cranked up loud. Pool balls clacked. The voices of men in different stages of high filled the stale air. The smell of spent beer, pickled eggs and sausages in large gallon glass jars sat on the bar, sawdust covered the floor. It all screamed roadhouse, an anomaly in Orange County.

A stout man in his thirties, wearing a torn black leather jacket, chaps, rough skin, and a mane of unruly hair and beard, took the stool next to Dakota. He pulled it down the bar a ways to accommodate his girth, sat, and ordered a drink with a flick of his thick wrist. Clearly a regular, the bartender knew his poison. She poured a shot of Jack Daniels before moving off, giving the men some privacy, with one ear perked.

After the biker made the shot disappear, he checked out Dakota through the reflection of the mirror that backed the liquor bottles. Finally satisfied this was the man they were waiting for, his body language changed as if he was gearing up for something, but not sure how to start.

A slight man standing in shadow behind the pool table slouched against the jukebox. He looked to be texting, but could've been grabbing video of the two men sitting at the bar across the room on his cell phone.

Dakota downed his drink and ordered another round, the big man included. Thought it might break the ice some. It worked.

The big guy started the conversation. "That your Bronco in the lot?"

"Why? I park in somebody's space?" No attitude, but wondering how he knew what he was driving. No one entered the bar behind him.

"No, nice ride."

"A classic."

"Good to have something waiting for you on the outside." Letting him know the bar had been alerted to his arrival and he was the designated mouthpiece.

"Battery was trashed. Surprised it's still running."

"They don't build 'em good like that anymore. How long you in for?"

"Six years and change."

"Tough ride."

Dakota nodded.

"So, hey, what can I do you for…?

"Just getting used to being on the outside. Get my sea legs. Take a few days, then look for work."

"I know the drill. Decompress. Get used to the wife and kids again, or whatever."

"Sounds like what I'm trying for." Wondering about the "whatever" comment.

"Never easy," he said, letting Dakota know he'd been incarcerated more than once. "Not for a few weeks. Then it's fuckin natural… but not really. Hey, you wanna get laid?"

Dakota's face darkened. "What'd you say?"

"You wanna get laid."

"Get the fuck outta my face."

The big man straightened. "You a wise guy?"

"You coming on to me?"

"Motherfucker." The big man slid off the stool.

Dakota spun and threw a roundhouse from the heels, hitting the man a clean shot to the chin. The guy's head snapped to the side, and two hundred fifty pounds of mean dropped to the ground before he'd even cocked his ham fist. It happened so fast, nobody in the bar was quite sure what the hell had happened, but all eyes were on the fallen man.

The bartender leaned against the bar, and, looking concerned, said in rapid fire, "He misspoke, rite of passage thing, guy getting outta jail."

"Shit." Dakota reached down a hand and pulled the burly, enraged biker off the sawdust floor. "Must a heard you wrong, boss. If you said that where I served time, you'd be pushing your guts back in your stomach about now. Lemme buy you another drink."

The bartender, playing peacemaker, pushed two shots across the bar. "On the house," she said. "Dammit Ralph, I would've hit you harder if you said the same thing to me."

"In your dreams, Trish," Ralph said, trying to shake it off, but the man was seriously pissed-off.

Dakota clinked his glass against the big man's and tossed it back.

Hard eyes knocked the dirt off his ass, wanting to cut Dakota's throat, but accepted the drink, and emptied it in one swallow. "No good deed, man..."

"I hear ya. Well, I didn't hear you correct. Sorry about that... Dakota," he said, proffering his hand.

"I know who the fuck you are, or you'd be picking glass outta yer skull," Ralph said, refusing the handshake.

"I guess we got off easy then," he said, ignoring the slight.

The big man cracked his neck, winced in pain, and hand ordered two more shots. "We'll see."

"You must be *the* Ralph, Turly said to connect with," Dakota said, trying to clear the air. "The brains of the organization." Ralph wasn't convinced, but he liked the sound of brains being attributed to him. He nodded in agreement.

A few more men drifted over, having waited to see how the skirmish would play itself out. It looked like things were almost back to normal, the new guy wasn't going to shoot the joint up, and so drinks were ordered and introductions made.

Detente, Dakota thought. It was a dangerous play that might pay dividends. He recognized a few of the men seated in a booth behind the pool table as Blackfox workers from Agent Steele's photos. They were aware of the new guy, but kept their distance. Reasonable. Maybe they'd report back to the powers that be at Blackfox, and help the cause.

Dakota begged off a last round that would've put him on his ass with promises of hanging out again in a day or so, after he got settled. He left a good tip on the bar, thanked Trish, fist-bumped Ralph who didn't yank his hand away and headed for home, one eye on the rearview mirror.

———

Ralph's two hundred fifty pounds of ugly was now two hundred fifty pounds of hurt. They closed the RockPile, and Trish handed a dirty bar towel filled with ice to Ralph, who balled it up, placing it gingerly against his neck and jaw.

"Son of a bitch was fast. I'll give him that."

"Turly warned us. Said, don't fuck with the guy," Trish said.

"Fuck Turly. I'll be dead by the time he gets out."

"Man's a powerhouse," she said with respect. "Damn smarter than you."

"Hey, don't kick a man when he's down," Ralph growled. "Gimme a shot."

"You, my friend are over your limit," Trish said, but feeling sorry for the bruised man whose ego had taken a hit, poured another shot. "Sip it."

The man, sitting next to Ralph, hadn't moved in fifteen minutes and stared blankly at the carved names on the mahogany bar. His head nodded as he decided to join the conversation. "Wadda you think?"

"I thought you were dead," Ralph said, and knocked back the whiskey eliciting an eye roll from Trish both men felt, but didn't see, and didn't give a shit.

"Resting my eyes." Nick was drunk, but had the ability to snap out of it, and not look wasted. A neat trick when he got pulled over by the bulls. That being said, drunk or sober, his level of hatred never wavered. The swastika that snaked above the neck of his t-shirt, and the flaming cross on his forearm told the story.

The only thing providing meaning to his life after being fired from his oil-drilling platform was the OC Wolf Pack. The group shared a loose ideology that preached overthrowing the illegitimate United States Government, starting a race war, and cleansing their America of all black, brown, yellow, Jews, and Muslim sounding people. A bucket full of hate made his world go round.

"Fucking dude was fast," Ralph said to Nick, repeating himself. "A man like that…" he flashed to the punch and got lost in his anger.

Ten seconds of silence and, "What?" Nick barked, irritated.

"We could use muscle like that. Plus, he's got the crossover look. Mean but smart. He's one Silver Star motherfucker. You got a question about that, Google him."

"He's got the look all right," Trish said, blinking the lights on and off, eliciting a grin from the men, because they were the only ones left in the room, and she did it every night. Groans and knees cracked as they stood and checked their level of inebriation, knowing damn well they'd be riding home with one eye shut to keep from running their Harleys off the road. Neither man could afford another DUI.

———

Agent Jean Steele threw her graceful legs off the side of her queen-sized bed, phone to her ear, switched on the end table lamp, and said, "Dakota, you did not say that?"

"I'd be willing to bet the guy's icing his jaw as we speak."

"Jesus."

It sounded to Dakota like the woman might have smiled.

"At least we can cross the gay community off the list. I came across as a raging homophobe."

Steele shook off her sleep fog. "This is not a sprint, Dakota," she said, covering her concern.

"I saw an opening and put on a show for the room. I think it worked out. Met some of the players after the dust settled. None of the Blackfox boys, but I caught a few grins from their booth. Trish, the bartender and only woman in the joint, played right into my hand and calmed the action… I've gotta crash. Not the kind of place I could order iced tea."

"All right. I'll set you up with one of our tech crew to install security cameras around your property."

"Let me do it. I don't want anything too sophisticated in case they come snooping, and I'm betting they will. Turly chummed the water, and I set the hook."

"Whatever you think."

"I'll give it a day, and then make another showing. I'll call you after."

"Twenty-four seven. And watch your back, Dakota."

"Okay, Agent Steele."

Dakota placed the phone on the new nightstand. He opened the drawer and pulled out his father's police-issue Glock 22, which sat next to a box of 40 S&W cartridges. Checked the load in the 15-round mag, satisfied he had ample firepower, he slid it back into the drawer.

The bedroom was so quiet he wondered if he'd be able to sleep. He flopped back on his pillow, thought about Steele's response, and fell out like someone had thrown a switch.

CHAPTER 7

Dakota backed the Ford Bronco, which was towing a twenty-foot, center console Boston Whaler down the concrete incline until the Ford's rear tires broke the water.

"Turn left, left," Billie shouted as she prayed her baby wouldn't run afoul. "Good. Straight down now, easy, easy, good." The boat floated above the tow-rig, and Billie tied off the craft as Dakota threw the car into drive, pulling the Bronco up into the parking lot of Redondo Beach Marina.

He ran down to the boat as Billie eased on board and turned over the engine. Dakota untied the craft, jumped over the side dragging one of his shoes in the water, and settled into the swivel chair next to the captain. Billie maneuvered the craft in reverse, and then slowly throttled forward, arced the boat around, and powered down the main channel of the marina heading for open water.

They cast their baited hooks into the water just off the cliffs of Palos Verdes Estates. There were a few small crafts fishing in a spot famous for its kelp beds that attracted the local fish. Mackerel, Yellowfin, Croaker, and the occasional White Sea Bass.

Billie was in her element. She sucked in the salty air, and shared a relaxed smile with her nephew. They cracked open two cans of beer, and enjoyed the view north to the Santa Monica Mountains.

"So, Aunt…" Dakota took a sip of Dos Equis and the slack out of his line.

"Drop the aunt, huh, Dakota?"

"It's in the muscle, Auntie. How old was I, six, when you took me fishing for the first time? Off the Manhattan Beach pier. Auntie, that's what I called you."

"Never liked it."

"You're tough. So, Billie…"

"Better," she said, cutting him off. "I've been giving your predicament a lot of thought."

Dakota gave her the floor. Knew it was the real reason for their outing. Get in a safe place, get honest.

"It's just the beginning," Billie said, with concern etching her brow. "And you already opened a can of worms." She struggled for a second, and took a sip from her beer. "Every morning when your eyes blink open, I want you to remind yourself that you're an imbed. And these assholes won't open up until you prove yourself, no matter what that Turly guy said. You're going to have to prove yourself in some way, and I'm afraid it will end up in a violent confrontation of some kind. If it goes wrong, they could toss you back in prison and throw away the key. That would kill me."

"It would kill me too, Billie," he said thoughtfully.

"Now, if these men are wannabes, you should be able to skate for a while. But that won't get you any closer to Blackfox. Your resume may be enough to open the door, but if the gatekeepers are the Wolf Pack shitheads, they might have to see you in action. That's a concern."

"I've got a handle on it."

"Bullshit. You might have to kill someone to prove your worth. To risk letting you into their cell. How in God's name do you handle that? And I don't want to hear you'll cross that bridge or any other bullshit. I'm serious, Dakota."

"I won't be pushed into anything I can't handle or live with. Won't happen. But I hear you, *Auntie*."

Billie flashed scolding eyes.

"All kidding aside, Billie. Point well taken."

———

Thomas Wentworth, CEO and owner of Blackfox Executive Protection, buckled into the lush leather seat of his Gulfstream G650ER. It was taxiing down the runway at John Wayne Airport in Orange County. The thrust pushed him back against his seat as his jet shot into the sky, revealing the deep blue of the Pacific Ocean, the scenic beaches and cliffs along the water's edge as it accelerated to its cruising speed of 704 MPH.

He caught his reflection in one of the eighteen windows in his private jet, and liked what he saw. People mistook him for Larry Ellison, but hell, he should be so lucky. As hard as it was to create the life he was living, Wentworth was feeling pretty damn good about himself.

He never lost his boyhood joy of flying. The whole concept of being able to travel anywhere on the planet, whenever he wanted, at any time day or night, made him feel like he'd arrived. He made an effort not to take anything for granted. Life was ephemeral. In his line of work, he knew it could all come crashing down in the blink of an eye.

He accepted a call he'd been waiting for from his employee, who went by the nickname of *Ant*. To each his own, Wentworth thought. Ant wore the moniker like a badge of courage, and he was one of the company's most valued assets.

"I'm sending along a video of Dakota Judd," Ant said. "It should be there now. He made quite the inaugural appearance last night at the RockPile. You might find the incident interesting."

"Okay, Ant, it's coming up." He played the digital scene in real time once, and then again in slow motion. It showed Dakota entering the bar. Ralph sitting down next to him. The men exchanged a few words. And then Ralph was on the floor, and Dakota was helping him up onto unsteady legs. After the slo-mo version, "Huh," Thomas said, his interest piqued. "Paint the picture for me."

"It cracked me up, boss, but anyway. Ralph was feeling Dakota out, making sure he was the man Turly gave the nod to. The whole event could have been even more embarrassing, if that's possible."

"Ant."

"So...the word is, and I got this from the bartender, Trish. Ralph was making small talk and found himself at a loss for words. So, he asked the dude if he wanted to get laid. Dakota – who's been in the joint for six years – took the offer the wrong way, and Ralph was on the ground before he knew what hit him, and anyone else in the bar knew what happened.

"It was over before it started, and Dakota showed some nuanced social skills, diffusing the violence and squaring things with Ralph, who was seriously miffed. Being bested in his own cave."

"What are your thoughts?" Wentworth asked.

"I think Dakota will be more valuable to us, in-house. He's a cut above the locals. A smart, Silver Star warrior who put the big man down like swatting a flea. It's one hell of a skill set. His tattoo has a skull wearing a maroon beret. Man's Airborne. Dude can parachute. He mentioned to Ralph he was looking for work. I'll send over the transcript of my conversation with Turly. Dakota appears to have the right stuff and proved it in his time behind bars."

"Send me his biography, and have somebody check out his living situation. I'll be back in town early next week. Give him some time to acclimate and prove he's a like-minded team player."

"Copy that, boss."

Wentworth closed the computer screen as an attractive flight attendant placed an icy martini on his teakwood tray. He smiled, took a sip, and said, "Thank you, Denise. It's perfect."

"Let me know if you need anything else, Mister Wentworth," she said with a coquettish smile and walked back to her station in the rear of the plane.

———

Dakota worked up a sweat, cleaning house. His parents' bed, their couch, a few living room chairs, and the bedroom end tables were stacked on the front lawn and being loaded onto the St. Vincent de Paul's donation truck. Dakota tossed three large plastic garbage bags overstuffed with his father's clothing into the truck's body, tipped the men, and didn't look back. He opened all the windows in the house to clear out the stale air.

Drop cloths on the hardwood floors; he painted the master bedroom a Greek blue. He liked it so much that after a bologna and cheese sandwich, he slapped on a coat of blue over the institutional green his father had painted his bedroom and turned it into his office.

Satisfied he'd gotten rid of the bad vibes, he sat on the front porch and cooled off with a beer. Twenty minutes later, he accepted delivery of a new mattress and box spring he ordered over the phone. It came with a metal frame, two sets of sheets, and two pillows. A good start, he thought.

He signed the invoice and the deliveryman rolled down the rear door of his truck, grabbed the paper, and jumped into the cab. As he pulled away from the curb an apricot poodle leaped up on Dakota's leg, and licked his hand. The dog appeared to be smiling.

"I am so sorry," the dog's owner said as she ran up, and grabbed the lead. "Get down, Lucky." The dog turned his head, looked at his owner and held on for dear life. She pulled the dog off and shook her head, slightly embarrassed.

"No harm," Dakota said. The woman was blonde, with bright hazel eyes, clear skin, and an engaging smile.

"He's a willful animal, and spoiled rotten," she playfully scolded the dog. "You can see how well he listens when I give him a command."

"I can relate to that," he said droll. "Are we neighbors?"

"We are. Four houses down, next to the monstrosity."

"Dakota Judd." He liked this woman, he thought as he extended his hand. She shook, and hers was warm, dry, and firm.

"I know who you are," she said. "The whole neighborhood does."

"Huh," he said, not sure how to process that piece of information. "Are they going to run me out of town with pitchforks?"

"Not everyone. Are you moving in or moving out, if it's not too personal a question?"

"Moving in."

"Good. The house has been empty since before I came to town. A nice woman came over every few weeks and kept the lawn manicured.

Everyone in the neighborhood appreciated it. We've had a problem with squatters in the hills. Hard to get rid of. Anyway, I think you might have already met another member of my family."

"No, you're the first."

"Really. I've got an overly friendly tabby who knows how to beg for food. The cat's fat and happy, and I've had to pull him off your porch more than once. He likes your metal rocker."

"He actually made me feel right at home."

"Just shoo him away if he becomes a bother. He won't listen, but he'll teach you patience."

"I'll remember that."

"And I'll let you get back to your painting."

Dakota raised his eyebrows.

"Blue paint. On your cheek."

"Oh," he said, the king of small talk.

"Nice color. C'mon, Lucky. Welcome to the hood. If there's anything you need while you're getting settled, let me know. I work from home, so I'm around a lot. It's the green Craftsman with brown trim. Name's Suzanne, by the way."

"A pleasure."

Suzanne stood in place, looking like she was searching for something, and came to a decision. "Two motorcycle guys were checking out your house. Took pictures with their phones and drove off. Nothing subtle about those men."

"Thank you. I know who you're talking about. I'll find out what they were up to."

She nodded and held back when Lucky pulled the lead.

"Really, thank you," Dakota said. "I'll be fine, but I appreciate your concern."

"Okay. I just know that where you've been, trouble is the last thing you need right now. Oh God, I'm talking too much."

"Just the right amount."

"Good."

Dakota watched as the apricot poodle dragged his owner down the block, knowing who was walking who.

———

Ralph was standing outside the RockPile, his hog ticking, and giving off steam in the cool night air. He was dressed in black. Top-to-bottom. Checking his cell phone for the time. Thinking about running into the bar for a quick shot when Nick rolled into the lot in a bruised Toyota Prius. Nick lowered the passenger side window.

"You couldn't a taken a bigger fuckin' car?" Ralph said.

"Get in. The line at Costco was around the building. We've probably got two hours before they even know their tin can is gone."

Ralph pulled his Ruger out of his hip holster and placed it under the passenger seat. Then grunted as he backed into the small cab, ass first, struggled to pull his legs in, cursing as he tried to get the seat belt around his gut, and snapped into the catch.

They were off and running. They passed a strip of ocean, and Nick got quiet.

"What?"

Nick was eyeballing an oil rig a quarter mile offshore in the Pacific. Lights twinkling. "Coon that fired me, hired a fuckin' wetback to work my job. I see an oilrig, it pisses me off. I told him he'd be better off if he moved back to Africa. Scumbag took it as a threat, which it was, and had me escorted off the rig."

Ralph had heard the story multiple times, but let his partner rant. Get the juices running. Knew it was only a matter of time before he paid his ex-manager a visit and sent him back to Africa in a box.

Sunset Beach to Lomita on the 405 to the 110 was a half-hour drive. They rolled along Lomita Blvd and passed a pure white Islamic temple with a blue tiled dome.

"I didn't know we had camel jockeys in the area. Put it on our list," Nick said.

"I'm your fucking slave now?"

"I'm driving, tossing out brilliance, and you're getting bent."

"I'm putting it on my to-do list, how's that. How the fuck are we going to forget seeing a raghead church that we wanna fuck up, or burn down."

"Maybe blow up. We should find out if Dakota knows how to build bombs. Too bad there isn't a synagogue nearby, we could start a towel head and yarmulke wearing Jew war. That'd make the national news."

"I gotta give it to you, that ain't bad, Nick." And then, "We're looking for the Marina Knolls projects. Where 'Marina 8' sells their drugs."

They continued driving on Palos Verdes N. past what looked like an old military housing project. "Gotta be it," Nick said. Multiple two-story tan structures. Separate housing units, surrounded by a chain-link fence. There was a basketball court lit at both ends, and a young man was shooting hoops.

"This has the look," Ralph said, agreeing. "Keep driving. Where the hell are the bangers?"

"Ant said to check out Marina Park."

Ralph tried to slouch down in his seat as they approached a small park with old-growth trees and wooden picnic tables. A group of five twenty-something Latino gangsters were sitting on the tabletops, smoking and drinking beer. Their heads swiveled, and they gave the car the once over and stink eye until it passed, and then back to their business not aware they had just been cased.

"I had an AK, could've taken 'em all out," Ralph grunted as he pushed himself back up in the tight seat.

"One at a time. Build the rage," Nick said, quoting Ant.

"And then we hit the 'Harbor Crew,'" Ralph said. "That should kick up some dust with the locals. Rev up the body count, the cops get physical, and they start burning their shit down and we've turned it into a fucking riot."

Nick liked the sound of that. He liked the sound of that a great deal.

"Turn around up ahead, and we can keep an eye out from the inter-section. If they separate, I'll make the move."

An hour later, Nick said, "I should've brought a few beers. This is taking longer than I thought."

"I prefer a clear head when I work. There."

The five men walked out of Marina Park oozing attitude. They eyeballed up and down the block, satisfied things were cool, fist bumps all around, and four walked back toward the projects.

A single banger walked up the street in their direction.

Traffic was light, and he jogged across the intersection, paying the Prius, no mind. The young man continued up Lomita Boulevard.

Nick started the car, shut off his headlights, and made the left.

They were on the hunt.

The banger crossed through a halo of light created by a lamppost, and kept up his cocky strides moving into shadow.

"Shit," Nick said.

Ralph pulled his Ruger 9mm from under the seat, powered down the window as Nick drove silently behind the man, who was unaware that he was being followed.

The Prius pulled alongside the man.

He felt their presence.

His eyes narrowed as he fumbled for his weapon.

He snapped his head around, raising his pistol.

A bright flash of fire from Ralph's barrel was the last thing he saw.

The bullet penetrated the man's forehead. His knees buckled, and he dropped sideways onto the concrete, his gun clattered across the sidewalk.

Nick tossed a black cap with "Harbor" stenciled in red on the brim into the street and drove away, making a blind turn on the next block before snapping on the headlights. When they were sure all was clear, Nick slowed their speed, blended with traffic, and headed back toward the 110 freeway.

The men sat in silence until they hit the 405 and their adrenaline started to wane.

"I've got to give it up to you, Nick. The Prius was fucking genius. Did you see the look on his mug when he saw the gun? He never heard us coming. You are the man."

"I need a drink."

CHAPTER 8

The Federal Bureau of Investigation, Orange County Resident Agency, was located on 4000 W. Metropolitan Drive. Steele's boss had a corner office on the second floor with a view of the towering Crystal Cathedral in the distance, and looked down on the planned communities and vast Irvine sprawl.

Agent Will Chase looked harried as he glanced up from his computer and waved Agent Steele into his office. He saved his work as she took a seat in front of his desk, littered with paperwork.

"If I have to input one more report, just so it will go into some bureaucrat's computer file to be forgotten, I'm gonna effing scream."

"You're not a screamer, Will. It's why I like working with you."

"I prefer silent but deadly. Wait a minute. Maybe I should rephrase that," he joked.

"Please," she said straight-faced, used to his attempt at humor.

"What do you have for me, Jean? And I wanted to share something that just came across my desk. There was a gang shooting last night near the Marina Knolls projects. A twenty-three-year-old Marina 8 gangbanger. A "Harbor Crew" baseball cap was found in the street near the body. The saga continues. First responders chalked it up to business as usual.

"Our guy, Trammel, showed up and got a bad feeling. Like it was all too pat. Kid was shot in the face."

"Drive-by?"

"Looks that way. Trajectory of the bullet, and distance to the vic. Coroner guestimated five feet give or take. Hard to get that close unless he knew the shooter."

"Drug deal gone bad?"

Chase answered with a shake of his head. "He had a few dimes of crack in his pocket, and two hundred in cash. Kid's gun was found in the gutter."

"Huh," she said, rolling around the possible implications. "Any prints on the cap?"

"Nothing but car tracks. It was pretty well chewed up."

"Too bad."

"So…how's our Dakota guy working out? I don't have to tell you, my phone is ringing day and night. I expected a call from you beginning of the week, but what the hell. Heads will roll if the guy was just dogging you for a get out of jail free card. And when I say heads…"

"You mean my head."

Chase nods. "And don't report me to business affairs, but you're looking good, Jean. I don't know when you find time to work out. I'm sitting on my butt all day and putting on the L-B's. So, Dakota?"

"He's a serious player," she said, ignoring his sexist remark. "Full speed ahead. I'm trying to rein him in some. Don't want to put off our targets. He's stubborn, but up to the task."

"Hmm," Will said with a furrowed brow. "There's going to be blowback for the shooting, one way or the other," he said, switching gears. "And we've been suffering a slow drip of gang retaliation in Orange County."

"If the threats the Wolf Pack have been making on social media are turning to action, it might be their play."

"You read my mind." And then he added, "Hey, just know I trust your instincts, or we wouldn't be sitting here, and our man wouldn't be out of jail."

"Dakota's making progress at the RockPile. Ralph and Nick have taken him under their wing. They're introducing him to the San Diego chapter of the OC Watchmen tonight. He's engendered some respect."

"That's good. That's very good."

"I'll keep you up to speed as things progress."

"Even if they don't."

"Got it boss. Thank you." And she meant it.

"And Jean, keep up the good work. You're killing it."

Agent Steele walked out of the office pumped.

———

The basement of the RockPile was set up like a card room, liquor and dry goods storage, and clubhouse. A few ragged couches, folding chairs, and side tables with half-filled ashtrays. One window, painted black, three strips of fluorescent bulbs lit the space, and the jukebox vibrating on the wooden floor above provided the muted soundtrack. The place was damp, smelled of sour beer, weed, and tobacco smoke. The men drank longnecks pulled from the chilled cooler sitting on the floor next to the scratched wooden table that fronted the room.

Dakota was on the hot seat, standing in front of five men from the Wolf Pack and four OC Watchmen, the militia that drove up from San Diego. It was a meeting of the white supremacists called to share political philosophies, real-time actions taken, and a meet and greet for Dakota, the new warrior in their fold.

The men were scattered around the room with Ralph running the meeting, and Nick, clearly the second in command. It was a shaggy-haired, tattooed, and bearded group, except for one tall man, wearing a thousand-dollar leather jacket and giving off a lord-of-the-manor attitude. He seemed to be the head-honcho of the San Diego militia.

"This isn't an interrogation, Terrance," Ralph said, tight. "Meeting Dakota is just a formality. Do you think he'd be sitting in on our business if he wasn't invited by me, and Nick, and Turly?"

"All I was saying is Dakota here was a little late to the game."

And then directing his attitude directly at Dakota, he said, "When did you come to this conversion? It's not a hard question. You were in prison for more than six years, and Turly's blog only makes mention of you in the last six months."

Dakota locked eyes with Terrance, and then his eyes raked the room, letting everyone know he was a man to be reckoned with.

"Some men wear their affiliations on their sleeve," he answered. "Some men need protection, some men…not so much. I'm one of the latter."

Eliciting a laugh from one of the San Diego crew, and a sharp glance from Terrance that cut it short.

"We still operate under a chain of command. You've obviously had issues with that if I can believe what I've read about you."

"I'm not here to re-litigate my trial, Terrance. Or my career. My only regret is not killing the captain. I draw a line in the sand when it comes to murdering women and children. I've got no compunction about killing in the line of duty or following orders. Fighting for a righteous cause. Like this." Dakota slammed his hand down on *Siege*, the James Mason book that sat open on the table.

"You got a problem with me, bring it on. Right now, Terrance. In front of your comrades. Then you can tell me if I deserved my Silver Star. Show me what you've accomplished in your life or shut the fuck up. Get back to me when you've decided my worthiness. Because as of right now, it's you boys who are coming up short."

Ralph's eyes narrowed.

"The Wolf Pack aside," Dakota interjected, catching himself. "Turly's word is sacrosanct to me. Man saved my life. Didn't have to do it. He's a wise man who knows how to judge a person by his soul and his actions. He gave the nod to Ralph and Nick. Said they had the right stuff. I believed him. And I believe in them. I don't remember him mentioning you in our conversations. And we sat shoulder to shoulder."

"We've only met online," came off sounding lame, and Terrance knew it. And it pissed him off.

"You might give some serious thought to joining a glee club if all you're good for is singing your own fucking praises. What the hell have you ever done to prove yourself?"

"I don't have to prove squat to you," he said with condescension, trying to get control of the conversation, but Dakota was just getting warmed up.

"I'll bet you shot video of yourselves, out in the woods, dressed in store-bought camo. Shooting automatic weapons at targets, and cans of cherry and grape soda, so it looked like blood if you were lucky enough to hit the mark. Lookin' all macho for the camera."

Terrance stood silent – feeling every eye in the room on him – doing a slow burn.

"You wanna know who's enjoying you on Facebook and X and maybe 8kun when you post. Raising money for your violent revolution to start a civil war, overturn the government, and turn the new country into a whites-only nation. A philosophy I embrace. You wanna know who's watching your posturing, and laughing at you. The FBI, the CIA, the ATF. And crime reporters writing for the local press who just want you to pull the trigger and give them something to write about other than threats."

"You don't know shit."

"You're the fake news, Terrance. They've got your pictures on a federal website, hanging on their walls at headquarters, waiting for you all to shoot your wad and then shut you down. Let's see how committed you are to the cause when you're six years behind bars, motherfucker."

Terrance's face turned beet red, and then his ears, and then it moved all the way down his neck. He turned to face his guys, and spun brandishing a pearl-handled, shiny 38 like a studied gunslinger in a B Western.

Dakota grabbed the gun with one hand and dropped a vise grip on the guy's wrist with the other, twisting hard until the man groaned in pain, and spun in place, his wrist threatening to break. Dakota pushed him away, slapped the cylinder of his pistol open, and emptied the cartridges onto the concrete floor. The wild-eyed man spun as if to charge, but the look on Ralph's face froze him in place.

Terrance made the right decision.

Dakota gripped the Colt by the cold muzzle and handed the gun back to the man. "Next time you pull a gun, be ready to shoot, or it'll be your last bad move. I'm ready to fight shoulder to shoulder with warriors. I'm not sure you make the cut.

"Thanks for the invite, Ralph, Nick, gentlemen." He made eye contact with everyone in the room. "No harm, no foul." Dakota walked out the door, the echo of his footsteps pounding up the wooden stairs the only sound in the room.

———

Dakota was driving the Bronco down PCH on his way back to Redondo Beach. He called on the burner Agent Steele provided, and she picked up on the second ring.

"How did it go?"

"Before or after a San Diego dandy pulled his gun on me."

"Dakota?"

"I'm doing what I can. And I don't think our boys held it against me. I gave them support and called Terrance out for being a fraud. He was giving me the third degree, and the man couldn't shine my boots."

"You're supposed to ingratiate yourself, gain the group's trust, what the hell?" she said not pleased.

"They wouldn't have bought it if I didn't come back on the man. I'll work with the RockPile boys if it comes to that. But I think I'm speaking to the Blackfox organization. I think the information flows upstream and it might move things along. I'm gonna stop by tomorrow night and toss a few back. Make sure I didn't burn bridges. Can you get me info on Terrance, from the OC Watchmen out of San Diego? He's got money, and the ear of his boys. They're the kind of men who might start believing their own hype and act out."

"Will do." Steele also made a note to call Agent Chase and bring him up to speed. "How are things on the home front? Did you get the security cameras set up?"

"My aunt's stopping by end of the week. She's technologically savvy. If there are any issues, I'll call. But so far, all's quiet."

"Let's keep it that way. You've got enough on your plate."

"I'll get in touch if I pissed off the crew. Have a good night, Agent Steele."

"Jean." And then, as if she needed an explanation, "it's less formal."

"Night, Jean." And Dakota clicked off, smiling.

The Bronco's windows were open, the cool ocean breeze buffeted the 4X, and Dakota was enjoying the ride. Agent Steele was good, he thought. Kept him aware that he was still on somebody's hit list, and to grow eyes on the back of his head. He wondered if she cared or if she was just protecting her investment.

Hell, he'd take it either way. He was out of prison, single, healthy, and he planned on keeping it that way. Dakota clicked on the radio to Rock 105.3. The Stones were singing "You Can't Always Get What You Want." He checked his rearview mirror, and when the light turned green, hit the gas.

CHAPTER 9

Agent Steele, habitually early, was seated in the rear office at Peluso, Costa, and Litto. She pulled five books, a yellow pad, and pen out of her attaché case, setting them in perfect order on the polished mahogany table. She heard the rear elevator ding and looked up as Dakota stepped into the room.

Dakota had taken a circuitous route driving over to make sure he wasn't being followed. Billie's reminder to watch his back had struck a chord. "I come bearing gifts," he said, smiling, and set two grande Americanos on the table. He pulled two half-and-half creamers and a few sugar packets out of his jacket pocket.

"Wasn't sure how you take yours."

"One is perfect. No sugar." She pulled the tab, poured, and stirred as Dakota set himself up across the table.

"You look like a school teacher with your notepad and all."

Steele's eyes narrowed slightly.

"I meant it in the best possible way, Jean. Teachers are the future."

"No offense taken, my mother's a teacher. Middle School English. She taught me well."

"Did you bring me homework?"

"It's not me who's going to be testing you."

"What do you have?"

"Information you asked about Terrance Gorman, from the OC Watchmen. He runs a successful brokerage firm in San Diego. Old money. His family settled there in the twenties. He's a well-connected Republican donor and an avid hunter with political aspirations. He's never far removed from the political scene in the area, and a frequent face in the social section of the local papers. Voted most eligible bachelor in *San Diego Magazine* a few years back. Never been arrested, a picture-perfect resume."

"What the hell is he doing running a militia filled with low-rent talent?"

"Like-minded people that speak his language? Maybe he hunts more than endangered species."

"Something to think about."

"I brought *Siege*, the Mason book Turly used as his primer. Mason was a former member of the American Nazi Party and a Holocaust denier. He believes America can only become a whites-only nation through violent revolution.

"It can't hurt to have a few quotes from *Siege* in your quiver. Turly opened the RockPile's door for you. We think he's also got ties to Blackfox, because some of their men hang with the Wolf Pack at the bar."

"I've put a few faces with the photos you showed me. They're keeping their distance."

"I think that's about to change. Now… *The Turner Diaries* inspired Timothy McVeigh and other terrorists these men glorify and use as role models. The greater the body count, the more they deify the deviants. Patrick Crusius gunned down twenty-two people at a Walmart in El Paso. He posted his Hispanic invasion manifesto on 8kun the day before his massacre. Dylann Roof, a white supremacist who killed nine African American parishioners at the Charleston Church shootings. The list goes on.

"When you make it to Blackfox, you'll be climbing the food chain, with more intellectuals in the mix."

Dakota liked her positive attitude. When, and not if, he made it.

"They all want the same results, and will be on the lookout for nonbelievers. You're going to have to be able to quote the leaders of their movement to cement your place in the company."

"I get it. Thank you. Just know, I've been doing some of my own research."

"Good to hear."

"I thought about what went down last night, and got the feeling I'm gonna have to blow something up, burn something down, or shoot somebody before long."

"Don't let them force you into a corner unless we've talked first. You're an independent contractor who operates on his own timeline. They can't fight you on that after your time spent behind bars. And let's face it, you're the talent, their star. You're a means to an end, and they're aware of that. Ralph's nobody's fool. If you do well, the Wolf Pack stays in business."

"I hope you're right. We'll only get one shot at this."

Steele sipped her coffee, lost for a moment in his intensity, and lowered her voice. "That's right...and if you can't talk the talk, if you can't sell it, you won't make it out of there alive."

They sat in silence.

Dakota wasn't sure how to move forward with the conversation. And then, "How does all this insanity make you feel?"

"How does it make *you* feel?" she fired back with a passion that caught him off guard.

Dakota didn't like being pressed, and not one to share emotions with someone he hardly knew. But decided it was a reasonable question.

"It takes a lot of control to keep my mouth shut when these assholes are spouting their racist bullshit. I didn't put up with it in the Rangers... in my squad anyway. I didn't break bread with the hardliners, and they understood I wasn't buying in. It was all about the success of the mission with me. Fulfilling my orders. My mother taught me all men and women deserved a fair shot at success in this country, no matter what color they were. It made sense to me as a kid, it still does.

"When I walked in on Captain Mullrooney attacking that young Afghan boy who had just witnessed his mother getting slaughtered, I snapped. Did what I believed was right, and lost a big chunk of my life."

"Regrets?"

"None. The man deserved worse." Dakota took a sip of coffee and said, "Your turn."

"People like the captain motivate me," she said without giving it a second thought. "It's why I'm here doing this. This career. This case. To make sure people like him don't win."

Dakota nodded.

"My grandparents grew up in the Jim Crow South. My parents came up during the civil rights movement. They sacrificed a great deal to give my brother and me a better life and yet I put up with racists, and sexist assholes, every day in the FBI. These militia are trying to take us back to Jim Crow. And I'm not about to let that happen.

"We can't prove it yet but we think the Wolf Pack helped gin up the racist mob that stormed the Capitol on January 6, and Blackfox was involved with inciting the violence."

"What do you want? End game." Dakota asked.

"I don't want to just chase the mob back under their rocks, or wherever they were spawned. I want retribution."

"In what form?"

"A jail cell works."

Dakota locked eyes with Steele. Her determination was intense. He couldn't speak to her emotion, because he'd never experienced that level of hatred growing up white in America. But he was damn sure he'd help her in the only way he knew how.

"Let's take 'em down."

———

Dakota was balanced on a ladder screwing the Ring spotlight camera to the side of his house that would cover someone walking toward the garage from the street and alert-him on his cell. He'd already installed one on the rear of the house to cover the backyard and rear entry, while Billie installed the video doorbell in the front. Just enough to alert people he was watching, not enough to question where he got the money to install a sophisticated system.

He still had a feeling the Feds had checked out his house before he was released. He wasn't convinced they wouldn't bug the place given a second chance.

Billie was holding the ladder and admiring her blue Vette in the driveway.

"I've been doing some research into the white nationalists, armed militias, and white supremacist groups in Orange County. The numbers are staggering. Not a surprise, really. The John Birch Society was rampant in the sixties. A lot of the cops on the force were members. Tried to rope me in. No interest. Too much hate already on the streets.

"But the card-carrying members had kids, and you know how that goes. Most people learn to hate from family and friends. Things get tough, there's always someone to blame for their lot in life."

"I'm getting better with the jargon," Dakota said. "I've got to learn how to hit it so it's natural. I sold it okay the other night."

"Half of those guys are unhinged. Your display of anger was probably perceived as a badge of courage. They talked about you all the way back to San Diego, where they'll crawl back into their caves."

"As long as I'm on track with Ralph and Nick, I think I'm good to go. And Ralph got to see what I can do physically, instead of being at the wrong end of the action."

"Just remember you're playing a part. It's gonna get tougher. They've got you under the microscope. Don't let them turn you into an asshole, Dakota."

"I'll keep that in mind."

Dakota stepped off the ladder, carried it into the garage, and placed it in its designated space created by his father many years ago.

CHAPTER 10

Dakota was slouched in the back seat of a brand-new Chevy Impala. Nick was behind the wheel, and Ralph was sitting shots. Nobody in their right mind would see the clean ride and think drive-by vehicle. The three had done reconnaissance of the target area in the late afternoon, and with intel the men had gotten their hands on, knew the address of the house where the "Harbor Crew" hung at night.

The men ate Mexican for dinner and parked two blocks away, with a view of the modest house and detached garage. They were waiting for the gangsters to settle in the backyard and enjoy their high. People came and went, and then the rap music was cranked up.

"That would piss me off, every night, loud nigger shit," Ralph said.

"Goes with the neighborhood," Nick snapped.

Ralph turned in his seat, stroking his beard. "We're ready when you are, Dakota. Let Nick know when it feels right and we're good to go."

Dakota nodded, his adrenaline spiking. He checked the load in his Glock and took a deep breath. He checked his watch, and at the same time the hand sprung to nine an African American wearing a black hoody turned the corner and sauntered toward the house holding a brown bag with two six-packs of beer close to his chest.

"Now," Dakota ordered, powering down his window.

Nick pulled away from the curb and drove comfortably toward their target.

The Black gangster glanced at the car and looked away, not bothered.

The white Impala was ten yards away. Then five. Dakota's arm snaked out.

Dakota fired!

The bullet hit the man in the chest. His hands flailed open and pinwheeled as he fell. Blood stained his white t-shirt red. Bottles of beer hit the concrete sidewalk and exploded as the surprised man went down.

Nick hit the gas as Ralph witnessed the action in the rearview mirror, "Fuckin' A!" They made a hard right, caught the light at the intersection, and blended with nighttime traffic.

"Motherfucker," Dakota shouted, letting off some energy as he fought to slow his breathing.

———

A black SUV with tinted windows screeched to a stop next to the shooting victim. The back door of the car swung open. The downed man sprang to his feet and dove into the 4X. The vehicle sped away before the door slammed shut.

———

The "Harbor Crew" poured out of the backyard, weapons drawn. They looked up and down the empty street, trying to make sense of the gunshot they heard and the broken beer bottles on the sidewalk. They lowered their weapons and scattered before one of their neighbors called the police.

———

Four blocks away, Agent Steele stood next to her car, checked her watch, radio in hand. Waiting for her team to call in.

―――――――

"You okay?" Agent Terry Stevens, the driver of the black SUV asked, breathing heavily, glancing in the rearview mirror at his partner in the rear seat.

"That was great! My heart's pounding like a son-of-a-bitch!" Dion Mitchel, the young FBI agent said as he slid out of his hoody and pulled the blood-stained t-shirt over his head. He ripped the blown squib off his chest, and the detonation device out of the hoody's sleeve. He wiped the fake blood off his skin with his balled-up t-shirt. "What a rush," he said, changing into a clean shirt.

"You done good," Stevens said. "I'll call Chase and report in, then give Steele the good news."

"Shouldn't you report to Agent Steele first?"

"Oh, you poor, naïve agent."

"Really? Next time I'll drive, and you can take the hit."

"Dream on, Mitchel, I don't have the acting chops you do, but I'm smart enough to know who to dial first."

―――――――

Steele let out the breath she'd been holding and clicked off the radio. Her face creased into a tight smile as the black SUV came to a squealing stop in the parking lot where they had deployed from. She called off the backup cars that surrounded the perimeter of the neighborhood, and fist-bumped Mitchel and Stevens when they dismounted the SUV.

"Talk to me."

"Went without a hitch," Stevens said. "Nobody in the rearview. All is well. Let's hope they bought it."

Steele was doing more than hoping. This was her mission and the first trial by fire for Dakota Judd. She wouldn't relax until Dakota checked in.

—————

Agent Steele was sitting on her overstuffed couch in her first-floor condo in Manhattan Beach. It was a half-mile from the pier, no view, but damn if the air wasn't clean. She was living in a beach community and loved her modest patio with purple bougainvillea and her Weber gas grill.

Her flat screen was on MSNBC, sound off, and she was trying to read a dog-eared copy of *O* magazine, but couldn't concentrate. Agent Chase had given her a major job well done over the phone, but she was concerned.

Steele reflexively checked her watch for the umpteenth time, and took a sip of wine, tamping down her growing concern. She should have heard from Dakota by now.

A year of pitching her idea, finding the right man for the job, selling it up the FBI hierarchy, and for what? Call for Christ's sake.

She jumped when her private line rang and grabbed the phone, "Are you okay?"

"Fine. All's good, Jean."

"That's great, Dakota. That's good."

"Were you worried?" he said with a smile-tinged voice.

Steele realized she was, and wasn't sure how to deal with her emotion.

"Don't flatter yourself, Dakota," she covered. "There were a lot of moving parts, and I'm very pleased. Any issues, anything I should warn Agent Chase about?"

"Just share the good news. Agent Mitchel was spot on. I bought the act, and so did Ralph and Nick. Make sure the kill is reported."

"It's set for the afternoon news. We've got an editor who owes us big-time."

"Perfect."

"Take tomorrow off and…what am I saying. You've been trained to take these kinds of risks. You know how it feels when the adrenaline disappears. You do whatever you want. This is good, Dakota."

"Thanks, Jean. I'll check in tomorrow and make sure you've recovered."

"Nobody likes a wise-ass." She clicked off and took a long sip of wine.

Dakota barked a laugh, flipped the top off a Dos Equis, and strolled through his living room and out onto the front porch. He sat on the metal rocker, took a sip, and heard the deep purring of the first friend he made this side of prison walls.

The tabby leaped onto his lap in one silent motion and burrowed down. Dakota rubbed the back of the tabby's neck and the purr rose in volume, joined by a mockingbird's late-night song. A perfect end to a damn good day. And then his cell phone beeped.

He checked the number. It was a text from Turly. "You made the cut. Don't fuck up."

Dakota typed, "Anything I can do for you?" and hit send.

"I'm solid," Turly texted back.

Dakota found himself grinning as the tension of the setup dissipated. He was feeling the pump. He was back in the game. That muscle had been in stasis. Biding its time until he was able to cut loose again.

His father had been pissed off when he signed on to the Rangers and turned his back on the police force. But Dakota knew when the Rangers were deployed, it was all action all the time. Looking at his father's life in the police department, it was six months of monotony, and reports, and taking orders, and an eye-blink of combat. His father never forgave him for being a young man with his own dreams.

Dakota took stock, looked at his potential moves from all sides of the game board, and was reminded of Agent Steele's earlier admonition...someone out there still wants you dead.

CHAPTER 11

Blackfox Executive Protection was located in a five-story cubist structure built into the hills of Orange County. The silver-glass reflective skin that wrapped the building made it blend, almost disappearing against the blue sky and cumulous clouds that were ever present in Irvine, California. Just the way Thomas Wentworth, the CEO and owner, envisioned.

Blackfox was a private company Thomas ran with an iron fist. He paid top dollar to talented men and women who made their bones in law enforcement and military deployments the world over. No contract was too small or too large if the money was right. He never contractually signed on to break the law, but the line between right and wrong was hazy in the jungles of Niger in West Africa or the Amazon rainforest in South America.

Blackfox had relationships with the CIA, the military, the senate, and the DOJ. He could dispose of left-leaning patriots who were thorns in the side of totalitarian governments worldwide. If the price was right, and the bonus checks readily shared with his warriors, all bets were off and the job was professionally dealt with.

He was loyal to his team and demanded the same. It was a win-win and created a successful business model.

Dakota had worked with men like Wentworth in the military, he thought as he listened to the man extol the virtues of his organization. Wentworth's eyes were dark, his long hair dark with a light dusting of gray, and his physique trim but muscled for fifty-nine. He exuded strength befitting his status on the world stage.

"You've been fully vetted."

"I understand the need."

"Just to be clear, Turly vetted you. And now Ralph and Nick vetted you. They put their names, and more importantly, their lives on the line for you. And we vetted the hell out of you," he said, smiling at his understatement.

Was Wentworth the puppet master pulling the strings of a vast right-wing militia army? It could be a formidable power if there really was an American Civil War in the offing. It seemed a reach, but even if it was aspirational, he knew Blackfox would stop at nothing to protect their secret.

"I could continue," Wentworth said. "But, if you still have any questions about signing on, I've invited someone who might be able to close the deal.

It was a damn good trick because right on cue ex-Ranger James Marshal entered the spacious office.

Dakota was out of his seat, and the two men bear hugged. Dakota lifted James off his feet and set him down, stepping back.

"Damn I'm good," Wentworth said, taking focus.

"That you are, sir," Dakota said and couldn't hide his grin. And then to James, "How the hell are you?"

"It's you I was worried about, but I can see there was no cause. You fucking look great."

"James, why don't you show Dakota the lay of the land? Bring him up to speed on how we do business. I'm sold. His history speaks for itself. I just need all of my men to have the same level of commitment. Take a few days, Dakota, and let me know what your thoughts are. If you're ready to work, available to travel, I can keep you busy."

Dakota walked over, proffered his hand, and the two men shook. "Thank you, sir."

Wentworth didn't dissuade him from the formality. He lived for it. It stroked his ego in just the right way.

"Let's start at the commissary," James said on their way out the door. "We have a great chef. We'll work our way around the campus after we eat."

———

The men were sitting in a booth in the Blackfox commissary that could've been a high-end restaurant in Newport Beach. Their plates were empty and they were nursing espressos.

"So, the eight-hundred-pound gorilla…" James started.

"Where is that motherfucker?" Dakota, said cutting him off.

"Captain Mullrooney retired three years ago. Settled in San Clemente. Thought if it was good enough for Nixon, it was good enough for him. I don't know if you followed his career, but Mullrooney got a lot of bad press after the trial."

"Only bits and pieces from my lawyer. Didn't lose any sleep."

"His career was over after the local press dug deeper into Mullrooney's past. Freedom of Information material. They discovered his record of violence went far beyond what we testified to."

"Not surprised."

"The man took his pension and moved on. I was on his shit list after the trial."

Dakota felt something dislodge in his chest, reliving that moment in time, his personal nightmare. It looked like James took a personal hit, too. He sipped the espresso, and as he set it down, James continued.

"I've been living with incredible guilt not visiting you in prison, no excuse," he said, maintaining eye contact. Ready to take whatever blowback came his way.

"You stood up for me during the court-martial. One of the few," Dakota said.

Words escaped James, he sat in silence.

"How'd you end up here?" Dakota asked.

"I stayed in another two years after they put you away and then mustered out. The writing was on the wall. I testified against the captain, and the powers that be decided I'd testified against the United States Army."

"You look like you weathered the storm."

"I landed on my feet. It took a few months to figure out what I wanted to do with the rest of my life. Money's great here, and I mean great. And I didn't have to go back to school and reinvent myself. No regrets so far. You?"

The answer came easily, "None. I did the right thing when I broke that motherfucker's arm."

The two men walked through the vast campus. An indoor shooting range in the basement, the size of a bowling alley. The weapons arsenal was massive; the fully equipped gym was high-tech and impressive. They passed an office with an intimidating double mahogany door.

"This is our war room. Can't take you in unless you end up working here."

"Makes sense."

"We offer protection for politicians coming into town, or we'll travel to huge rallies wherever we're needed. Sometimes it's one-on-one, or up to a few hundred lending support to the National Guard. We travel in groups set up like we had in the Rangers if there's political trouble the government doesn't want to dirty their hands with. We step in, take the heat, and they pay through the nose."

"Guns for hire," Dakota said without attitude.

James nodded in agreement and grinned.

They walked past an office that looked like something out of Comic-Con. Movie posters of monsters, heroes and buxom maidens. A life-sized model of the Creature from the Black Lagoon, and two ornate, medieval long swords hung on the wall behind a slight, young man, dwarfed by a massive array of computers and monitors. He glanced up and nodded hello before diving back into his work.

"That's Anthony Bernacki. He goes by 'Ant.' He's our technical genius."

"He's a kid," Dakota said, thinking he picked up a flash of recognition from the guy.

"Can't argue with his success."

"Looks like his name."

"It was his video-game nickname, and it stuck. The boss recruited him after he became a grand master at the age of nineteen. He designs video mockups for our sorties, and intricate game plans for our moves, with contingency plans in case things go to hell. And I'm here to tell you, the kid has saved my life."

James went on, "So, we've got Ant, the camera drones, the best new weaponry money can buy, and of course, the talent." He raised his eyebrows and grinned.

Dakota had to smile. When James was deployed in one of his groups, he always felt safe. Never questioned his resolve, bravery, or ability on the battlefield. They never talked politics, race, religion, or shared their personal lives outside the Rangers. It was all about the combat mission. But if Blackfox was as bad as Agent Steele and the FBI thought, and James had gone over to the dark side for a buck, he wouldn't think twice about dropping the hammer.

Dakota understood if he was successful with Blackfox, the chance of taking the organization down and getting away clean was going to be the hardest challenge he'd ever faced.

Dakota decided Thomas Wentworth's offer – to take a few days before responding – was the way to go. He wanted to drive to San Clemente and see where Captain Mullrooney landed. The captain was high on Dakota's list of men who had a grudge to bear. And with his sociopathic tendencies, the captain has had plenty of time for the hatred to fester.

He'd call Agent Steele on his way home, fill her in on the job offer, and get any intel she might be able to share on the captain.

———

Steele was sitting in her office talking on the phone when her private phone trilled. A call she'd been waiting for. She signed off on her conversation and tapped the cell. "How did it go?"

"We have a personal connection between Blackfox, the Wolf Pack, and Turly. Directly from the mouth of Wentworth. And there's a kid that works there, name's Ant. It looks like he might be good for generating the intel Ralph and Nick used on the Harbor City Crips scam. He's someone to keep an eye on."

"That's amazing, Dakota. Jesus. Let me know when you've signed on the dotted line. Agent Chase will be to the moon and back."

"That's your bailiwick. I just need to keep you happy."

"Chase writes the checks. And we need all the support we can muster from the FBI moving forward. It's not going to get easier, just more dangerous."

"Point taken. And on that note, I need a favor. Can you get me Captain Mullrooney's address? I learned today that he settled in San Clemente. One of my old Ranger buddies is working at Blackfox. Wentworth used him to sweeten the deal. Name's James Marshal. He was a good soldier who testified on my behalf at the trial. He filled me in on the captain's whereabouts, I didn't want to push."

Steele gave that some thought before answering. "This will be on the QT. You can't go to this 'well' again unless your life is in danger. You're not the only one living under a microscope. And Dakota, look, but don't touch."

"No worries, Jean. I just want to do reconnaissance. I'm not going to shake the fool down."

"Give me a few hours. I'll text you by the end of the day. And Dakota…fine work. It sounds like Wentworth is all in."

———

Dakota poured himself a scotch, set himself up at his desk, and dove into the alt-right books and manifestos Steele provided for his reading pleasure. A tutorial in hate. The written screeds of killers and miscreants, sure to haunt his sleep. Twisted minds with dreams of civil war and a white-washed America. The terror of losing the majority that had once been theirs. It was driving them crazy.

He took a sip, decided to check out Ant on the internet and discovered he was a major talent, a gaming savant. The young man had an analytical mind and turned a couch competition into a million-dollar enterprise. He had his own Wikipedia page.

His bio explained after enormous success in international competitions that gave him a net worth in the millions, high-tech recruiters offered him jobs at Apple, Google, Nvidia, and Blackfox. He reported choosing Blackfox because the CEO of the company spoke his language. Respected his philosophies, and allowed him to create real-time scenarios that were only fantasy in the gaming world.

A heady experience for a twenty-three-year-old who'd spent most of his life locked in his bedroom playing video games.

Ant was someone Dakota would have to stay on the right side of if he was going to have success at Blackfox. He decided to let Steele's tech crew sweep his home and protect his devices. He'd been vetted by Blackfox, but needed reassurance his home was a safe electronic domain and hadn't been infiltrated.

He never got comfortable with the digital revolution, and Dakota now understood there were many new ways Big Brother could keep an eye out on his personal life. Even the security cameras he and Billie installed could be breached and used against him.

He felt a wave of paranoia, accepted the emotion, and tamped it down using his training. Primal reactions to unique situations could be the difference between life and death.

CHAPTER 12

Dakota was surveilling Captain Mullrooney's house in his mother's silver BMW convertible parked on Coyote Bluff, a suburb of San Clemente. He decided her ride would blend with the upscale nature of the community. The car's black soft-top was up, and he'd parked in a spot two blocks down from Mullrooney's sprawling California ranch that offered a clean view of the driveway and the captain's front door. A black tile roof accented the sleek, dark blue-shingled house. It was perched on a quarter, acre lot that afforded him a pastoral view of rolling hills.

Where did he get his money was Dakota's first question.

The second: Why the hell was he sitting with eyes on the captain's house in the middle of the day? What was he trying to accomplish? There was no activity on the property, and if the captain was home, it was news to him. A few dog walkers and gardeners paid him no mind as he faked a phone conversation. He'd give it another few minutes and hit the road before someone got suspicious and called the neighborhood's vehicle security company.

He contemplated knocking on the captain's door and confronting the man who ruined his life, but knew it could generate a restraining order from the police department and the wrong kind of publicity. Or he might snap and finish what he started. A losing proposition. He ultimately wanted to see the man in the flesh and get it over with. He'd allowed the killer more than enough time invading his subconscious. Take him down, or cut him loose.

The moment he decided to call it a day, an SUV approached from the rear, turn signal blinking. Dakota slouched in his seat and snapped a picture of the car's license plate as it passed and pulled into the captain's driveway.

A young man hopped out of a matte-gray Mercedes and walked up the stamped concrete path toward the front door. There was something familiar about the man's gait, but Dakota couldn't get a full-face view. The front door swung open as the man reached for the bell.

Captain Mullrooney stepped out onto the covered porch, his ruined right arm had atrophied and hung by his side. He smiled and fist-bumped the man with his left. The visitor had the countenance of a soldier. No surprise there. The captain turned and was followed into the house by his guest.

Dakota's heart pounded as he started the car, executed a tight U-turn, and stilled his breathing as he headed down the hill toward the ocean. He one-handed dialed his aunt's number.

"Dakota, what's up?"

"Hey, Billie. Can you trace a license plate for me? Car's a matte-gray Mercedes SUV."

"Why the interest?"

"I'm in San Clemente doing recon on Mullrooney's crib and don't want to get the Feebs involved."

"You okay?" she said, picking up Dakota's energy level.

"Fine, just trying to get a feel for what the captain's up to, or whether I can cross him off my list. A young dude showed up at his house. I'd like to discover the who, and maybe the why."

"Did he look dirty? Just a friend?"

"Looked military. I doubt Mullrooney has too many friends unless they're like-minded people, or on his payroll.

"My guess, if the captain wrote the check for the contract on my life inside, he knows I've been released. And it doesn't take a genius to find out where I live. The reason Steele hired me in the first place was concern about leaks possibly coming from retired FBI agents."

"Text me the number, I'll see what I can do."

"I'll also send along the captain's address. Love to know how a retired officer can afford the pricey location. Maybe he's got family money. I don't think his Army pension could handle the zip code."

"I'll get on it. Watch yourself."

"Thanks, Billie."

———

There was only one way to the major thoroughfares from Coyote Bluff, and Dakota decided to sit at the end of the road. From there, his target could take the 5, the 405, or PCH. There was a good chance he could catch the Mercedes SUV when the man left the captain's house.

Dakota grabbed an iced Americano and a sandwich from Starbucks and settled into the mall parking lot with a view of Coyote Bluff. He was just bagging the dregs of the ham and cheese sandwich when he picked up the matte-gray car heading in his direction. Dakota tossed the bag on the passenger floor, turned the key, and when he knew what direction the car was headed, pulled out of the lot, and followed, keeping a five-car distance from the target.

The traffic on the 405 was heavy enough to keep an eye on his target, but remain out of the SUV's sightline. Forty-five minutes later, the man exited on Rosecrans heading toward the beach. He pulled a jarring left on PCH and an immediate left on Pine Road.

Dakota slowed on the PCH and eased across Pine, in time to see the taillight of the Mercedes disappear into a building's subterranean parking. Dakota pulled onto Pine, slid to the curb past 369, a four-story upscale condo building. He jumped out and snapped photos of the address on the side of the tiled building, and then a series of unit numbers on the security intercom. He left the scene, pulled to the side of the road, and texted Billie the photos and new information before heading home.

Dakota pulled the BMW into the garage, hit the remote, lowering the metal door, and carefully covered the vehicle. He locked the side door and entered the house through the rear entrance. Dakota re-checked the security alert that arrived on his phone while he was wolfing down his sandwich. He watched a hefty box being placed on his front porch. The man who rang his bell and made the delivery was dressed in street clothes. No UPS or FedEx uniform.

Dakota made a quick stop in the bedroom, grabbed his 9mm, walked out back, and quickly eased down the driveway. His eyes raked the street in both directions. Nothing out of the ordinary caught his eye.

He turned his attention to the package that was secured on the side of the metal rocker out of view of passersby. It looked expensive and was carefully wrapped in silver paper. An envelope was attached to the black ribbon that bound the parcel.

Dakota gave one more look up and down the block, walked onto the porch and carefully untied the ribbon. The envelope was embossed with the Blackfox logo.

He sat on the rocker, opened the envelope, and read the handwritten note from Thomas Wentworth. *"I'm an optimist, Dakota. Come on board. I think you're a perfect fit for my organization, and you'll do well for us both. We'll discuss the signing bonus when next we speak. The swag is yours to keep, whatever you decide. Yours Truly, Thomas Wentworth."*

Dakota walked the box into the kitchen and opened it on the table. There was a black leather jacket with Blackfox discreetly monogramed in black thread on the front. A Blackfox sweatshirt and four Blackfox T-shirts.

Dakota slid into the bomber jacket and wasn't surprised when it fit like a glove. He knew Wentworth had gotten his address from Ralph or Nick, and wasn't worried about the intrusion. His training as a Ranger stressed precision in every move and every waking moment. It was clear that's how the Blackfox organization was run. He could relate.

The kitchen hadn't been fully stocked yet, so he threw a chicken pot pie in the oven and opened a beer. The sun was falling below the tree line and the temperature in Redondo dropped a few degrees. Dakota decided to relax and call it a day.

He'd call Wentworth in the morning, thank him for the gift, and accept his offer. Then reach out to Steele, knowing it would make her day. And tomorrow night, drinks would be on him at the RockPile.

CHAPTER 13

Dakota tucked his Blackfox t-shirt into his jeans, slipped a blue work shirt over it, made sure the house alarm was set, his cell phone charged, and headed out the door. 9:00 p.m. He jumped into the Bronco and backed out of the driveway, executed a two-point turn, and headed down the hill.

A new, white Honda Accord's lights snapped on, and followed the Bronco at a discreet distance.

———

Dakota was standing at the packed RockPile bar. Trish filled the glasses of bourbon and passed the bottle around the room. Dakota pulled back his blue work shirt, revealing the Blackfox logo on his black T-shirt and raised his glass. "To the Wolf Pack!"

The house raised glasses. Ralph locked eyes with Dakota, "To the Wolf Pack!" he intoned. The room repeated the toast. Nick tossed back his shot and shouted. "Wolf Pack!"

"I wouldn't be here without you," Dakota shared with the crew. "I want to make a toast to the man who brought me into the fold. Who saved my life, and paved my way."

Trish filled his shot glass again, smiling with pride.

"To my mentor, Turly. May his last years behind bars go without a hitch, and continue our work!"

"To Turly!" the men shouted.

The bottle was shared and the men moved back toward the pool table and spread out throughout the room. Steppenwolf's, "Born To Be Wild" was blaring on the jukebox.

Dakota took his seat at the bar next to Ralph and Nick and clicked glasses with them. He lowered his voice, "Thank you. You're my brothers. You offered me a new life and paved the way for a job that can help me make up for time lost. I'm in your debt."

The three men clicked glasses and tossed back the bourbon. Trish was on the spot, filling the men's glasses, when the front door opened, letting in a gust of sea air. A scent caught Dakota by surprise, and he went silent. His smile evaporated, staring into the mirror behind the liquor bottles. He wasn't sure at first, and then his eyes narrowed as Sarah Moore entered the room.

Trish asked him, "Are you all right?"

"My ex-fiancé just walked through the door."

Dakota looked at his friends. "I've got to run," he said, knocking back his drink. "Not sure how the woman found me. But no good can come of it. I'll call you. Shit," he said, and dropped three crisp hundred-dollar bills on the bar, slid off the stool, and stepped up to Sarah who looked startled and confused.

"Dakota," was spoken like a question.

"We can't talk here," he shouted over the music. "Please, let's go outside." He held her arm like an old dance partner and guided her out of the raucous bar.

"Fucker looked like he'd seen a ghost," Nick said.

Trish leaned in close to the men. "Said it was his ex-fiancé. Couldn't have ended well, huh? All that time away. Sticky."

"I don't know…could've introduced us," Nick said.

"Cut the man some slack. Christ, Nick," Ralph sneered.

———

Dakota and Sarah walked around the corner and stopped in the parking lot filled with Harleys, muscle cars, trucks, and 4Xs. The sound of Steppenwolf bled out of the bar.

"What are you doing here, Dakota?"

"What are you doing here?" he argued. "How'd you find me?" he said, trying to tamp down his conflicted emotions.

Sarah looked lost, and Dakota's heart throbbed in his throat. She was as beautiful as the day he was dragged out of her life.

"Someone called yesterday. He sounded friendly, like someone I knew, or who knew me, and asked if I'd seen you, that you were back in town. It caught me totally off guard, and I said no. I was about to ask who I was speaking with when he apologized, very politely, said he had an important call on another line, and he'd ring me right back. He didn't." Before Dakota could speak, she went on, "What's up with your new friends?"

"Sarah, this is very important. How did you find me here?"

"I'm embarrassed, but I went to your place. I was afraid to knock on the door and then I saw you drive out in your father's car. I followed. I wasn't thinking straight, I'm sorry…I had to see you."

Sarah stepped closer, and Dakota put his arms around her and pulled her in tight. "Jesus, Sarah. My God." Dakota was at a loss for words. Not surprised at the instant attraction, their chemistry was the cement that bound them together. But he wasn't sure how to move forward. He didn't know what to say, how much to reveal. All the things he couldn't explain without jeopardizing both of their lives. "Where did you park?"

"Down the block."

"Let me drive. I know where we can talk with a little privacy."

Sarah followed him to the Bronco. He opened the passenger door and helped her into the cab. He slid behind the wheel and glanced at the woman who haunted his dreams. He felt her pain, but knew he couldn't reach out. The engine roared to life, and he eased the Bronco onto the street.

He did a slow drive up and down the PCH looking for anyone out of place. Anyone too interested in the RockPile. Satisfied Sarah hadn't been followed to the club, he did a U-turn and powered down the road.

———

Dakota parked the Bronco on the far end of an empty lot at Sunset Beach. The conversation had been sparse on the drive over. Sarah gave him iceberg-tips of her life over the past six years. Married, divorced, no children. She was a buyer in women's fashions at Bloomingdale's, South Coast Plaza, and liked her job. She took full responsibility for the divorce. Said she was trying to find a replacement for a man who couldn't be replaced.

Dakota didn't know how to respond to that piece of information. Six and a half years disappeared for a moment. Left him breathless. He powered down the windows and let the sound of the surf calm them as they stared at sets of waves breaking on the shoreline the way they had during their courtship. It was a spot they'd frequent when important issues were on the table. It wasn't a haphazard choice.

"Aunt Billie called me radioactive the other day," Dakota started. "That about sums it up. I didn't call when I was released because I'm damaged goods, Sarah."

"I don't understand."

"There's a contract out on my life. I cheated death twice in prison, two attempts on my life, and it's followed me home. The call you received, it was a message. They know my history, where I live, who I care about. You. It was a warning. And now you've been pulled into their game."

"Jesus, Dakota."

"There are some people I can contact. I need the exact time the call came in and your phone service. I think we can set up a trace."

Sarah paused for a second. "Yesterday, at seven. *Jeopardy* had just started. And my landline is AT&T."

"Did you notice anyone when you pulled out of your building. Anyone following you? Anyone following you here?"

"No."

"What time did you head over?"

"What time did I head over?" frustrated now.

"Is there someplace safe you can stay for a few days?"

"No!" she snapped, her eyes starting to well up as the dire nature of her situation sunk in. "Jesus, Dakota. What the hell?" She traded her tears for anger, "And you never answered my question. Why were you in that bar? Who are your new friends?" she demanded.

Dakota blew off her question. "Let's get your car, I'll follow you home, and you can pack a bag. Billie has a spare bedroom. She'll be happy to help, and I'll work at getting to the bottom of this. I'm sorry, Sarah. There's nothing else I can say, or do."

"I think you've done enough," she said.

Dakota felt the chill and fought the urge to reach out. Sarah swiped at an errant tear and leaned a stiff back against the seat. "Why the hell did I care? You walked out on me! I should've hung up on the guy."

Sarah got no argument from Dakota whose racing mind tallied the implications of the phone call. None of them were good. He accepted the cold shoulder, started the Bronco, and hit the gas.

———

Billie Judd's house was in Torrance. A nice two-story rambler with white wood-lap siding, brown shutters, and a manicured lawn. The shrubbery was well maintained, and just like a retired cop, the house had an unobstructed 180-degree view of the road in both directions.

Dakota pulled to the curb as Sarah drove her Accord onto Billie's driveway. He opened her door, grabbed her bag out of the back seat, and gave her a piece of paper with his cell phone number on it. "Please use this only in case of an emergency," he said. She tossed it into her purse and followed him up the path toward the house. Billie opened the door, a warm smile on her face, and ushered Sarah in.

"Thank you," Dakota said, handing off her bag and left them to it. He knew Sarah was in good hands.

Billie was a woman who understood if you spent twenty-five years of your life putting away scumbags, one might decide to come back and bite you. "I made up the guest room with clean sheets and towels," she said to Sarah, who was seated at her kitchen table. "Make yourself at home. I know you've had a shock, but things will work themselves out. Dakota filled me in on the situation, and we have to be careful until we know who or what we're dealing with. Not much consolation, I know, but it's the best I can offer. Can I pour you a glass of wine?"

"That would be nice, Billie. Thank you." Sarah looked emotionally drained. Not what she anticipated sitting in front of Dakota's home, wondering what it would be like to rekindle their relationship. It felt like a week ago, but it was only a few hours.

"Red or white?"

"White if it's open."

Billie went to the fridge and grabbed a chilled bottle of chardonnay. She uncorked it, poured two healthy glasses, and joined her at the table.

Sarah took a drink and let out the breath she'd been holding. "It's my fault," she said quietly. "Now they know where Dakota lives. They could have followed me there. I didn't see anyone, but I wasn't looking. Why would I?"

"My best guess, as an ex-cop, they already knew. Whoever it is, they want to punish him. Not just kill him. Dakota is one of the best. He'll figure it out.

"One thing I do know… he won't share any personal information with you. Not now. He'll be operating as a lone wolf until he's got solid answers. Until he's sure of himself, you can't be seen together. It would only put both of your lives in danger. You did nothing wrong, Sarah. You led with your heart. Don't beat yourself up for that."

Dakota was back at Sarah's condo complex. He finished his second drive around the area, in concentric circles, and came up empty. The parking garage was gated and keypad secured. He walked the perimeter of her building and came up empty.

He drove toward his house and parked two blocks away. Pulled the 9mm out of the toolbox he'd locked in the trunk, snugged it in the small of his back, and walked. The neighborhood was quiet at midnight. A few barking dogs, a few night birds, parked cars, nothing out of the ordinary. Nobody was sitting surveillance or hiding in shadow. He circled the block, jumped into the Bronco, and drove home.

Dakota thought it was too late to call Steele, but he'd text her and set up a meeting at Joseph Peluso's office for the morning.

Billie had emailed a name she put with the address on Pine Street, using the reverse phone directory. Doug Darby, ex-Army Ranger, 75th Battalion Sniper. Not much of a surprise there.

Billie was trying to fatten out the man's resume after leaving the force, but came up short. The Army wasn't forthcoming sharing information about their men. The FBI had the reach to help with that. It was time for Agent Steele to lend a hand.

Billie also hit a dead end researching Captain Mullrooney's financial status. Said the banks were tighter than their locked vaults when it came to sharing clients' financials. The search was made more difficult not having the power of the gold shield. It pissed her off.

Dakota knew if Steele agreed to trace the call to Sarah and it matched Doug's cell phone, he'd have a game plan. If not, it was all about keeping his eyes wide-open and expecting the unexpected. Business as usual.

Steele already delivered Mullrooney's street address, with the admonishment that his life had to be in danger before she'd let him go to the FBI "well" again. It wasn't *his* life he was worried about. Sarah was another matter. If the phone call was just a warning, a shot across the bow, to put Dakota on edge, make his life miserable before killing him, she might be okay. Her usefulness already exhausted.

Or…worst case, they might attempt to grab her. Use her as a hostage. He had to run it all by Steele. Sarah was safe with Billie tonight. Tomorrow, he'd see if Steele could assign an agent to watch her condo, something.

Dakota poured a glass of scotch and sat at his computer. He queued up his security camera app, started an hour before he left the house, and watched passing cars through the camera lens with a view of the road.

Nothing caught his eye until he watched himself back out of the driveway and take off for the RockPile. A few seconds later, Sarah's white Honda followed in his wake.

And then nothing. A few neighbors' cars, a few unidentified vehicles that whizzed past, not paying any attention to the house. He fast-forwarded the digital tape, and a half-hour in, a matte-gray Mercedes with dark-tinted windows obscuring the driver did a slow roll up to the house, paused for a moment, and continued out of frame.

Dakota's heart rate quickened. The SUV couldn't have followed Sarah to the RockPile, and then driven back to his house in the documented timeline. This was the first good news of the night. One less thing to worry about.

———

Dakota was scheduled to start work on his first assignment for Blackfox in two days. Senator Bradley and his wife, Shirley, were hosting a fundraiser at their estate in Pasadena. Four hundred guests at a thousand dollars a head, to support his mid-term election. There'd be speeches galore, a jazz band, dance floor, drinks and hors d'oeuvres, leading to a sit-down dinner under the stars.

There were already warnings Black Lives Matter were planning a demonstration outside the front gates of the estate. Dakota was assigned security detail, and would be responsible for checking people off the guest list as they arrived. No name, no entry.

Valet parking would be on scene, and after being cleared by Dakota, the guests would drive up the long cobblestone lane where they'd be greeted by more Blackfox men and women, and the valets would drive their cars back down the rise and park on the street.

A lot of moving parts, a great deal of unknowns.

No way he could be a no-show on his first assignment without getting fired. They'd come a long way in a short amount of time. If it fell apart now, he'd be back in lockup.

He'd check with Billie first thing in the morning, copy Agent Steele on the intel they'd collected to date, and see if she'd lend a hand.

CHAPTER 14

Agent Steele had been aware of the attempt on Dakota's life before she met with him at Greeley Federal Penitentiary. Before she offered him a way out of prison, dangling the chance of a new beginning. His history and response to the attack was part of the equation that made him a premier candidate. She bet her career on it.

And now, he was succeeding beyond expectations. Best laid plans…there are fuck-ups. Goes with the territory. And then there was that unspoken attraction she felt for the man. An attraction she knew could never come to fruition without destroying her career and possibly his life.

So, why was she second-guessing? Was she feeling vulnerable because she'd bared her soul to an ex-convict? Was she losing her edge?

No, no way, she decided. She was schooling Dakota because he was risking his life for her cause and his own self-interest. If he understood her motivation, it would motivate him. That's how a good leader operates.

Dakota walked into the conference room carrying coffee, and ham and cheese croissants.

Agent Steele snapped out of her self-recrimination, grabbed a croissant, and took a hefty bite. "Thanks, I missed breakfast."

"That's what I do."

"What?" she said as she took a sip of coffee.

"Deliver." He grinned and brought her up to speed on the events of the last twenty-four hours.

"You never mentioned Sarah."

"Would it have made a difference?"

Steele gave that a second's thought. "No," she said. "You did the right thing trying to keep your distance. Protect her, protect yourself, and protect the operation. What transpired last night was not on you."

"Good to hear. I think I got a stink eye from Nick, but Ralph and Trish were all in. I picked up the tab and got out clean. Didn't stop Sarah from grilling me later."

"How late?" she asked immediately, regretting the question.

"About eleven. I answered Sarah, by not answering. She took the hint and didn't pursue it any further. She wasn't happy being dropped off at Billie's, or the situation she's caught up in because of me. And became downright prickly when I asked her to stay put at my aunt's until I got a handle on things. Who could blame her?"

Steele gave a commiserating nod. "I'll have to run it by Chase, but under the circumstances, I don't think the boss will say no to tracing the call. The threat's real, and I'm sworn to protect you. It might take a few days once approved, but I'll get back to you on that."

"Sounds good."

"I'll try and cut Mitchel and Stevens loose. Let one of them stake out Sarah's house, and the other, keep an eye on Billie's the next few days."

"Thank you."

"Let me know how it goes when you speak with her. Best-case scenario, she stays with Billie, where she'll be safe. But she can't get in our way."

"I'll do my best." Dakota didn't sound convinced.

"You know I've got to run the information you texted me up the flagpole. Excellent work on both of your parts. Billie must have been a good cop. I'll try and keep control of the new case. The fact the SUV was caught on tape scouting your house overlaps with Blackfo*x*, and makes it my case. You won't be any good to me dead. But I can't promise Chase will let me run with it. He won't want me stretched thin. There's too much at stake."

"I love it when you get all analytical on me," was met with chilly eyes that made him smile, and Steele not.

"I start at Blackfox in the morning," Dakota reminded her.

"Don't I know it? I don't want you worrying about Sarah tomorrow. I need you clearheaded. I'll make sure she's well taken care of. As long as she's not aware you're working for the FBI, we should be okay. Good work, Dakota. And knock-em-dead tomorrow. The senator's fundraiser is the big leagues. And you're ready for the challenge."

––––––––––

Agent Will Chase looked pensive, drumming his middle finger on the desk strewn with paperwork. Steele wasn't sure what his response to her requests was going to be, but wasn't about to interrupt his thought process.

"I'm going to give you some good news, and then walk you back a few steps, Jean. I'll give you Mitchel and Stevens for a few days. Use them as you see fit. The trace on the phone, a no-brainer. Go for it. We knew the risks when we hired the man. I agree, through no fault of his own, our entire enterprise was put in jeopardy. But it appears we've come out of it unscathed."

"So far so good, Will," she said, waiting for the bad news.

"Dakota and his ex-cop aunt have to stop moonlighting. If he won't let us take the lead and run with the good work he's already done, we'll pick him up after the fundraiser tomorrow and he'll be headed back to Greeley."

"He's got to be able to protect himself if it comes to that."

"No argument there. But he must be willing to curtail any offensive moves, and call you first if there are any issues that endanger his life, or the life of Sarah Moore."

Steele rolled that around for a moment too long. At least she wasn't pulled off the case.

"It's non-negotiable, Agent Steele."

"Understood," she said, and turned to leave before he heaped on more restrictions.

She was stopped in her tracks: "Try and keep things as simple as this complicated case will allow. I think Dakota understands what's at stake. Let's hope he's able to control his instincts and put his trust in the company."

"Your words to…"

"The FBI's ears," he said, finishing her thought.

―――――

"Bullshit," Dakota said to Agent Steele who was driving her brown, Government-Issue sedan from FBI headquarters to her condo in Manhattan Beach. It was the end of her day, and she found herself locked in traffic, and being squeezed in a conversation that set her nerves on edge.

"We've got the man's name, address, the car he drives, and his connection to the captain. He's an ex-Ranger for Christ's sake." Dakota glared at his "special" cell phone and looked like he wanted to throw it out of the Beemer's window.

"Billie did terrific work," she said. "She's a great ex-cop. And that's another part of the equation that has to stop. Today. She's being ordered to cease-and-desist."

"Billie will love that."

Steele soldiered through the sarcasm. "You've done exemplary work, Dakota. I understand the impulse, but you're working with the FBI now, and you have to let the FBI do what we do best. And that's run the guy to ground, if he's our man. Agent Chase is fair, but intractable. No wiggle room."

"By the impulse, you mean trying to save my own life?"

"If our suspect comes after you and you're in immediate, life-threatening danger, then, of course, protect yourself with any means possible. Any other situation, Dakota, if you get jammed up, you contact me. Me," she repeated. "I'm your first line of defense. I will rally the troops. Protect your cover. Keep you alive. But you can't go looking for trouble."

"Or what? Your boss will pull the plug. With the relationships we've forged and success we've already delivered."

"You'll be back in the federal pen folding sheets before the wine glasses are bussed tomorrow night. I'm sorry, Dakota. Too many man-hours in, too much money spent, and now, the added liability of Sarah, a civilian."

"They would destroy your career?"

"In a heartbeat."

"That's harsh."

"That's my life. But hey, we're putting a trace on the call to Sarah, and Mitchel and Stevens have been assigned to keep an eye on Billie's house and Sarah's condo. Hopefully she'll stay put, and we can keep her safe."

They sat in silence for a while, waiting for the other to speak. Dakota blinked first.

"You keep Sarah alive, I'll keep my powder dry."

"Good to hear, Dakota."

"Keep your phone charged." He clicked off and watched through the car's windshield as the matte-gray Mercedes pulled out of the condo building's underground parking, drove up Pine Street, and disappeared in traffic on the Pacific Coast Highway.

"Son of a bitch!" Dakota shouted. He fumed for a few minutes, sucked in a breath, turned the radio to KJazz 88.1, and headed for home.

———

"We're off the case," Dakota told Billie as he powered down the Pacific Coast Highway. "Steele complimented the work you did, but we were handed a cease-and-desist order from on high. They threatened to send me back inside if they discover I'm not in compliance."

"I'm not surprised," Billie sounded deflated. She was in her den, sitting in front of her computer reading an archival *LA Times* story, and hit delete. "The Feds are good at what they do. They might be able to shut the guy down; if it turns out he's our hired gun."

"Were you able to talk to Sarah about taking vacation time, or sick leave at Bloomingdale's? I know the job's important to her."

"I tried, she said no. Went upstairs to take a nap, and came down to say, yes. She called in sick, said they were great about it, and it made her feel guilty. We're going to drive over to her place and let her pack a few more things. She's a doll. Are you going to call her?"

"Not right away. There's nothing I can say that'll make things better."

"I tried to explain that to her last night. I think she heard me."

"And FYI, Steele set up an agent with eyes on your house, and another at Sarah's place. So don't go rousting anybody. That's all we'd need."

"I can smell a Fed a mile away. Watch your back tomorrow. Keep your guard up and your head low. This is your first test at Blackfox. You'll do okay."

"Better than sitting around, waiting on a bullet."

"Man speaks the truth."

"Out."

CHAPTER 15

Senator Jack Bradley's estate was located in the hills of Pasadena overlooking the Rose Bowl. The twenty-thousand-square-foot Spanish Revival sat on eight opulent acres with an Olympic-sized pool, manicured gardens, and two tennis courts that were set off in one corner of the massive grounds.

Tables were arranged in a semicircle around the dance floor and raised podium. Four bars spaced on the four corners of the lawn, poured premium liquor and the sound of margaritas being blended filled the air, along with the twelve-piece jazz band that played in the background.

Black-tied waiters delivered hors d'oeuvres and champagne to the couples as they stepped from the house onto the lawn, checked their table numbers, and looked for their names on their place settings. Some donors were pleased, others, necks swiveling, were ready to lodge a complaint.

The well-dressed donors in attendance were there to write checks, curry political favor, and support their favorite United States Senator that was willing and able to keep the selfie camera shuttering. They also knew, he and his wife Shirley threw one hell of a party and if the social gods were shining, their faces would appear in every local newspaper and magazine in Orange County.

———

Dakota Judd leaned toward the Bentley convertible as the tinted window rolled down. His face split into a grin. "Terrance Gorman."

"Why am I not surprised," Terrance said without rancor.

Dakota checked him off the list. "You're good to go, Mister Gorman."

"No harm, no foul?" Terrance asked, repeating the phrase Dakota spoke in the basement of the RockPile at the joint militia meeting.

"Sounds about right to me, Terrance. Enjoy," he said, letting the leader of the Wolverine Watchmen off the hook.

Dakota straightened up and watched the Bentley roll past the iron gates and up the trail toward the house, and caught the vanity plate on the rear of the car. T-Gorman. Dakota turned and waved a Jaguar forward.

The shouted cries of the Black Lives Matter group fought against the smooth jazz emanating from the party above. The wife of Senator Bradley sauntered down the granite stairs, tossed her red hair off her shoulders catching Dakota's eye, and waved him over. She was a woman who lent credence to the phrase fifty is the new forty. Stunning, he thought.

Dakota handed his leather-bound clipboard to James, who was showing him the ropes, and stepped up to the host of the party.

She glanced seductively at Dakota and read his embossed nametag. "Hi Dakota, my name is Shirley. And you work for me today."

Dakota flashed a relaxed smile. "Pleased to be here, ma'am."

"Good to hear, son. Question?"

"Ma'am."

"Could you do something about those people down on the street, causing trouble for our guests?"

"I'll do what I can," Dakota answered smoothly and started walking down the driveway toward the protesters.

"Dakota?"

He turned on his heel.

"Blue pill or red pill?"

"Oh… I've been red-pilled, ma'am. All the way."

"Good to hear, Dakota. And great name, sir." Shirley glanced down at the placard carrying African Americans. "I find them so unattractive," she said, and winked. It was the subtlest sexual move he'd ever experienced, and it dripped with comfortable racism.

Dakota accepted her come-on with grace, and headed down the driveway to check out the protesters. He made a mental note to thank Agent Steele for her reading material.

Red pill was a reference to the movie, *The Matrix*. In the film, the blue pill designated living a life filled with comfortable lies. The red pill was living with difficult truths. For the racists, the red pill was code for a society that conspired to keep the white man down.

Dakota paused in the driveway as the valet parkers rolled down the exit curve in the cobblestone road, drove past the protesters, and parked in an ever-expanding line of luxury vehicles.

He heard the Wolf Pack's Harleys before he saw them, as they rounded a curve in the road. Six tattooed, bearded men, on tricked-out motorcycles, revved their throaty beasts and pierced the crowd, causing them to split ranks and let the marauders pass. Ralph, in worn leather regalia looking like a wild man, and Nick in a Hawaiian shirt, with two full sleeves of tattoos, locked eyes with Dakota without a sign of recognition, as they drove past, leaving rumbling exhaust and angry protestors in their wakes.

Dakota walked up to the African American woman who appeared to be in charge of the twenty-or-so marchers.

"Hi, my name's Dakota."

"Sherry," she said with veiled suspicion, glancing at the Blackfox T-shirt under his black sports jacket. And a familiar bulge under his arm she recognized as a concealed weapon.

"You all have every right to be protesting here. I'm aware you have valid paperwork. I'm wondering if you would do us a favor and stand on either side of the road, making it easier for the guests to get into the party. It will save you a ton of hassle. And trouble's the last thing I want to see on such a beautiful day."

Dakota spoke with such sincerity and strength; Sherry fought the urge to resist his request. Instead, "Believe it or not, I just don't want to see anyone get hurt. I'll see what I can do."

"Thank you. Stay safe," Dakota said and walked back toward the entrance of the compound. He glanced over his shoulder and saw Sherry speaking with her group, and then the protesters moving to the sides of the road allowing the donors' cars to drive smoothly into the event.

Dakota relieved James and took control of the list, as a bright electric-green Lotus pulled up to the gate and rolled down the window. "What the hell did you say to them?" Ant asked, amazed.

"That there'd be hell to pay if they didn't calm the fuck down."

"Damn." And Ant drove past the gates.

Shirley stood at the top of the stairs and watched the action below. She liked what she saw. A man with finesse, hmmm. She turned, raked her long red hair with a delicate hand and manicured nails that matched her lip gloss, and walked back into the house.

———

The party was in full swing. Dinner plates were being bussed, the wine was flowing freely, and the band amping-up the already festive mood. Senator Bradley and Thomas Wentworth were doing a walk and talk away from the tables. The senator picked up a yellow tennis ball his wife's pro left after her tri-weekly lessons. She wasn't getting any better, but it kept her body in shape, his libido in high gear, and was well worth the investment.

He squeezed it like a stress ball: "I'm fielding at least six phone calls a day. Wives, lawyers, kids, family of the men, all crying, demanding I do something. Anything to get their men out of that stinking Venezuelan prison and home. Jerry Moran has a bad ticker and has lost twenty pounds. If he dies behind bars, I might as well give my donors back their money, because I'm going to lose the election. Bill Vincent has four kids, all girls, who've set up a website to keep their father alive. The site has been visited over a million times, and growing."

"What does the White House have to say?"

"Say? You really think they're going to take responsibility for backing Nicolas Guaido? And since when did Maduro's government have issues accepting five million dollars delivered in brown paper bags? They created the La Mordida business model. Bribes are their fucking middle name. Now they've got the temerity to use it against us. Taking the high road."

"What about the Secretary of State?"

"He's in Afghanistan, and after his visit to Iran, he goes back to Israel, and promises to get right on it. It's been two months of asks. The man doesn't get right on anything unless it's on presidential orders. He's like a damn lap dog. We need muscle. And we need it soon."

"I'll come up with a proposal and have something for you next week."

The senator nodded his head and went on, "I mean we backed the wrong horse, and we're stuck holding an empty saddle, and down five million.

"I had to cajole six senators in the Appropriations Committee to dig into their slush fund and do the right thing, and now I've got egg on my face. My name's all over the Rentex Petroleum deal, and their stock has dropped twelve percent in the fourth quarter. Insult to injury. I need a drink."

He got no argument from Wentworth.

The men strolled off the tennis courts and started walking across the lawn toward one of the portable bars.

————

Dakota and James were headed in the men's direction. Wentworth wanted to introduce Dakota to the senator after Shirley extolled the new hire's virtues.

"Is that the new man Shirley spoke of?" the senator asked.

"Name's Dakota. I think he's going to work out."

————

Dakota was enjoying the festive mood, and James was keeping him on the straight and narrow. They were the hired help. Nothing more, nothing less, he repeated for the umpteenth time. He checked his watch and leaned into Dakota, "Shake the senator's hand, and then we'll blend with the crowd," he said and stopped in place, letting Dakota walk ahead and take center stage.

Twenty-five feet from the senator, Dakota felt the hair rise on the back of his neck.

A mirrored flash of light reflected the waning sun from the ridge above.

Dakota started running. Sprinting toward the men who looked a question, and then shock.

He dove. Collared both men around their waists, his momentum knocked them to the ground.

Wentworth fought as the cracking sound of a high-velocity round punched a large divot in the green grass sending a shower of dirt flying, where the men had been standing.

A second shot rang out.

The bartender dove for cover as his bar exploded. Glass, bottles, and champagne flutes, stacked pyramid high, shattered.

The panicked crowd screamed and knocked over chairs and tables, sending plates flying as they ran for the safety of the house.

Dakota jumped to his feet, "Call in a bird," he ordered James, who had drawn his weapon and pulled out his phone while Dakota took off running for the back wall.

Dakota leapt onto the eight-foot stone wall, rolled over and down, setting off an alarm that pierced the cries of the panicked crowd.

The climb up the ridge through a copse of trees, and a thicket of bushes, and undergrowth made the fifty-yard climb to a neighbor's mansion more difficult. Dakota pulled his 9mm out of his leather shoulder rig, and stopped for a second. Listened. Then continued on.

He blasted up the final twenty feet, scaled the neighbors' wall landing in a garden. The imposing house was set back from the slope. He heard and saw nothing. He spoke into his radio, "James, let the cops know I'm here, and armed. Nothing yet."

"Our team's on the way. I'm locking the scene down."

"Block all the exit roads, and get a bird here ASAP."

"Out!"

Dakota moved along the ridgeline looking for a nest, the place where the shooter made his assault. At the end of the property, there was a firebreak in the overgrown foliage, which had a slight view of the senator's tennis courts and a narrow piece of the grassy area leading up to the tennis courts. On the backside of the fence, he discovered an area the sniper could have set up. The wild grass was bent, and there were two indentations where the shooter could have been kneeling when he pulled the trigger. He stepped back from the wall and discovered a footprint the shooter might have left behind as he leapt over the wall and made his escape.

Dakota snapped a photo with his cell phone and stayed clear of the scene, not wanting to contaminate any evidence left behind. He ran toward the mansion that appeared to be empty, and made his way along the side of the brick wall toward the front of the property and the road beyond.

A car filled with kids drove past, and then two more. People oblivious to the terror-filled party below, and the attempt on the life of a United States Senator.

An SUV came careening around the corner and skidded to a stop as eight Blackfox employees dismounted and hit the ground running, weapons drawn. Dakota gave them an instant briefing, warning them away from the back wall until a forensic team arrived. The men spread out, hunting for the shooter.

A Pasadena Police Department helicopter arrived on scene, roared overhead, flying low, detritus churning into the air as a thousand-watt spotlight raked the shadows of the old-growth trees surrounding the mansion and the neighboring properties.

The senator's head of security arrived. Derik Traina was a worried man. He listened to Dakota and followed him to the possible shooting nest and the footprint. "My men have been up here scouting the ridge multiple times, and never caught this angle. Heads will roll."

The alarm from the senator's property echoed across the ridgeline of multi-million-dollar estates as Traina got the sheriff on the phone. He requested a full forensic team, and backups for the Blackfox group to interview every household, check every security camera of every estate up and down the hill, and then start on the retailers on the main drag below.

Dakota fielded a call from James as two local news choppers started circling the area. He filled him in on the details as neighbors from both sides of the mansion started congregating, checking out the intrusion, and found themselves being interviewed by Blackfox employees.

"As soon as the dust settles," James said. "The senator wants you to stop by the house. He's in shock, but wants to personally extend his gratitude."

"How's Wentworth holding up?"

"Better than I expected. You knocked the piss out of both men. I saw Wentworth struggle with you until he understood the situation. Didn't know he had it in him."

"I was on autopilot."

"You haven't lost a beat."

"Thanks, man."

"I'll let you get back to it."

Dakota walked over to the senator's head of security.

Derik Traina was wringing his hands, his brow furrowed with deep slashes, waiting on the PPD, the FBI, and the PPD's forensic teams to arrive. The man had a lot of explaining to do.

"I'm going to need you to stick around," he said. "They'll all want a preliminary report. Damn fine work, Dakota."

Dakota nodded his thanks and took a step away from the action. His heart rate had slowed some, and his breathing returned to normal. His response had been instinctual. He was only doing what the United States Army had trained him to do.

One of the television birds came in for a closer pass. Dakota stepped into shadow. No need to have his face plastered around the country. Any news coverage could only bring up his past and complicate his mission. He'd give all the credit, if asked, to Blackfox.

CHAPTER 16

I t was still and quiet in the hills of Pasadena by the time Traina dropped Dakota at the front door of the senator's home. Dakota had given the Feds a preliminary statement with a promise of a second, the financial donors, the jazz band, the valet drivers, and the caterers were long gone. A few of the Blackfox crew were walking the perimeter of the property. They looked Dakota over and hand signaled the okay sign. He wondered if it held the same double meaning he came to understand in prison, and decided yes, of course it did.

He rang the bell, which set off a series of deep melodic chimes. The thick, carved, mahogany door was opened by Shirley herself. Her eyes were red, and she forced a polite smile as she straightened her back, challenging her emotional state. "Thank you, Dakota. Jack's in the den waiting for you. What a day."

"We've had better."

"It could've been so much worse." Wet tears filled her hazel eyes. "Let me take you back," she said.

Dakota followed Shirley through the massive house he was seeing for the first time and it was clear the senator came from old money. The craftsmanship was beautifully rendered. The rooms, larger than expected. The intricate Spanish tile work and chiseled wood beams, impeccable. The rugs, finer than he was accustomed to. The furniture and art, surprisingly modern, he even recognized a few of the artists. And they were all originals.

"Beautiful home," he said to Shirley.

"It all means nothing," she said, tearing up again. "Did I thank you?"

"You did, ma'am."

"Please don't call me ma'am," she said without any anger, more a touch of humor. "Shirley works just fine. Or Mrs. Bradley, if you're really inclined. I won't hold it against you. Here we are." She opened the door a crack and said, "Dakota's here, Jack…"

"Send him in, hon."

Shirley pushed the door open the rest of the way and let Dakota enter the finest den he'd ever walked into.

Senator Bradley stood, glass of scotch in his hand, looking none the worse for wear. "Come in, Dakota. Your boss here made me open a bottle of 25-year-old Macallan."

Dakota smiled at Thomas Wentworth, who looked like he'd imbibed more than a few drinks. He stood, but let the senator have the floor.

"How do you thank a man who has just saved your life?"

"Well, first, offer the man a drink," Wentworth barked, eliciting a laugh from Bradley.

"Right you are. I was going to get all poetic on you, but I'll just go and pour you a drink, if that's to your liking."

"The day we've had, I think it's perfect."

"Well spoken," the senator said, and poured more than two fingers into a crystal glass. "Rocks?"

"No sir. Neat."

"He passed the test, Thomas."

"I told you he would."

The senator handed Dakota his drink, the three men stepped close, and clinked glasses. "To life," Senator Jack Bradley said, with a resonant voice. Not sappy, just a recognition that the three men had been through one hell of a day, and life was better than the alternative.

"To life," Dakota and Jack intoned.

The three men took a sip of ridiculously fabulous scotch and appreciated the moment.

———

Billie walked into her living room carrying a bowl of fresh popcorn with melted butter. Sarah grabbed a handful and glanced up at the television screen for a second time.

"Was that Dakota?" she asked, startled.

Billie read the NBC crawl reporting an assassination attempt on the life of Senator Jack Bradley occurred at a fundraiser at his compound in Pasadena.

"I wasn't looking at the TV."

"Play it back," Sarah demanded.

Billie tamped down her knee-jerk reaction to the attitude, grabbed the remote, hit rewind, and waited for what seemed like forever, until the crawl ran again.

An on-air reporter, standing outside the senator's estate, turned toward the camera in a studied move: "This afternoon, during Republican Senator Jack Bradley's fundraiser, being held at his estate in Pasadena, there was a foiled assassination attempt on his life."

The screen cut to a jerky cell phone video that captured crazy mayhem as panicked men and women stampeded across the lawn running for their lives, out of range of the gunman's deadly bullets. "The senator and Thomas Wentworth were escorted into the house by security guards as police hunted for the sniper."

The story cut to the upper ridgeline, where the killer might have laid in wait. The helicopter's camera traced back and forth across the mansion that provided cover for the shooter, and the arrival of the Sheriff's department and the FBI.

"There," Sarah shouted.

A man who appeared to be Dakota, lowered his head and stepped into shadow as the camera lens panned across the scene, pushing in on the arriving sheriff's vehicles and the uniformed men and women who disembarked and fanned out, searching the neighborhood for the shooter.

The channel cut to a commercial.

"Might have been," Billie said noncommittal.

"It was Dakota. Why was he there, Billie?"

"Not sure. But it damn well could've been him."

"It was Dakota," Sarah hammered.

"He just got hired by a security firm, and today was his first day at work. He didn't tell me what he was up to, what the assignment was, or any more than he felt the job would help get him back on his feet."

"I like you, Billie. You've reached out at a time of need. But if you lie to me again, I'll leave tonight."

Billie didn't appreciate being pressed, and let loose with twenty-five years as an LAPD detective. "That's up to you, Sarah. I can't stop you. I will not speak for Dakota. I owe him that much respect, and from where I sit, so do you. He's got important work to do, and when he's ready to share, if he wants to share, he will. If you keep prying, you'll put his life in danger, and yours. The man's been locked up for six years and three months."

"I know how long he's been locked up!'

"Then you'll understand when I say he needs space and time to work things out. If you ever cared for the man, now is the time to prove it."

Sarah accepted Billie's dressing down and wasn't sure why she was so emotional. Dakota was his own man. She was the one who infiltrated his life. She was responsible for the danger she found herself in and Dakota, and Billie, had already given more than was required.

Billie switched channels and they watched *Jimmy Kimmel Live*, and ate popcorn. Eventually, they laughed at one of his one-liners.

"Sorry," Sarah said.

"Apology accepted."

———

Agent Steele was tense, leaning forward on her couch watching the news on CNN when her phone rang. She knew it wasn't Dakota because it was her work line. Agent Chase's private number. She clicked on, and before she could speak:

"Have you been watching the news?"

"It's on," she said a little terse.

"I fielded a call from Ted Larrabee, nice guy out of the Pasadena office. He was on scene. Good to have friends."

"What do you have, what do you know?"

"Wasn't Dakota supposed to be working there today?"

"What's up boss?" She said knowing damn well he knew, and tried to keep the frustration out of her voice.

"Blackfox was there doing security?"

"Will!"

"Our boy's a hero."

Silence, waiting for more, and then, "You're serious."

"Tackled the senator and Thomas Wentworth at the same time. Knocked them to the ground, saved their lives, then ran up the hill, found the shooter's nest, and well, the damn guy saved the day. Unbelievable. You still there, Jean?"

"I'm here. It's a lot to process."

"All good. And good on you. Get together with our boy ASAP. He's in like Flynn at Blackfox now. Any word from Mitchel and Stevens?"

"I just sent them home for the night. All clear at both locations."

"Some more good news. Sleep tight, Jean. We'll talk tomorrow."

Steele went into the kitchen and poured herself a glass of wine. She toasted the television screen, paused the picture, a second before Dakota stepped back into shadow, and knew she wouldn't get any sleep until her private line rang.

———

Steele didn't hear the phone on the first ring, but fumbled for it and placed it to her ear. She wasn't sure how long she'd been asleep, but was ready to talk.

"Jean… I wish we could hang out," Dakota said, his voice husky.

Steele took in the import of the statement. And before she overthought her reply, said, "I know."

Dakota and Steele sat in silence. Breathing on both ends. He could hear her intake of breath, and she could hear his slow exhale. He gently broke the silence.

"You've taught me things that saved my life today. Allowed me to be in the right place to change my life, and save another. I don't know what it means or how it happened. But I'm grateful."

Dakota clicked off, and Steele set down her phone. Making a mental note to remind herself she hadn't dreamt the conversation.

CHAPTER 17

Thomas Wentworth, never a man at a loss for words, looked across his power desk at the man who might have saved his life, along with the senator's.

"Just know, Dakota, I let the senator have the floor last night, but I have much to be grateful for. If I had taken one step ahead or behind Jack, the bullet would have cut us both down.

"And between the two of us…the bullet might have been directed at me. Running Blackfox, I've made more than my share of enemies. It was just a passing thought…one that I've heard occurs in men involved in near-death experiences. My guess…they wanted the senator.

"And I take no joy in that," Wentworth said, flashing a smile that met his eyes. "How are you holding up? Any damage?"

"A few cuts, some bruises. You put up quite a fight."

"And then I heard a high velocity round whiz past my head. Shocking. Heart stopping. I loosened my grip."

"I appreciated it, sir."

Both men smiled. One cheated death; the other foiled the attempt. They were both winners.

"So, where do we go from here?" Wentworth said. "Your first day will be hard to replicate. And I usually work my men and women for six months before I hand out plum assignments."

"I've spent so much time behind bars, whatever you've got, wherever you need me, my bags are packed. I know you won't waste my training."

"You're right about that. I've been looking for someone to move up through the ranks. And after last night, I think I've found my man. After your exemplary show yesterday, you are now at the top of my list. You've got the skill set, and if all goes according to plan, we can change the world. Make me believe. Let's make this work."

"I'm all in, sir. The last six years I lived with a spike in my heart. I'm grateful for the opportunity. And I'll work my ass off to make you a believer."

"Senator Bradley's sold. And we have a mission that needs your kind of talent and background. I won't go into it today, let's take some time to recuperate, and we'll continue this conversation."

"Thank you, sir."

"And stop by Ant's office on your way out. Young man was impressed beyond belief. He's smart and a serious player. Someone who's essential to the success of our team."

"Will do, sir."

Dakota turned on his heel and headed for Ant's office.

———

Ant was sitting at his bank of screens. He glanced up, and a big smile lit up his young face. "You are the fucking man. I could not believe my eyes. I saw you sailing through the air like a damn rocket, and taking down the boss and the senator, and you all lived to tell the story. I was so pissed."

"Why is that?" Dakota asked, not knowing where Ant was going.

"It happened too quick to pull out my phone. I got some real-time images of four hundred tables being emptied in one massive stampede that made the news, but I missed the real action. I hate when that happens."

"I'll let you know next time I'm in the thick of it."

"Trust me, Dakota. When you work for us, you'll be wearing a camera, and you and I will be in communication if things go sideways. I'll keep you alive, and you'll come out looking like the fucking hero you are."

"Let's not get ahead of ourselves."

"Right," he said as if he was privy to information that hadn't been shared with Dakota yet.

"I'll let you get back to it. I look forward to working together."

"Back at you, Dakota. Back at you."

Ant dove into his computer screen and was lost in his work before Dakota had cleared the doorway.

———

"What did he say?" Steele asked as she knifed a smear of cream cheese across an onion bagel and took a bite. They were back at Joseph Peluso's office, and Steele was executing a casual deposition of Dakota.

"Thought I might have saved his life, and as payback, he was ready to change mine."

"Does Wentworth think he was the target?"

"Not really. But he knows if he'd taken a wrong step and I hadn't been there to make a difference, one bullet could have taken them both out."

"A reasonable assumption."

Dakota nodded. "Dangled moving me up through his ranks. Fast-tracking me. I think the man's looking for the son he never had, and I might be the anointed one. I'll have to prove myself, but he believes things happen for a reason. I didn't dissuade him."

"This is impressive."

"The bagel? I thought we should broaden our culinary chops."

"Funny man. What did he have in mind?"

"I'm not sure. He's working on a project with the senator. Didn't go into details but thinks I'm a good fit."

They ate in silence for a moment. The intimacy of the late-night call was on the back burner. This was a business meeting, and they both respected the parameters of that relationship.

"Ant is big-time in the organization," Dakota said. "Too smart for his own good, but a reputation and skills to match that are important to Blackfox. He's already a fan, but someone I can't take for granted. You should check him out. Alt-right social media sites, the whole nine yards, because I think he's going to be the difference between life and death on my next mission. I'd like to know if he's on any of the FBI files. And just a thought... I need one of your men to check out my house, my computer, phone, cars, and security system. Ant is so good, he could become dangerous."

"Done. Have you spoken to Billie?"

"Next call I'm making."

"Let her know I can keep Mitchel and Stevens in play for a few more days. So far, so good. Let's hope the interest in Sarah just fades away."

"What if it doesn't?"

"It has to."

"Hmm. Any word on the phone trace?"

"It was made from a burner."

"Shit, what about Mullrooney's financial status? Is there any way we can get a look at his bank statements?"

"Not on a hunch. On a positive note, Agent Chase is a big fan of yours as of yesterday. You're making him look good."

"As long as it works for you."

"It does, Dakota. I'm proud to be in business with you."

"It's a two-way street, Jean."

"Did you save a bagel for me?" Joseph Peluso appeared at the door, interrupting their conversation and insinuating himself into the bag of bagels. "I was watching the news last night," he directed at Dakota. "And saw a man I thought I recognized"

"Really?"

"Who looked a lot like you. At the scene of an assassination attempt on Senator Bradley."

"Really? Looked like me?"

"Guy never really showed his face, almost like he knew the chopper was shooting overhead and didn't want to be seen."

"Strange." Dakota was playing it serious. "Indigenous people believe if you let someone take your picture, they'll steal your soul. There might be something to that."

"Good bagel," Peluso said, wiping cream cheese off the side of his mouth. Knowing he wasn't going to get the real story until he cornered his old friend alone.

———

Dakota and Steele stood in silence at the elevator. The doors whooshed open, they stepped in and the doors closed. He walked Steele to her car. "We'll talk," she said.

Steele was about to get in but turned.

Dakota stepped close and kissed her.

Steele gave way to the moment, wrapped her arms around his waist, and pulled him in tighter. She kissed Dakota with a passion that caught them both by surprise. They broke the clinch before losing control. Steele took a step back. "That will never happen again," she said, her gaze tight.

"Damn," Dakota said, breathless, knowing there was no other reasonable decision to be made.

Steele slid into her car and shut the door. She turned over the engine, glanced out, locked frustrated eyes with Dakota, pulled out of her space, and drove down the ramp, tires squealing on the tight curves.

CHAPTER 18

Billie pulled her Corvette gingerly into the lot of Red's Tow and Police Impound. There were scattered potholes that kept Billie on her toes not wanting to stress her vintage car. She pulled to a stop at the small flat-roofed, cinderblock structure that served as Red's office.

Red stepped out wearing a big grin. "Lieutenant, you moonlighting?"

"Fishing for a favor, Red."

Red's hair was one shot short of rust. His face, a mass of freckles that overpowered his pale white skin. His accent was Cockney but his manner upper crust.

"I owe you a few. I won't kill anyone though."

"Hah! Not on my list. I'm in the market for a beater that might not make it back alive. And then again, eh…hard to say."

Red didn't have to think twice. "'83 Chevy Cavalier. I let my nephew drive it when he's in town. You wouldn't notice it being out of place, because you wouldn't notice it. And I won't miss it, one way or the other."

"Sounds like a winner."

"I wouldn't go that far, but it'll take you to Vegas and back and when you're done, text me the address and I'll have one of my men pick it up."

Billie pulled out her credit card, and Red waved it away. "Your money's no good at my shop."

"Thank you."

"You were a good cop, Billie. Keep yourself in one piece."

Billie nodded and got into her car. "I'll be back in a few days."

"Your chariot awaits, ma'am. You ever want to sell your baby, put me on the front of your list. I'll pay over the going rate."

"I'm gonna be buried in this sweet ride."

"Not too soon, I hope."

"I'll do what I can, Red." Billie turned over the V-8. The throaty sound echoed as Billie rolled off the lot and left a tire-burning strip of rubber as she hit Grand Avenue.

———

Sarah's white Honda darted in and out of traffic. She drove with a heavy foot and Billie cursed below her breath as she tried to keep her distance, but not lose her. Not an easy feat driving Red's, '83 Chevy Cavalier.

Sarah had spent three more nights at Billie's, and the following day the FBI pulled Mitchel and Stevens off surveillance. Sarah had to have been on the same wavelength because she announced at breakfast it was time to go back to work and time to move home. She fought the urge to reach out to Dakota, taking heed of Billie's advice.

Dakota was furious. Billie had mixed emotions. Her house seemed to lose square footage with the opinionated young woman living in the spare bedroom. She told Dakota she'd follow Sarah home from work and take over the FBI's place on the street. She never minded sitting surveillance, but her bones got stiff sitting in a lumpy bucket seat, and she felt every year of fifty-eight.

Nothing was happening, but Billie refused to give up the assignment until she felt sure the young woman was out of danger. She knew the men hunting for Dakota wouldn't give up the fight if they believed

Sarah was the key to setting him up. If they killed her, it might be the death of her nephew. Just the notion, too much to bear.

"Shit," she said, when the Chevy got locked in behind some boob who stopped on a yellow light. She hit the gas when it changed to green and tortured the four-cylinder engine, rattling the old car's frame.

She pulled onto Sarah's street just as the Honda disappeared into the parking structure of her building.

An electric charge surged down Billie's neck as a matte-gray Mercedes pulled to the curb a few doors down from the condo.

Billie had the make, model, and license memorized and eased to the curb, waiting.

The man in the Mercedes turned off his engine, and the rear brake lights blinked off.

As the door to the Mercedes cracked open, Billie hit the gas. The four cylinders responded, moving toward 25 mph.

The old Cavalier smashed into the rear of the German SUV.

Billie was prepared for the impact. The driver, not so lucky.

The airbag exploded into the stunned man's face. White powder blinded him. The force of the collision swung the door fully open as a passing gardener's truck ripped it off its hinges.

Billie ran out of the Cavalier with her Colt Detective Special held at her side, while the truck kept right on down the street.

"What the fuck?" the startled man asked.

Billie backhanded her pistol across the man's forehead. Blood spurted from the open wound. She pressed the barrel of the Colt against the man's temple, and as blood streamed down the man's face, Billie caught her breath and started talking through clenched teeth.

"We know who you are, dipshit. Who you work for. The platoon you were connected to, and where you were deployed the last four years."

"You're dead," sounded weak coming from a Ranger who'd been bested by a woman, and was bleeding all over his sixty-grand car's leather seats.

Billie continued undeterred. "Time for you to find a new line of work, douchebag. You suck at being muscle."

"I'm calling the police."

"I am the police dickwad. Now stop talking and listen. It's the only way you'll come out of this alive."

Billie exerted extra pressure with the cold metal of her Colt, marking the man's temple, forcing his head toward his shoulder.

"We have more friends than you. If you bother my people in any way, the next accident will be your last. Do you understand what I'm saying?"

The man blinked his eyes twice, afraid any more motion might cause the gun to discharge, and scatter his brains over the burl wood accents in his car.

"I want you to explain all of this to Captain Mullrooney. Tell him he's got one chance to cease-and-desist or he'll lose his other arm. We know where he lives, we know where you live. And the police and the FBI have all your information. Just waiting on a phone call to take you down, make sure you're unemployable, and embarrass you in front of your family and friends. You're outnumbered and outclassed. Are we clear, Doug Darby, ex-Army Ranger, 75th Battalion?"

"Yes, ma'am."

"Good."

Billie stepped back from the Mercedes as a passing car rolled down the window and offered to help.

"Police are on the way, thank you."

The good Samaritan flashed the peace sign and continued down the road, as Billie jumped behind the wheel of the Cavalier, and turned the key. It started on the first attempt. She jammed the transmission into reverse, and the Mercedes rear bumper fell to the curb. Billie executed a tire-squealing U-turn and drove away from the scene.

She called Sarah, who said she heard a collision but was afraid to look out her window. Billie told her to stay put, lock the door, and she'd be back in an hour or so to check on her, but all was fine.

———

Sarah ran up the stairs, cracked open her vertical blinds, and started shooting video of a matte-gray Mercedes that was parked near her condo. A man with a stark, white face muscled the destroyed driver's side door into the trunk of the SUV. He grabbed the rear bumper from the gutter and tossed it on top of the wrecked door, and tried to close the back hatch, but it wouldn't lock. He left it open, jumped behind the wheel, and drove slowly past her condo, glanced up, not making eye contact, and continued down the street, out of Sarah's line of vision.

Sarah dug into her purse and grabbed the crumpled piece of paper Dakota had written his phone number on, typed a text message into her cell, attached the video, and hit send.

———

"Son of a bitch," Billie grumbled, as smoke started pouring out both sides of the Cavalier's hood like a comic book dragon. She was able to coax the car a few more blocks before the Chevy gave up the ghost, and Billie coasted to the curb in neutral. She made note of the cross street and texted the information to Red.

Billie was feeling pretty chipper. It had been a long time since she'd seen any action, thought she'd acquitted herself quite well, but the waning adrenaline made her jittery. She crossed the street toward a taco joint, ordered a spicy shrimp burrito, a Corona Extra, took a seat at the outdoor picnic table, and ate while she waited for her heart to return to normal and her Uber to arrive.

CHAPTER 19

D akota found himself sitting at the right hand of Thomas Wentworth, which elicited mixed reviews from James and three other warriors who were going to be taking orders from the newbie at Blackfox Elite Protection.

The lights were dimmed in the war room at the corporate campus in Orange County. The action played on two 98-inch ultra-high-def, wall-mounted screens, and was following a virtual helicopter as it powered over a dense rainforest in Colombia. The picture was so authentic it gave the four men and the only woman at the table a feeling of vertigo. The hidden surround sound speakers thundered as the bird's rotors filled the room with thrumming bass, causing ripples in the team's water glasses and vibrations felt in their abdomens. Each member of the team had lifelike, computer-generated, virtual humans, playing their part in the presentation. The virtual team was strapped to the bench seats in the chopper, wearing pensive expressions, thanks to advanced facial animation systems and AI.

The digital artistry and visual war primer, were created from the fertile mind of Ant.

Dakota had never seen his facsimile portrayed on screen before, and it left him feeling exposed.

"The assault team just crossed the border of Colombia into Venezuela, over the State of Zulia, where the Táchira Annex Prison is located, and our primary targets are being held," Ant explained with disciplined authority, as he watched his handiwork over his laptop, and continued the briefing.

The bird dove low banking to the right, and everyone at the table – except Wentworth and Ant – leaned slightly into the turn, as the chopper sped through a clear-cut channel between dense trees, and set down on a tight, open field surrounded by protective rainforest. The team dismounted and watched the chopper lift off and return to the squad's base camp.

A camera drone followed the team across the border and continued recording the terrain in live action, showing the team the lay of the land and a safe route that would lead them to the prison unassailed.

Kathy Nalven was a retired Air Force officer and an expert in drones. She'd been deployed for three years in Las Vegas, where she destroyed human targets in the Middle East. A moving blip on a computer screen, a button pushed, another human turned to dust. The irony of personally burning out, after incinerating hundreds of soldiers in Iraq, sitting in an air-conditioned room in Vegas, wasn't lost on Kathy.

To deal with her demons, she zero-balanced her salary every week, and leaned on gambling, coke, and booze, to get straight at the end of each day. Her retirement was a mutual arrangement between the Air Force brass and the brassy woman who had been such a decorated and successful asset. They counseled her to enter rehab and let her muster out without reprimand.

After hitting rock bottom, a friend introduced her to Thomas Wentworth. Kathy mentioned missing her multi-million-dollar drones, and Wentworth, more than happy to exploit senior talent, helped the woman reinvent herself.

The other two men at the table glanced from the screen over their shoulder to check out the man sitting next to their boss, whom they'd just been introduced to, and learned was going to lead their squad. The information dropped like a bag of nails.

Dakota's first sortie out of the gate. The stories they'd heard about his prowess in the field, most recently at Senator Bradley's party, preceded their meet-and-greet. The men didn't look impressed and struggled to control their bruised egos at being passed over.

Gary Janko was six-foot-two, weighed in at one 195 and had the neck of a defensive linebacker. Trey Avila was Hispanic, five-eleven, with zero body fat, and the long sensitive fingers of a piano player. He was an explosives expert.

Dakota had spent a career leading men in the field and was more than up to the task. He'd picked up the strained vibe and would take it slow, knowing he'd win the men over by example. It was how he operated, and success in this engagement would be a big step toward his personal freedom.

The camera drone revealed ancient trails through the dense forest, the safe path down a rock-strewn gully, where to cross a raging river, and where to scale the cliff face.

The drone shot skyward through a clearing and displayed an overview of the well-fortified prison they were being handsomely paid to launch an assault against. Then the camera honed in on the exact location of the isolated bunkhouse within the prison walls, where the American oil execs were being held.

"The prison's perimeter is patrolled twenty-four seven," Ant went on. "It becomes lax between 2:00 a.m. and 4:00 a.m. Then two men walk the length of the rear walls every twenty-five minutes. You can see it butts up against the jungle. There's usually a twenty-minute piss and smoke break at 3:00 a.m., which leaves the rear wall unprotected for close to a half hour. That gives Avila time enough to work his magic. I want five C-4 satchel bombs to be set along the wall, to be detonated in progressive order. Starting at your entry point on the north side of the prison, and moving down the line away from our targets.

"Piece of cake," Avila said without ego.

"In a coordinated attack, and on Dakota's signal, Kathy will blow the main entrance to the prison with enough firepower to wake the dead, and simultaneously, Avila will detonate the first satchel bomb and start the progression. By the second explosion, you should be able to gain entry into the prison and the cellblock where our prisoners are being housed.

"While Dakota and James deal with our execs, I want Janko to blow as many doors to as many cell blocks as is reasonable and let the prisoners, who have plenty of motivation to fight their way out of the hell hole, keep the military guards active, and cover your retreat. By the time the last satchel bomb explodes, your team should be out with our hostages and moving away from the facility."

The drone was on the move again, showing the point where Dakota and his team would have to be ready to hold off army or security forces that might be on their tail.

"Kathy's drone will follow your movement, and be ready to come into play if things get out of hand.

"From there, Dakota, you'll move the team and the American hostages to our final location, where you'll get one shot at being extracted by the chopper and flown to the safety of Colombia and our base camp."

————

The lights went on in the room. Wentworth seemed satisfied with the presentation and his assembled team. It would be a tough mission, but a proving ground for what he thought might become his A-team. "No one is to be left behind," he said, his face stone serious. "I have the utmost faith in each and every member of the team, and know you won't disappoint.

"We've just received a report from our man on the ground," Wentworth continued. "The hostages will stand trial in a new location, sometime by week's end. Everything is fluid down there. It's a formality, and if things go as we assume they will, the men will be found guilty and transported back to the prison to continue serving their sentence.

"We'll have a 48-hour window to extricate our hostages. I want you ready to deploy on a minute's notice. Our private jet will take off from John Wayne and land in Colombia. As soon as the sun sets, you'll be flown into Venezuela and deploy."

Ant stood and took over. "You'll have at least a week to review the digital movie on flash drives I've provided. Memorize your maps, get comfortable with your individual assignments, and get familiar with each other. Like Mr. Wentworth said, it's fluid down south, but we're on a tight schedule. So, keep your bags packed, your guns loaded, and cell phones charged. Feel free to use me as an asset twenty-four seven.

"Kathy, you'll be working from here while our men are deployed in Venezuela. Your room is already set up. I've designed a new program on our computer simulator you can use to familiarize yourself with the payloads and our next-generation drone. I think you'll be pleased. Your work is invaluable and can make the difference between success and failure in this extraction."

Wentworth didn't like the sound of Ant's final statement. He corrected: "You will succeed and save the lives of both American citizens. Their families are being torn apart. Failure is not an option."

Dakota nodded and told the men they'd begin their training at 0700 at the Blackfox outdoor facility in the hills of San Bernardino. And he looked forward to working with them.

Everyone stood, grabbed their packets of intelligence, and headed out of the room.

Dakota's cell had vibrated during the presentation. He decided to keep his powder dry and wait until he was on the road before checking it out. There were surveillance cameras all over the campus and he knew his every move was being recorded.

———

Dakota pulled out the phone on his drive home and hit play, waiting on a light. It was the cell phone video Sarah shot from her second-floor bedroom. His face darkened as he watched Captain Mullrooney's hired hand, Doug, go through his histrionics, clean up all the pieces of his car that could lead back to him, and drive away.

When the light changed, Dakota pulled a tire squealing right, coming to a chattering stop at the curb on the Pacific Coast Highway. He punched in Billie's number and took a deep breath.

"Billie," he said.

Billie felt the chill but wasn't sure what motivated it. "Didn't expect to hear from you so soon. How'd the meeting go at Blackfox?"

"Is there something you want to share with me?"

Busted. "I don't think so." But she knew Sarah had spilled. Funny how she didn't mention it when she checked in on her.

"Come again?" Dakota asked, tight.

"Dakota," Billie said, trying to lighten the mood, and when that didn't elicit an immediate response, she resorted to cop speak. "When someone I love is in jeopardy, I go to the mat for them. I send a warning, and then I get serious."

"Right."

"I caught the enemy, Dakota. I pulled up to Sarah's condo, and Doug started to get out of his German car. I put a little crimp in his attitude. If you want, I'll bounce ideas off of you before going to DEFCON 1. But I will take the motherfucker out if need be."

Dakota sat for a while. Listened to the white noise of passing traffic, before going on. "I appreciate you, Billie... Ah, hell. Thank you." As the picture got clear, Dakota realized he would have done the same. And more.

"Just one of life's little complications," Billie said. "We'll handle it. You just go about your business and stay in one piece. I'll keep my eyes on that little turncoat, Sarah."

"She's a handful."

"Women."

Dakota's face relaxed, and creased into a grin, "I'll call you when I get home and fill you in on my meeting. I'm heading south of the border."

"Signing off, hombre."

Dakota started the car and kept driving.

Dakota was sipping a few heavy fingers of the eighteen-year-old scotch – one of Peluso's homecoming gifts – on his front porch. His cell phone was planted against his ear.

"Did you not think I would get this far?" he asked, measured.

"Not this soon," FBI agent Jean Steele said, staring out her office window at the lights emanating from the parking lot. She was working after hours, and not pleased she had to make this phone call.

"So, my ass is in a sling one way or the other? If I back out of Venezuela, I'm dead to Blackfox, and if I deploy without the FBI's approval, they'll send me back to prison."

"No. Not on my watch," she said with a shade of defensiveness. "I promised to have your back, nothing has changed."

"Hmmm."

Steele didn't like his response. "Nothing has changed," she repeated with an edge.

"Well." There was a sexual tone to his response.

"That being said, I have to run it up the chain of command. Know full well that I understand the ramifications. I'll call a meeting and let you know when the decision is rendered. If they say no, and I'm not expecting that, not with the response Agent Chase had to your success with the senator and all you've accomplished, but, if it's a no-go,"

Dakota cut her off with, "Don't go all silly on me, Steele. You've got time in…that means something. It means everything. Just know I'm in it to win. All the damn way. You have yourself a good night, agent."

"Don't play me, Dakota."

"Never. You hear me? Let me know what the suits have to say. I'll respond accordingly," And he clicked off.

Steele wasn't sure what the hell he was inferring. Would he step down if ordered, or gamble on the extraction being the ultimate winning hand?

Dakota pushed back off his metal rocker, finished his drink, and headed for the bedroom. Dead on his feet, he lay on top of the sheets, just to rest his eyes, and when his head hit the pillow, he fell out into a deep REM sleep.

Dakota was being led out of a packed courtroom, the sound of shouted questions from reporters was hushed as a thick wooden door banged shut, and the military police allowed him five minutes to say goodbye to his fiancée.

Sarah Moore, fragile, looked at him with unbelieving eyes, her world destroyed. Dakota understood that after numerous deployments overseas, his seven-year sentence was more than the young woman had signed on for or could bear.

His own words were etched in his subconscious.

"Don't write, don't visit, don't try. You've suffered enough from my actions. I won't take you down with me." Sarah started to protest, wet eyes implored, taking a step closer. Dakota's glare stopped her short as he head-nodded the military police, who grabbed each side of his handcuffed arms and led him out of the antechamber. The light smell of her perfume lingered and almost caused him to break down as he walked into the garage where the armored van stood, waiting to deliver him to purgatory.

CHAPTER 20

The plan was for the men to show up at 7 AM, and hump a hundred pounds of gear including body armor, batteries, and assorted weapons of their personal choice on the company's practice field in the San Bernardino hills.

The outer perimeter of the prison walls was measured out to the millimeter, and the schematics of the interior of the prison walls were turned into prefab buildings arranged to mimic where the hostages were being held.

Dakota was the first to arrive at the training field. He got down on the hardened dirt, and started cranking out his daily workout routine, honed to perfection in prison. The three men arrived a few minutes late, and Dakota expressed his disappointment with a curt glance at his watch. No need for words, the men got the point.

"How many satchels can you hump with the rest of your gear?" he asked Janko, who was the last to step onto the field.

"More than you."

"Really? Do we have issues?"

"You asked, I'm just saying."

"One?"

"Two."

"Two, James," he said, grinning. "Gimme three, and hook up the hotshot." And then to Janko, "Twice around the track."

Janko nodded, flashed a wolf grin as he secured the backpack that carried the exact weight of two satchel bombs, along with seventy-five pounds of his regular equipment.

Dakota slid into his expanded pack and nodded to Janko. "Have at it."

Janko started running. Pounding the dirt track. Dakota gave him a ten count and followed the big guy up the hill. As they made the first turn, the two men were shoulder to shoulder. Janko grinned, thinking he could crush the newbie. As they rounded the last turn and readied themselves for the second lap, wiseass gave Dakota a sneer, thinking he was wearing him down.

He didn't know Dakota had a second gear. It kicked in and powered him three heads in front as they hit the rise in the course. Janko was dripping sweat, his face red, but keeping his own pace. He was getting pissed as Dakota, carrying more weight, kept increasing their distance until he was half a circuit in the lead.

By the time Janko crossed the finish line, Dakota had stripped off his backpack and stood there looking at his watch.

"Good time, Janko. All right." And then to James and Avila he said, "You two, gear up, and twice around." When the men started their run, Dakota waved Janko over.

"Do I need to replace you?" No anger, just waiting on an honest response. "I don't go into the field with anyone who might endanger my men."

A long silence…too long. "You're out. Get the fuck out of here."

"My fault," Janko said. The first sincere words out of his mouth. "I'm good at what I do. I won't let you down."

"Fuck with me again, or anybody on my team, and you're gone. You've got a week to change my mind."

"Got it."

"And you better get your ass out here before I arrive in the morning, or we'll have issues."

"Roger that."

"Okay."

The team started running a designated line, dropping their satchel bombs in pre-determined spaces, as Avila wired them and made it back to the starting line, waiting for Dakota to give the order to detonate the explosives.

"That took thirty minutes," he said. "We've gotta get it down to twenty."

No argument from the team. Success would depend on teamwork and timing.

"I'll drop the farthest satchel and sprint back to position one, and let Avila get started wiring the explosives, James drops the second, Janko the third, and the fourth will be in place as soon as the guards turn the corner of the prison walls. The first bomb explodes while the front gate is vaporized, and we're in through the opening."

They ran the exercise, and ran it again, and again, until they whittled it down to seventeen minutes.

"Great hustle, guys. Let's get some rest and start again at 0700. Tomorrow we'll enter the prison walls and get a feel for blowing the doors off the captives' isolated bunk house, while Janko blows open as many cell blocks as he can and lets some angry inmates out of their cages. You all know I've spent a lot of time behind bars, and the one thing I'm sure of…those motherfuckers will be very motivated to exact some retribution as they run for their lives."

Dakota had set up a meet at the RockPile on his way back from San Bernardino for a few drinks and to shoot the breeze with Ralph and Nick. Keep things on track and the up-and-up. The FBI's reality of what was up-and-up.

The bar's anthem, "Born To Be Wild," was jamming at ear bleed volume, accented by the sound of pool balls clacking, and players cursing, as one man after another lost a game to the local shark who took them on a rocky ride at the table and made enough on a good night to pay his electric bill.

Dakota was the first to the bar and glanced up as Nick sidled up next to him. Strange vibe, but then, Nick was a strange man. Trish, the bartender, poured another round for Dakota, and off his hand signal, a shot for Nick.

Dakota scraped his hand across the scarred wooden bar top again like a man asking for cards at a blackjack table as Ralph banged through the front door, gave him a friendly slap on the back, and slid onto the stool on the opposite side.

"How'd it go?" Ralph asked. "We heard nothing but good from Ant."

"It went," Dakota said, grinning, first time he heard Ant was the Blackfox connection to Wentworth. "I'll be hitting the road in a week or two. I've got a few issues to deal with, but everyone appears to be happy."

"Not everyone," Nick said, icy. Accusatory.

Dakota didn't appreciate the attitude or know where it was coming from. "I put in a hard day's work," he replied in a don't mess with me voice. He took a sip of bourbon and gave the man a minute to spit out whatever was on his mind.

"Right," was his only response.

The vibe in the bar was chilly, and after the second round of drinks, Nick looked ready to get down to brass tacks. He opened his mouth to speak, and Dakota held up a hand cutting him off. He ordered another round of drinks, and then flipped his hand in a tell-me-more fashion. Not about to put up with any shit after the day he'd just had.

Nick, miffed at being cut off, led with attitude. "Remember the banger...you know." Nick lowered his voice and head swiveled to make sure no one was in earshot. "The banger you fuckin' shot? Kinda cementing your place in our business?"

"Didn't lose any sleep over that one, or give it a second thought," Dakota said, though he had a good idea where this was headed, and kept his cool.

"You created some tension down in the basement when Terrance and his boys drove up from San Diego? He did some digging...and couldn't find a body to match the name of the deceased in the *Tribune* obits."

"If the prick's so interested in my business, have him talk to the cops. What does his paranoia got to do with me?"

"Not sure," Ralph's voice rasped like broken glass. "I saw it with my own eyes. Terrance told me to keep my mouth shut, but it's strange. Thought we'd run it by you. See if...I don't know...strange though." Ralph didn't seem all that worried about it.

"You wanna know what else is strange?" Nick said, clenching his jaws and sucking his teeth before going on. "We took care of the beaner the week before. Your kill should've raised retribution or some shit. Far as I can see, there was a whole lot of nothing in response. Not a damn fucking blip, or drive-by...nothing."

Dakota, cool, even, "Don't have a clue. All I know is cops don't give a rat's ass bout dead spades. Could've tagged the wrong toe."

"Wouldn't put it past 'em," Ralph said, the man of reason. Nick looked like he'd been chewing on the information for a few days and was having a hard time putting it to rest.

"Another?" Dakota asked, knowing the answer.

Ralph nodded.

Trish sashayed down from the end of the bar, a seductive look on her face and a bottle of Bulleit in her hand. Slid the three shot glasses together, and off a flick of Dakota's hand, added one for herself. Trish shook her bottle-blonde hair off her face, her eyes on Dakota, poured down the line without spilling a drop like a bartender in a '60s western. The four of them toasted the Wolf Pack, Dakota's success at Black-fox, and knocked the liquor back with practiced ease.

———

Dakota punched in Steele's number on their private line and woke her up. Groggy, she smiled as she answered the phone. Her good humor faded.

"You better find an African American John Doe, and put the guy's name you posted in the newspaper on his toe, or I'm toast. Terrance Gorman is snooping around my story," he explained. "Started digging into my drive-by kill and couldn't find a body matching the name printed in the *Tribune*. I may have convinced Ralph tonight, but Nick is still a question mark. He's a pit bull. Might not let go of the bone until someone has a definitive answer."

"I'll get on it ASAP." Steele jumped out of bed, her mind working a mile a minute. "They've got cadavers stacked with the gang war escalation. I'll reach out when I have an answer."

"And Nick confessed to killing the Marina 8 gangster."

"You're the gift that keeps on giving."

"Sleep tight."

"Not likely." Steele clicked off, ran into her office, and pulled up contacts on her computer. She punched in a number on her land line. "Charles, it's Agent Steele…Yes, I know what time it is but we've got a major problem and I know you'll have a solution. It relates to our John Doe story. We need something in the morning edition ASAP. All right, make some coffee, and call me back in ten. It will save a life, Charles. I'll give you the exclusive when the dust settles. I know, I'll owe you big-time. And you know I always pay my debts."

Steele hung up and ran into the kitchen to put on a pot of coffee.

———

Dakota tapped in Billie's number.

"It's late, you in trouble?"

"Sorry," he said, and he brought her up to speed on Terrance's sleuthing. "He could blow up a great deal of work, and put my ass in a sling that might prove fatal."

"Why don't I take a road trip down to San Diego and sniff around. All background stuff, just get a feel for his universe."

"I wouldn't tell you not to."

"I'll get on it. I've still got his contact information from the intel after your first run-in with the guy. Would've thought you'd be gold after he witnessed your action at the senator's party."

"The man's dirty. He doesn't trust anyone because he can't be trusted."

"Don't get pulled over. Sounds like you've been over-served."

"I'm sitting in my driveway. But, thanks for your concern. Talk to you tomorrow."

CHAPTER 21

Agent Steele stood at the head of a conference table at FBI headquarters. Five other agents seemed eager to please. Agent Chase was holding court because of a special guest.

Agent Stryker had flown in from Washington and had the ear and the support that ran all the way to the top of the FBI hierarchy. His hair was silver with strands of black, and full for a sixty-year-old man who had been in the trenches of the war against homegrown terrorists for twenty-eight years. He'd been instrumental in the takedown of Timothy McVeigh and kept a watchful eye on this particular case.

"Dakota has exceeded expectations," Steele began. "He worked his way up from infiltrating the white supremacists in prison, where you first agreed to commission him. Upon his release, he befriended the Wolf Pack and earned their trust and respect. Not an easy feat in and of itself. Enough so that the militia shared their vetting process with our ultimate target, Blackfox Elite Protection. Thomas Wentworth has now taken Dakota under his wing after the man's exemplary performance, saving the life of Senator Bradley. That's impressive, gentlemen.

"The FBI has been trying to get a foothold into Wentworth's organization, and their reach and influence over our local militias operating in and around Irvine…ever since, well, ever since I started working in the Orange County Bureau. Dakota proved there's a connection between Blackfox and the Wolf Pack. Our first direct link. Add to that his relationship with Senator Bradley, who personally requested Dakota head up the extraction operation. Oh, and a possible inroad into the dark money that may be bankrolling the mission, and his reelection campaign, and you're really questioning whether or not we should let Dakota deploy?"

Before her boss could respond, she continued, "The blowback from off-lining our CI would be catastrophic and undermine thousands of dollars spent, hundreds of man-hours, put your careers in jeopardy, and Dakota Judd's life in mortal danger."

Steele's eyes connected with each agent at the table. "We can't let that happen," she said and nodded, letting them know she was finished presenting her case.

"Thank you, Agent Steele," Chase said. "We appreciate your hard work. It hasn't gone unnoticed. I'll call you after we've run it up the flagpole."

Steele knew what was in play, but felt confident the men would see it her way. The senator's input might just be the winning hand. If the extraction were a success, they'd all move up a pay grade. If it failed, Dakota could end up back in prison or buried in his family's plot in Redondo Beach Cemetery. She expected them to do the right thing.

Steele had withheld Dakota's explosive information of Nick's taking responsibility for the murder of the Marina 8 gangster. She wasn't sure if she could trust everyone at the table with the new intel, and one false move could bring heaven's fury down on Dakota. Steele wasn't ready to gamble his life on unknowns.

———

Chase waited until he was sure Steele was on the elevator and about to leave the building before reconvening the meeting.

Agent Stryker sat opposite Chase, a pensive expression on his face.

Chase began the conversation. "Okay, so…where do we stand?" he asked, and then started talking. "Dakota's in bed with killers on our offer, our contract, Agent Steele's forward-thinking idea. After the local scumbags trusted him enough to share trade secrets, if he pulls up his tent the man's as good as dead, and so are we."

Mitchel, the young African American agent Dakota "shot" in the field, offered, "But, we can't sanction an embedded confidential informant, under contract, to get involved in a life-threatening situation with our knowledge."

"That ship has sailed," Stevens piped in. Glib.

Stryker ignored him, narrowing his eyes, like he was mentally playing a scenario in his head and had come to a decision. The table waited for the man from Washington to weigh in.

"I don't know if any of you are going to like my solution, but it just might work. It could protect our charge, Dakota, and the FBI's potential culpability. He's already given us the local militia, entree into San Diego's OC Watchmen, and been anointed by the CEO of Blackfox. He's earned the senator's goodwill. I say cut him loose."

"They'll kill him," Chase reiterated.

"The man has fulfilled his contract," Stryker went on. "We sign off on him. He walks away a free man. If he wants to see his assignment come to fruition, we can't stop him from going to Venezuela. But now…it's his call. He can stay. He can leave. He's no longer an employee of the United States government."

"Cake and eat it too," Stevens tossed in. He got no eye contact from anyone in the room, and wished he'd kept his mouth shut.

Agent Stryker continued, "I wasn't sold on Steele's idea from the get-go, and I've been proven wrong. Sign off on Mr. Judd's contract. As a free man he'll find a way to make it out alive. It's in his DNA. And we can put the squeeze on the local militia groups with his intel, and continue to let Dakota generate insight into the inner workings of Blackfox. I want you to make it clear; he can lean on the FBI for protection if things go south. His choice."

The room sat in silence, surprised by the big man's decision.

"The man had issues with a killer in uniform," Stryker went on. "I don't condone his actions, but it's clear to me, Dakota is a patriot who's paid his dues. What say you?" he delivered to Chase, the only other agent at the table who had a vote, and career money in the game.

"I say call his lawyer, and let Agent Steele deliver the good news."

————

Billie was driving her convertible like just any other beach hipster in the upscale town of La Jolla. Her brown hair was wrapped in a silk scarf, and her oversized Tom Ford sunglasses were styling. She decided to wear a designer skirt with a subtle floral pattern and a blouse she bought on sale at Bloomingdale's. With her clothes and makeup, she could follow her mark wherever he decided to land. Billie didn't get much chance to dress up anymore and enjoyed the process.

Twelve miles from San Diego, she was hanging far enough behind Terrance Gorman's Bentley not to raise suspicion. The man was on the phone the entire drive from his office, and Terrance was so self-absorbed, he wouldn't have paid any notice to Billie in her vintage car.

Billie pulled to the side of the road when she saw the Bentley's brake lights strobe as they rolled onto Prospect Street in La Jolla Village. The Bentley's convertible top slid into place as he pulled to a stop at the valet station at Duke's La Jolla, situated next to the historic fig tree and a statue of Duke Kahanamoku, the father of modern surfing. The view of the cove from the restaurant was killer.

————

Billie found metered parking, gave Terrance ten minutes to get settled, and decided to grab a late lunch at the bar. See who the lucky woman was.

She took a bar stool with a view of the ocean and the outdoor patio which was in high gear with patrons eating, drinking, laughing, and taking in the unobstructed view of La Jolla Cove. Terrance worked hard for his money, because his phone never left his ear. He checked his watch a few times, and a forced smile appeared as his lunchmate arrived.

Every once in a while, surveillance paid dividends. Billie contained her excitement, pulled out her phone, and pretended to be texting. She recognized the man who walked past by his lame arm hanging loosely at his side, and his left-handed fist-bump when he reached his destination.

Billie got two clean shots of Captain Mullrooney when he sat down at the table across from Terrance Gorman.

This was such an interesting turn of events; she ordered a glass of chardonnay and the poached salmon lunch. Might as well make an afternoon of it, Billie thought. Just wished she were sitting closer to the men who were already engaged in serious conversation.

————

Mullrooney slammed his frozen margarita on the table. His voice colder than his drink. He tossed a folded copy of the *Tribune* onto the table for dramatic effect. "The body turned up at the morgue," he said, spitting the excess rim salt onto the table. "Your intel was faulty."

"Can't argue the point. It's my good name that's taking the hit. Not yours," he said having sucked up just about enough attitude from the man who was living in one of his investment properties, and paying him chump-change.

"Dakota has the ear of the senator and Wentworth," the captain said tightly. "He's on to me, and Doug. Threatened to call in the Feds if we don't back off. I want him dead. I'll back off when he's six feet under. His mouthpiece threatened to take my other arm."

"That's harsh. We can't let that happen."

"Really, that's all you've got, Terrance?" He made his name sound like a slur.

"Calm down, or you'll end up in the street. Really, show some respect. You're a pariah; I'm your link to reinventing yourself. So, calm down and we'll work this out."

The captain didn't look convinced.

The waiter read the chill at the table, and silently set down a fish platter in front of Mullrooney, and a bloody steak in front of Terrance before scooting back to the kitchen.

"Bide your time Mullrooney, and rethink your relationship with Doug. He missed his target and almost shot the senator," Terrance said, cutting into the meat and watching the blood red juice bleed into his fries. "We've got something in the works that should motivate another Black Lives Matter rally we can exploit. The senator is giving a campaign speech in Old Town. Blackfox will have a security presence there. We can take him out when the rioting begins and place the blame on Antifa."

———

Billie paid the bill, and as she finished her wine, a good-looking older gent stepped up to the bar and asked if he could buy her another round. The offer surprised Billy in a good way. Her face creased into a genuine smile, "I'm late for an appointment," she said. "But you made my day. Thank you, sir." And she left the restaurant thinking she ought to get out more.

She was sitting in her car when the two men exited the restaurant, and stood in withering silence waiting for their vehicles. Billie's impulse was to tail the captain, and see what he was up to after watching him belt down his fish, and rise from the table before Terrance had even pulled out his wallet.

She couldn't read lips, but was sure she'd been part of the explosive conversation they shared. The captain was furious and might show his hand. Worth the effort, Billie thought. But not today. She'd have to trade in the Vette for something non-descript to surveil the captain, who was probably running scared and driving with one eye on the rear view. She decided to take PCH home and fill Dakota in on the surprising turn of events.

CHAPTER 22

Dakota agreed to an afternoon meeting with Agent Steele after he finished working out with his Blackfox team. Janko had been the first to arrive, as promised, and was on his best behavior. A move appreciated by Dakota who felt they'd turned a corner in their relationship.

Billie's news about the connection between Mullrooney and Terrance was confusing. He'd have to give it some thought, because James' connection to Blackfox and Blackfox's connection to Terrance and the Wolf Pack was reasonable in the white supremacist playbook. Everyone was in the chain of command, except Mullrooney and Doug, who were hidden outliers. He'd have to dig deeper.

Dakota wasn't sure what kind of mayhem he was walking into as he stepped off the elevator at his lawyer's office. The phone call from Steele had been strained. She wanted a face-to-face and refused to discuss the agenda over the phone.

Joseph Peluso sat at the conference table across from Steele. Never a good sign. The air in the room felt stilted. Serious. And so, he poured himself a cup of black coffee and sat at the far end of the table, in silence, waiting for the verdict. He wasn't going to make it any easier on them if he was being sent back to prison.

"You're probably wondering why I called this meeting," Steele said, not sounding like herself. "I wanted your lawyer to be here, so there could be no mistakes, and it was all done according to the law."

Dakota wasn't sure what had to be done, according to the law, but, Steele, true to her name, had her FBI shell firmly in place again. It was only her light scent wafting across the expanse of mahogany that gave him some hope.

"All right, give," he broke down and asked. "I'm a big guy, I can take the bad news. Am I off the extraction? Or is it worse than that?"

Steele took a moment to compose herself. "It's not bad news, Dakota. It's very good news," she said gently.

Joseph's face creased into a relieved grin.

"What the hell?" Dakota asked, not enjoying the game.

Agent Steele pulled a contract out of her attaché case and pushed it down the length of the conference table. It spun to a stop in front of Dakota. Steele's eyes were bright, appeared to be welling. What the hell?

"You're a free man, Dakota," she said simply.

Dakota glanced at his lawyer, who nodded agreement. "Signed, sealed, and delivered from the United States Government. For services rendered."

Dakota couldn't talk.

If he had been standing, his knees would have given out.

Six years, and six months, to the day.

His eyes felt wet, but he wasn't about to cry. He was a Ranger. He didn't know what the hell was dripping down his cheeks; his stone face belied his emotion. He sucked in a few breaths, nodded his head yes, and took another sip of coffee.

Steele's face softened, and if he wasn't mistaken, she looked at him with love in her eyes. "Take a few minutes to catch your breath, there's a lot to discuss, but I think it's all good. You'll let me know, because as I said, as of today, if you put your signature on that contract, you are a free man. I'm very proud of you, Dakota, and in all honesty, still in shock myself."

"This is well deserved and high time, my friend. Congratulations," Peluso gushed. And Dakota watched his lawyer get all sappy too.

Okay, he thought. It was a cry fest, for a few minutes, and then they got down to business.

"First of all, thank you," he said to Steele. "And second, how do I get out of this alive."

"Agent Stryker's point of view, and he's now a staunch supporter, is that nothing would have to change immediately. Unless you wanted it to. Because you're a free man. But..."

"There's always a but."

"But it's clear to everyone it wouldn't be safe for you to just walk away. And so, you may want to let everything roll. You deploy to Venezuela, stay safe, and live this life you've created for as long as you want to. As long as it suits your needs."

"What are the FBI's needs?"

"Information that could help law-abiding American citizens live in a democracy without fear. We will guarantee protection if and whenever things get too hot to handle. Agent Stryker thinks you're a patriot, and smart enough to figure out an exit strategy that was sorely missing in our initial agreement."

Dakota had played all the possible scenarios of winning this game in his mind, in many sleepless nights. He was stunned it appeared to be working out in his favor.

If he didn't stay in the game, the list of men who would hunt him down started with Turly and would grow every day. If he stayed, he could help take down some real scumbags, fatten his bank account, and wend a way to retirement, without burning bridges.

"Like I said to you the other night, Agent Steele, I am all in."

CHAPTER 23

VENEZUELA

The seven-hour flight from John Wayne airport to Colombia in Wentworth's Gulfstream was uneventful. The jet was cushy, no flight attendant, but the galley was fully stocked.

They landed in Colombia as the sun disappeared behind the tree-line, and were immediately ushered onto a refurbished Army Chinook helicopter. On the trip across the border to the drop-off point in Venezuela the heavens opened up and torrential rain pounded the steel skin of the bird like a bass drum. The sound was deafening. The atmosphere among the men, subdued. This was supposed to be the dry season.

The Chinook set down, and the men offloaded in the Perija National Park, and started humping their gear into the safety of the thick rainforest's canopy. The men were drenched, the ground covered in decomposing leaves, bark and detritus, which had already turned into thick, boot sticking, mulch that smelled like a rotting greenhouse. The sound of frogs, insects, birds, monkeys, and parrots was ear-piercing. The humid air was thick, the temperature in the high nineties. The men were hot, clammy, and dripping wet, and they'd only been in Venezuela for ten minutes. An inauspicious beginning.

Janko slapped his neck so hard it stopped their march.

Avila said, "I told you to use the spray."

"Ant swore it wasn't the season."

"Then what the fuck is biting you?"

"You, if it's my ass."

Dakota continued leading the way, and after a half hour of fending off mosquitoes and branches that left welts on the men's exposed faces, they arrived at their first position, where they would start the descent into the gully. He motioned for the men to wait and walked ahead to clear the footpath that led down the side of the hillside into a deep gorge. It had a layer of moss growing on it, and the incessant rain had rendered it slippery and treacherous, but doable. It was the least of their problems.

The river swelled with the downpour and inundated the boulder bridge, making a crossing impossible without putting his men with their explosives, automatic weapons, handguns, and food supplies in jeopardy.

Dakota pulled the men back and ordered them to stand down while he called Blackfox and spoke with Ant, who was following their every move on the men's body cameras, projecting digitally on the computer screens in his office, and the large double screens for Thomas Wentworth in the war room at headquarters.

"I'm on it." First thing out of Ant's mouth. "I had the South American weather service on the line the moment the storm struck. The storm cell should pass in about twenty."

Dakota hoped he meant twenty minutes, and not twenty hours.

"It hasn't rained there in a month," Ant went on, not able to contain the frustration in his voice. It was the first chink in the little man's armor, Dakota thought. But hell, it was weather.

Dakota shared the conversation with his men, and told them to hang tarps and sit tight. They were settling in until the rain subsided, or Ant re-routed them.

Janko made short work of unfurling his tarp, while Avila tied off the end between two trees.

"What the hell kind of bird is making that low, weird sound?" Janko asked while he slid under the safety of the plastic tarp and checked out his RLCS, Ranger Load Carrying System. It was his vest that secured magazines, grenades, hydration squeeze pouches, the works.

"It's not a bird," Avila said as he joined him and wiped the rain from his face.

"What is it, big-shot?"

"It's a monkey."

"Bullshit," Janko said.

"A howler monkey. You've never been in a rainforest?" he said as he used a piece of a branch to pluck out the thick mud that stuck to the corrugated rubber soles of his field boots.

"No. Afghanistan, Iraq, Iran. Never ran into a monkey in the desert. I hate monkeys."

"How high up are they on your list of most hated things?"

"Shut up."

Avila didn't try too hard to stifle his laugh and it pulled the big man's tight face into a grin.

"This is the shits," Janko said, speaking to the entire team.

"Can't argue that," James agreed.

"I just want to get in, grab our guys, and get out of here alive."

"That's the plan," Dakota added.

The men were very aware of their tight schedule. If they were rain-delayed for too long, they'd have to hunker down and try again the following night. And as much as Janko hated monkeys, he really hated snakes.

The shrill squeal of the Amtrak train braking to a stop next to the parking lot was a distraction for Captain Mullrooney, who parked and headed in the direction of North Beach in San Clemente.

Billie had switched out her car with her late sister-in-law's BMW. Dakota left the keys to use while she was on the road. It blended better than her Corvette while sitting surveillance, and no one would look twice at the aging 3 series with tinted windows. She watched the commuters step off the train and felt liberated, not being part of the rat race. Doing what she was doing now didn't feel like work. She was still plugged in and felt engaged, interested, jazzed even.

She grabbed her belongings and was about to exit when a car she didn't recognize pulled tight into the space next to the captain's vehicle. When the man dismounted from the black Audi SUV, wearing mirrored sunglasses and a swollen gash on his forehead, Billie knew immediately it was Doug Darby. The creep whose SUV she'd trashed outside of Sarah's condo. She watched Doug rubbernecking, his eyes checking the parking lot. The man was definitely paranoid, Billie thought, and it put a satisfied, mean grin on her face. Doug checked the text message on his phone that pointed him down the path toward the ocean.

Billie had parked on the far side of the lot. She jumped out, walked across the black macadam, and stepped behind the two vehicles, snapping a few photos of their license plates. She checked out the interiors, and not seeing anything of interest, strolled toward the beach and stopped on a grassy knoll overlooking the Coastal Trail that ran along the coastline all the way to the south end of San Clemente. Just beyond, she watched Doug kicking up sand as he approached Captain Mullrooney.

Billie had dressed down for the occasion, no makeup, her hair pulled back fastened with a scrunchie, wearing a faded cap, torn jeans, her gardening sunglasses, and a well-worn pair of sandals. She carried a dog-eared paperback, a brown-bagged lunch, and looked like just another retiree, one step away from living in her car.

She could see Mullrooney in the distance, seated at a green picnic table, oblivious to the majestic waves crashing on the sandy beach in front of him.

Billie pulled out her cell, took a few shots, wishing she were carrying a zoom lens, but caught Doug as he slid down on the bench next to the captain. No niceties were exchanged. The two men started talking. No eye contact, both men staring blindly toward the perfect baby-blue surf, furious they'd been discovered, and hoping their plan would come to fruition.

Billie took a large bite of a ham and provolone sub with extra onion, and then tapped a number into her cell:

"Diedre, long time."

"What you want, girlfriend?" Diedre was from Jamaica. She moved to the States when she was twelve, but held onto her lilting accent, because it made her smile and reminded her of home. Women were in the minority in the OCPD, and the two women had forged a personal workplace bond. "Miss your sorry self around the precinct."

"It was time. After Harry passed, I wasn't right."

"You know what they say?"

"Get out, before the job gets you."

"You bet, but you were good. What can I help you with that could make your life in retirement easier?"

Billie read the license plate number off the car Doug was driving.

"Just need the name of the owner. And an address wouldn't hurt any."

"I'll get back to you, honey. I'm up to my ankles in alligators. You

know how it is. Give me a few hours, and let's have lunch sometime."

"Nothing would make me happier."

"Stay out of trouble, my friend."

"I'll talk to you soon, Diedre." And she clicked off, a big smile on her tanned face.

———

The day hadn't been a total bust, Billie thought as she drove home with the convertible top down. The sandwich was great, she got a little sun, read a bit of John Sandford she picked up in a second-hand store for a buck-and-a-half, and oh, by the way, Doug and Mullrooney looked miserable. Billie decided she had put the fear of God in their killer minds, and damn it felt good. She hoped that would be the end of them.

Her cell phone chirped, she checked the number, and smiled as she answered her cell. "What news do you have for me, Diedre?"

All business now. "The car is registered to a James Marshal. His address is 369 Pine Street."

Billie's smile faded as the implication of the name sank in.

James Marshal. One of the men deployed with Dakota in Afghanistan who testified at his trial. James, who is Dakota's second in command in Venezuela.

If James was friends with Doug and Captain Mullrooney, Dakota could be in more trouble in South America than he'd signed on for. She thanked Diedre profusely with a promise of lunch and pulled the car into Dakota's garage.

She parked, covered the Beemer, hit the remote, and watched the door roll down and lock. She punched in Dakota's number as she exited the side door of the garage and stepped into the backyard.

The phone was ringing and Billie's stomach lurched as her mind raced through multiple possibilities. All of them bad. The cell rang eight times, and went to voicemail. Billie looked up from the phone before clicking off, not leaving a message. She thought she'd heard a faint ringing in the background and dialed the number again. Shit!

Dakota's phone was ringing in the house.

Billie tried every number she'd ever had for Dakota and realized her nephew was probably offline during the sortie. In a worst-case scenario you wouldn't want to get caught with a cell phone that held secrets and contact numbers that could be damning.

Billie got into her Vette and headed down the hill toward home. The only way to reach her nephew would be through Blackfox. That call could blow Dakota's cover and put him deeper in trouble. She wouldn't be able to live with herself if she were responsible for Dakota's death.

CHAPTER 24

The rain stopped as abruptly as it started. The men took the tarps down, and after twenty minutes, descended the slippery path into the gully and the river's edge where they dared to cross. The water was running fast, but only an inch above the face of the boulders. Dakota took the end of a nylon rope, knotted it around his waist, and started walking. The rubber soles of his boots held firm, and he negotiated the expanse of water without incident. He got a good foothold and with Janko acting as the anchor, Avila and James started across. The rope helped their balance, and they scrambled up the far side of the river.

Janko started moving hand over hand on the nylon rope. A large emerald green macaw flew along the river, its shrill, squawking, cry, echoed against the walls of the gully. He glanced up and his foot slipped off the boulder and he slid into the river. He fought to keep his head and ninety-pound pack above water.

Dakota braced himself and all three men pulled the slick rope, hand-over-hand until Janko made it to the far side and scrambled onto shore on all fours. He stayed in place sucking in air for a few moments, jumped to his feet, nodding his thanks to the team. They continued to traverse the river's edge until they arrived at the ancient switchback trail used by hunters and their prey that lived in the rainforest.

The weak moonlight fought through intermittent clouds and was enough to light their way along the river, but humping ninety pounds of gear and twenty-five pounds of wet clothes up the cliffside slowed their progress. Dakota set the pace and the men rose to the occasion.

After they arrived at the top and entered the thick forest, the men pulled on night vision goggles and their world turned an eerie green.

They'd lost an hour and would have to double-time it to arrive at the prison walls at 0200 hours, set the explosives, and pull off the impossible.

———

The ambient sound in the rainforest was 130 decibels, muting the sound of Dakota's men getting into formation on the edge of the rainforest that ran the length of the prison wall.

Two prison guards were shooting the shit as they smoked, laughed, and strolled along the wall, oblivious to Dakota and his team lying in wait. We'll give them something to laugh about, Dakota thought as he checked the load in his M4.

As the guard glanced at his watch and nodded to his comrade, the man flicked his lit cigarette into the damp weeds, and they both disappeared around the prison's stone wall.

Dakota, James, Janko, and Avila immediately moved out of the forest as one and secured their explosive satchels against the wall. Avila, starting at the far end, wired each bundle with nimble fingers until he joined Dakota at the front of the line, and their first charge. The C-4 charges were sequenced to pull the security forces away from their targets in the bunkhouse where the American prisoners were being held.

Kathy's drone hovered and she watched the men's movements in real time from her cubicle at Blackfox headquarters. The prison was on her screen. Her multi-million-dollar drone hovered in place. Her computer-guided missiles were primed and ready to fire.

Wentworth sat behind the mahogany desk in the war room and

watched the mission unfold on the massive high-def screens. Ant was in his office, also viewing the action in real time on his computer, and wired into the men's radios ready to lend support if needed.

The second hand on Dakota's watch counted down toward 0300. He did a mental five, four, three, two. "Fire!" he shouted. Kathy launched her missile as Avila plunged the button on his detonation rig.

The forest went still as if in anticipation of what was in store. The explosions were deafening. The prison's front gate was blown off its hinges, taking sections of wall with it. The lights in the complex went black. Each man in Dakota's team knew their orders and moved to fulfill their mission.

The first satchel bomb had blown a hole in the old stone wall. Janko was the first through the opening, as dust, dripping water, and a sour smell like a zoo gone bad filled his nostrils. He ran down the length of the cellblock, and using small C-4 charges, blew the locks off the steel doors as he moved back toward the first explosion. Crazed men flooded out of their cells not knowing if they were caught in an earthquake or the end of the world.

The second charge exploded. The building shuddered, pipes in the old structure cracked, water rained down on the fleeing men. Dakota's night vision goggles tracked from face to tortured face as desperate men fought their way past him, exiting the opening in the rear wall, running for their lives.

A klaxon wailed impotently, the damage, the dust, the surprise attack, were more than the sleeping guards had expected or were trained to handle. Prisoners spilled out through the front gates, savaging the stunned guards as they fanned out down the dirt roads in all directions.

Dakota and James reached the bunkhouse. Dakota attached a C-4 charge over the lock and detonated the explosive. It blew the door open, and left it hanging off its hinges.

The American hostages, Jerry Moran and Bill Vincent, were cowered in the corner of the room. Their heads covered in burlap sacks. "We're Americans, you're safe," Dakota said as he and James took the bags off the men's heads, pulled the tape off their mouths, and cut the plastic ties that bound their wrists. Both men were clearly in shock. One man looked skeletally sick and was shaking uncontrollably.

Dakota was calm in the storm. "We have to leave now, sir. Just follow my orders and we'll get you out of this hellhole." They left the bunkhouse and were inundated with screaming, shouting, and cries for help. Inmates were meting out payback on the hapless guards caught in the middle of the violent melee.

The fourth charge exploded, rocking the building again. The weaker hostage fell to his knees. Dakota reached down and pulled him to his feet as Janko joined the crew, covering the men's escape as they rushed through the breach in the stone wall. Dakota led his team into the dense jungle as the mob of prisoners stampeded throughout the dark prison, escaping out the jagged openings in the back.

Hundreds of prisoners poured through the destroyed front gates, out through the five holes blown in the rear of the prison walls, running in all directions, fighting prison guards who were outnumbered and firing blindly into the fleeing crowds, cutting down men in the process.

Avila detonated the fifth bomb and joined the team. The sound of the explosion and stones toppling, and gunshots, and screams diminished as they cut deeper into the rainforest and their new route away from the gully toward a cleared field where they would be picked up by helicopter and flown to safety.

Kathy followed her retreating team with her drone's thermal imagery system which could detect the escaping team and their hostages under the rainforest's canopy. She moved the drone ahead of the men and set up in her secondary position. She was ready to clear a hundred-yard radius around the small landing area, and offer help if the shit hit the fan before the chopper arrived.

Two military vehicles filled with Venezuelan soldiers skidded to a stop at the prison walls, just as the backup generator restored partial light in the devastated complex. General Felix Ramirez jumped out of the truck before it had come to rest. He pounded through the dust, rubble, and weeping pipes, making his way toward the building where their million-dollar oil executives were being housed.

The General ran toward the room, kicked the door that was

partially blown off its hinges, finishing the job. He cursed the empty room, and his men stepped back, giving him a wide berth.

He stormed past his soldiers and out through the first hole that had been blasted from the wall. His eyes raked the jungle that was filling with fleeing inmates. His head snapped in both directions shouting orders to his men, who followed their leader as he ran back through the complex toward their trucks.

The General strode up to an inmate who unwittingly blocked his way. He smashed the man in the back of the head with his 9mm, splitting the man's skull, and sending the convict to the ground unconscious.

The General was on the hunt for the oilmen and the unknown army that cut them loose. It was a professional job, Americans, he suspected. If the hostages got away his career and his life would be in serious jeopardy. He was in charge of prison security, and the American company Rentex Petroleum had just agreed to pay the fifteen-million-dollar ransom for their executives' release.

"Don't kill the hostages!" the General screamed red-faced as he leapt into the lead armored truck. The vehicles took off on opposite dirt roads, hoping to run down Dakota's team.

CHAPTER 25

Dakota was feeling the time crunch. His team was making slow progress, slogging through the rainforest in the direction their maps and GPS locators prompted them. The rain had loosened the soil underfoot, and the oil execs weren't in any shape to run.

Dakota could hear shouted voices in the distance, and the faint whine of truck engines moving in their direction. As they cleared the rainforest, they could see the open field a quarter mile away. Dakota radioed Kathy for support.

———

The General was standing upright, holding on to the windshield of the truck as it powered up the dirt road that ran parallel to the forest. His demeanor changed when he made out Dakota's team in a copse of trees in the distance, just off the road. He shouted into his radio, giving the second truck his coordinates, and ordered the driver to go faster as the truck lurched through potholes closing in for the kill.

———

Kathy sighted in on the one-inch blip as it moved across her radar screen in the direction of her men. Her face was etched in granite. She could see Dakota and the team bunched near the forest, firing rounds at the armored vehicle that skidded to an abrupt stop.

———

The General's angry voice filled the thick air as he shouted in broken English through the vehicle's megaphone, "Let the hostages go, and I'll let you live!"

———

Kathy fired. Her guided missile left a contrail as it zeroed in on its mark. The target was hit, the explosion rose in a mushroom cloud. The General, his truck, and six Venezuelan soldiers were torn apart in a blaze of fire and fury. All that was left of the men and their vehicle was a large crater and singed, smoking foliage on the jungle floor.

———

Dakota waved the team deeper into the cover of the jungle, moving toward the field, as the second armored vehicle skidded to a stop next to the crater. The soldiers jumped off the back and fanned out, firing automatic weapons as they ran.

Dakota's men were forced to stand, fight, and hold off the attack until the chopper arrived. Janko stepped from behind a tree and let loose with a burst of rounds from his Army M4 automatic. The Venezuelan soldiers returned fire but were caught by surprise, and fell back. Janko exploited the weakness, pushing them behind the armored vehicle and burning through the entire magazine.

Dakota, Avila, and James covered the warrior as he ejected the spent clip and slammed in another. The battle was fierce, with rounds slicing through the jungle.

"We need support, Kathy!" Dakota shouted into his radio. "Now!

The armored truck inched forward; the Venezuelan soldiers used it as a shield. Dakota's men returned fire. Rounds pinged off the truck. It continued to roll in their direction.

Moran and Vincent crouched behind a thick group of trees. Shaking with fatigue, fear, and sickness. Their bodies shuddered with every rifle blast. James stepped out of view of the other teammates. He grabbed a handful of mud from the rainforest floor and smeared it on the lens of his body camera. He raised his automatic, his sight painting Dakota's back.

James jerked the barrel away as Dakota shouted: "Kathy! Come in! Kathy, where the hell are you?" James knew they were in deep shit. Without air support, the team would be lucky to make it out alive. James's furtive move wasn't lost on Dakota, who would've cut the man down if needed, but had his hands full trying to save the hostages.

———

Ant's voice bellowed over the men's radios. "What the hell! Fire Kathy. ASAP!"

Instead of the promised missile strike, Kathy cried: "Hey! Hey! Get your fucking hands off me, Goddamn it! They're arresting me, Dakota," Kathy screamed. "You're hurting my wrists..." Kathy's signal went dark.

———

"Shit!" Dakota shouted. He'd seen James's movement, but needed every gun if they were going to succeed in the mission. "We're on our own, James. Get your ass up here!" he shouted menacingly.

———

Ant's voice broke, "Get out of my room! What the fuck're you doing? The Feds are arresting..." Ant's signal was cut off.

———

"Over your left shoulder," James yelled. Dakota turned and cut down a Venezuelan who was sighting in on him. James fired his M4. His burst cut across a soldier's chest, knocking him back against the armored truck, bleeding out as he slid to the ground.

————

Thomas Wentworth watched Dakota and the squad's firefight in real time. Alarm etched his face. He stood as the ATF kicked in the door to the war room. "You're putting my team in mortal danger," Dakota's men heard him shout over their radios as his signal was silenced.

————

James stood shoulder to shoulder with Dakota. Safety in numbers, he thought, as they pelted the oncoming army with high-velocity rounds. Ejecting magazines and slamming home full loads. The advancing soldiers were pushing the team deeper into the rainforest and unknown territory, where they could be picked off.

Dakota hand signaled Avila and Janko, who were shielding the oil execs, with their bodies. Moran and Vincent held on to each other for strength as they watched their protectors step forward into the hellish firefight.

"Double up on grenades," Dakota ordered. The team pulled hand grenades from their vests. Four men working in unison. "On a three count," Dakota shouted like a quarterback. "One. Two. Three."

The truck moved in for the kill. It was met with four airborne grenades, creating synchronized mayhem. The explosives hit their mark. The soldiers on the back of the truck dove for cover, and the truck's engine died. Smoke spiraled from under the hood.

Dakota's team hurled a second round of grenades, scattered around the burning hulk. The soldiers ate dirt trying to stay out of the explosive field of the grenade's shrapnel.

The team humped out of the forest double-time as the truck's fuel tank exploded shooting diesel flames and black smoke high into the air. Jerry Moran, who'd lost twenty pounds while incarcerated, fell to the ground. In one smooth motion, Dakota muscled him up, slung the sick man over his shoulder, and continued the hustle toward the open field.

James and Avila stood strong and held off the attack from the remaining soldiers.

———

Dakota and Janko hit the tight grassy field as the helicopter set down. The men lowered their stance, running toward the open door to evade the spinning rotary blades and the dust and leaves kicked up by the downwash. Janko jumped into the craft and helped the oil execs on board, strapping them onto the bench.

———

Dakota turned and ran back into the firefight to cover James and Avila, who were drained of ammunition and sprinting toward the bird. Dakota let out a final burst of his M4 sending three soldiers onto the dirt, and was the last man aboard as he dove onto the body of the chopper.

The bird lurched straight up and disappeared into the early morning darkness. The sun was just piercing the horizon as the helicopter broke above the rainforest canopy and the team and their grateful hostages crossed the border into Colombia.

CHAPTER 26

At Blackfox headquarters, Wentworth and Ant were seated side by side, cuffed in the war room, watching the action on the wall of screens, as the ATF special agents tried to cut off the transmission and failed.

They watched murky images on James's body cam as Dakota lifted Jerry Moran and tossed him over his shoulder like a sack of linen, and ran toward the empty field. The bouncing picture filled with the helicopter setting down, the team boarding the body of the bird, James and Avila firing, holding the soldiers at bay. Dakota covered his men as they slid into the beast. The bird lifted safely off as the screens in the war room blinked to stark black.

Ant head signaled his boss, and they watched Kathy glance into the war room, her cold eyes brisling with anger as she was led past the open door, in handcuffs.

The arrest warrants charged Blackfox with conspiracy, trafficking in illegal firearms, explosives, and terrorism. Blackfox was engaged in an illegal action on foreign soil, not sanctioned by the United States Government, or the Venezuelan government, for that matter.

"You're making a terrible mistake, gentlemen," Wentworth said, trying to control his rage. The mission had been a great success. The oil execs and his men made it out alive, but now was the time for politics to be played and the collection of favors owed, to clean the trail that led to the American hostages' release.

———

When the helicopter set down in Colombia, the team and their American hostages were immediately boarded onto Blackfox's corporate jet where two paramedics stood by to attend to the oil executives as they headed for the States. Doctors and hospital beds were waiting for the men upon their arrival at John Wayne Airport.

Dakota and the team sat in the front of the jet. Their automatic weapons, and heavy gear had been stowed in the hold, and they took turns in the bathroom, cleaning off as best they could. The flight attendant wasn't on board because of the delicate nature of the trip, but the galley was fully stocked with food and drinks for the men. The adrenaline rush of the firefight had worn off and left the men feeling spent. The arrest of Wentworth and their Blackfox support team in the heat of battle was hard to swallow. Someone set the team up. The men wanted answers but knew it was best to keep their powder dry until they touched down.

The premium liquor and gourmet food eased some of the tension in the cabin, and everyone settled in for the flight home. Janko was snoring. It was a bass rumble, like something an aging tiger might emit. Avila was playing video poker, staring at the screen, his piano hands flying over his cell phone's keypad. He'd occasionally utter, "winner, winner, winner."

The co-pilot stepped out of the cockpit and waved toward Dakota, who got the message and stepped up to the cabin. He was handed a cell phone. "It's Derik Traina, Senator Bradley's head of security. He's got some intel. Just knock on the door when you're finished."

"Thanks, Frank." He placed the cell to his ear, and was brought up to speed on the ATF raid at Blackfox, and the arrests of Wentworth, Ant, and Kathy.

"It was harsh, Dakota. There's a blackout on intel going in or out of the Department of Justice. All things being equal, Wentworth shouldn't do much time," Derik said. "He has the best legal staff in California.

"Senator Bradley's on a flight to D.C. to meet with the Feds and the DOJ. Trying to work his magic, and loosen the noose. There's a press conference scheduled at John Wayne upon your arrival, trying to stay ahead of the news and control the spin. It's probably best for you and your men to stay out of camera range. The jet will pull into the hangar before offloading the execs. You can exit the rear door and pick up your vehicles without making waves."

"Any idea who set us up? Someone leaked the time and place, and disposition of the extraction. It was ugly, but could've been deadly."

"I've got my men working on it. They weren't picking up any chatter after the arrests went down. The ATF ran the show, but is staying tight-lipped, protecting their informant. If something comes to you, anything, call me. I'm available twenty-four seven, Dakota."

"Any movement on the attempt on Bradley's life?"

"The FBI's on the case, I'm hearing nothing but crickets. Stay in touch."

"Appreciated." The men signed off, Dakota rapped on the door and handed the phone to the co-pilot and then alerted his men. No one bitched. They all knew it was a good move that would keep them out of the public eye, and out of a federal pen.

Dakota walked to the rear of the jet to check on the hostages who were resting peacefully. The paramedics had done a good job cleaning the men up.

"How're you doing, Jerry?" Dakota asked.

Jerry Moran was being administered a saline drip, and antibiotics for flaming cuts acquired when he fell face first onto the jungle floor, and parasites that invaded his large intestines in his damp prison confines. "As good as can be expected," Moran said. "If it weren't for you, those animals would've let me die. And if I forgot to say thank you, blame it on my meds. Jimmy here," he said, referring to his paramedic, "tells me my heart rate has returned to moderately safe levels."

"Good for you."

"You're telling me. At this point, I'll take moderately."

Bill Vincent, the second exec, was surprisingly cheerful for a man who'd lived through an authoritarian, kangaroo court in Venezuela, and two months of hellish imprisonment.

"Same question to you, Bill, how are you?" Dakota said, trying to keep it light.

"Better than most," Vincent said. "I'm very pleased to have made it out in one piece so I can see my family, my girls and…" Vincent started crying for a few seconds, and then sucked it in. All he could say was, "I miss them." And then, "thank you."

Dakota sent the medics to the front of the cabin for snacks and shared a private letter with Moran and Vincent written by the CEO of Rentex Petroleum, and delivered to Dakota in the belief the extraction would be successful. "Welcome home gentlemen," he read. "At the press conference, please thank the Venezuelan government for your compassionate medical release. If asked, you were never introduced to any of the men who transported you from Venezuela to Colombia and the Blackfox jet. It was a whirlwind of activity, and the uniformed soldiers were all business.

"On another note, the company's board of directors has approved a stipend of four million dollars for each of you. Consider it well-deserved hazard pay. You've made yourself, your family, and the company proud."

Moran and Vincent understood their marching orders and would comply. They were profoundly grateful to be alive, and the money didn't hurt.

Dakota walked back up the aisle and slid into the thick leather seat next to James, who raised his glass of Stoli and air toasted the team leader. They sat for a moment, the sound of the jets easing the uncomfortable silence. Dakota turned and faced James. Laser eyes looking for a reaction.

"You want to tell me what happened out there?"

"Not sure what you mean, boss."

Dakota paused before going on. "Yes, you do, James. But you didn't pull the trigger."

"What? When I was standing to your right? I took the gunman down when he leapt off the truck. You witnessed the kill."

"The bullet was meant for me."

"You're crazy. I might have swung the barrel past your position as I dodged a bullet and lined up my shot. But that's it. Sorry, it made you nervous." And then, "I guess with you there's nothing in the bank, huh, Lieutenant?"

"Think on it. It's important you give this some serious thought, James. It will change your life, one way or the other."

"Pour yourself a drink, and get out of my face."

———

Dakota stood and sat two rows behind the man he had trusted with his life, and believed was a friend. He'd never make the mistake of giving James an easy target again.

The mission was accomplished but Dakota had personally killed three soldiers. Men who had mothers, and fathers, and wives, and kids, and lives outside of their uniforms. Young men who became soldiers because it was the only way to put food on their family's dinner table, and wouldn't make it home to enjoy the meal.

Dakota carried the added weight of knowing he was responsible for ordering the missile attack that liquidated seven human beings, like so many game pieces on a video screen.

It had been years since he was involved in an armed operation. But at the time, the kills were sanctioned under the banner of the United States government.

And although he believed this had been a righteous deployment, he was really just a gun for hire and it didn't sit well.

Someone tried to destroy the mission. And that someone had inside information. How else would they have known where everyone in a support position was located in the labyrinth of offices at Blackfox headquarters?

At the beginning of their relationship, Agent Steele shared there were suspected leaks between retired FBI agents working at Blackfox, and men still in uniform, or working for the Department of Justice. Old relationships. Stories shared over a few drinks.

Dakota thought about the sacred nature of trust and the importance it played in his own career as a Ranger. And what it took to turn that commandment on its head to gain his own freedom.

James had been a proven commodity. What would it have taken to make him flip? Dakota didn't have the answer, unless James blamed him for his fall from grace with the Army. That wound might have festered and turned to hatred.

Dakota wasn't in a forgiving mood and wasn't going to stop until he discovered who wanted him dead. Someone who was willing to sacrifice his own man to achieve that goal.

Captain Mullrooney's stench was all over it. Dakota felt it in his bones. Now he had to prove it.

CHAPTER 27

WASHINGTON D.C.

FBI Agents Stryker and Chase were seated in a private booth, with etched glass partitions, their eyes locked on the massive carved mahogany bar at the entrance to the Old Ebbit Grill. The restaurant was over a hundred and fifty years old, and walking distance to the White House. They were waiting on Ted Northrup, a highly placed lawyer at the DOJ, and Senator Bradley, who had been stalled at Reagan International and was ten minutes out. He told them to start without him and he'd play catch-up.

The men were surprised at the invitation to join the meeting. But Chase was leading the investigation into the attempted murder of the senator. Stryker had the bona fides that might impress the Department of Justice lawyer. And the FBI, being miffed at not being in the loop about the Blackfox raid, should work in their favor.

Stryker recognized Northrup as he walked through the door, and he raised his hand to let him know where they were seated.

Ted Northrup had a slight stoop to his gait, but his leather soles clicked smartly on the hardwood floor. Northrup was in his late forties and prematurely graying, but Washington politics could do that to the best of men and women. He stepped up to the table, a harried expression on his narrow face, and forced a power smile. Introductions were made, he ran a hand through his fine brown hair, and took a seat. They ordered coffee, and it was placed in front of them along with a basket of breakfast rolls and sweet butter.

Senator Bradley pushed through the brass revolving door, schmoozed a moment with the maître d, and headed in their direction. "I feel older than the grill," he said, eliciting a few light grins from the men. "I couldn't sleep on the flight, but I refused to miss this meeting."

"Just as you like it," an older waiter said as he put a mug of Irish coffee in front of the senator.

"Thank you, Roy."

"I'll give you gentlemen a few moments and then take your orders," Roy said, and left the table.

Bradley raised his mug, air-toasted the men, took a healthy sip and seemed to shred the effects of jetlag and instantly relax. "Should we order, or get down to it?"

"Don't take this the wrong way, senator, agents, but I'm on a tight schedule today and have to keep this meeting brief."

"No offense taken," Senator Bradley said. "I'll set it up, and FBI Agent Stryker can bring it home. I'm sure you've been apprised of the release of the two Rentex executives who were held hostage in Venezuela for the past two months, without any meaningful support from the administration. Jerry Moran, a father of three, has a heart issue and came close to dying in captivity. I'm also sure you've been briefed on the Blackfox raid and the arrest of Thomas Wentworth, the CEO. They've handled many touchy contracts on foreign soil and excelled on our country's behalf.

"In this situation, his company embarked on a dangerous mission with a talented crew. To free the hostages. They were successful. As the team was making their escape, heading toward their flight home, someone from the ATF intervened, served arrest warrants at Blackfox, and seriously hindered the play on the ground in Venezuela. They endangered the lives of all six men, who were lucky to have made it out of the country alive."

The waiter showed up at the table again, and the senator said, "Give us fifteen minutes, Roy. Thank you."

They waited for the old gent to move back toward the bar before continuing.

"What do you want from me?" Northrup asked. "I know the case, I'm aware of Blackfox's history. The arrest warrants seemed to be in order. I'm not sure how I can be of service."

Agent Stryker took over, "We need you to intercede with Mike Caldwell at the ATF. We've been running an ongoing case at Blackfox, and it's the wrong time to shut them down. We're close to something with international implications.

"And cutting to the chase, no pun intended," he delivered to Agent Chase and then shifted his focus to Northrup. "As you know, Senator Bradley is the Chair of the Senate Committee on Appropriations. We're aware the ATF is in line for a major increase to its bottom line. Money that will be well spent protecting arms that are flooding across the border. He'd be mighty disappointed to learn that the funds were withheld because Caldwell steamrolled an arrest without thinking about the ramifications of said arrests: the safety of the incursion team, the safety of the American hostages, both situations that could have been avoided if he had only shared intel before making a unilateral move."

Bradley piped in, "Let's not forget the negative impact his lack of communication will have politically, flying in the face of the American public's overwhelming support of returning American hostages to American soil."

"What can you offer if he agrees to back off?" Northrup asked.

Agent Stryker loved politics, and seasoned politicians who could take care of business. "I think it's safe to say, we can get an indictment on the number two man at Blackfox." Stryker glanced at Bradley, who nodded in agreement. "Young brilliant guy, named Ant. He was the brains behind the sortie, guided our warriors through the rainforests of Venezuela, into the prison, and back toward home base before his mike was cut off during a major gun battle when he was most needed. Our men were taking incoming, and ready to die to save the Rentex men, and return them to their wives and children. We've got digital video of the entire incursion."

"Is that all?"

"Excuse me," he said and turned to Bradley, "Senator?"

"I can guarantee full funding in this year's budget for the ATF. It's a great organization, and we support our first responders."

Northrop's cell phone beeped. He checked the text and leaned forward; his demeanor tight.

"It's too late, gentlemen," he said sotto voce. "The government dropped the hammer on the entire Blackfox organization and froze their assets. I'll do what I can and get back to you. But I'm afraid it's a fool's errand."

Ted Northrup stood, nodded to each man taking their measure, turned, power-walked toward the bar and pushed through the brass doors heading for 950 Pennsylvania Avenue.

Senator Bradley's brow furrowed, his bloodshot eye revealed his disappointment. He waved toward Roy, who delivered a second Irish coffee. Bradley took a sip, burned his lip, and said, "A red-eye flight, and we came up short."

The Feds sipped their coffee, no response needed.

"Question," Bradley continued. "Any movement on who took a pot shot at me?"

"I won't sleep until we find the shooter," Chase said.

"That's something anyway. Good to hear." And then collegially, "So, you're running a case with international implications against Blackfox?" he said, smiling now. "Do tell."

Stryker was well aware of the personal relationship Bradley shared with Wentworth. "Not a thing," he said clear-eyed. "I was negotiating, senator. Thought it might help. Wentworth doesn't have many friends in Washington. The Feds view… Blackfox is a necessary evil. But we've got nothing."

"You're good, Stryker. I'll give you that."

The backhanded compliment was duly noted.

CHAPTER 28

Janko woke up in the Blackfox jet. He slapped the side of his head, tried to make his ears pop, and realized the plane was losing altitude. He glanced out the window at a desert landscape. His eyes narrowed as he tried to make sense of what he was seeing. "Hey, boss, it looks like Barstow is coming up to meet us. What the hell?"

Dakota slid up the shade, glanced out the window, and saw the jet was flying at about a thousand feet, and in the base leg of the flight, preparing for the final approach to the runway at Barstow, Daggett Airport. He bolted out of his seat and pounded on the pilot's door. Frank, the co-pilot, poked his head out.

"You should buckle up, Dakota."

"What the hell's going on?"

"We've been ordered to land in Barstow and given instructions to taxi to hangar three."

"On whose orders?"

"The Federal Government. It's all I know but we're not about to question their orders. Go belt yourself in. I've gotta land this thing."

Dakota strode back to his seat and pulled his 9mm out of his rucksack. "The Feds have changed our flight plan," he revealed to his team.

"I'm not sure what we're in for, but we'll know soon enough." The team watched Dakota check the clip in his 9mm and slam it home. They followed suit.

The jet started its final descent, touched down, and squealed to a stop before the tower gave directions to hangar three. The jet rolled to the far end of the airport and pulled into the dimly lit structure.

Dakota touched his gun, ready to draw if needed.

Spotlights snapped on, revealing a second Gulfstream jet. This one had the official decal of the Venezuelan government painted on the fuselage. Five serious men wearing dark blue jackets with ATF stenciled in yellow on the left breast and across their backs, stood behind Ed Tilly, a honcho from the State Department. His eyes raked the windows along the Blackfox jet's body, his demeanor predatory.

"Stow your handguns," Dakota warned his men as Tilly waited for the co-pilot to open the hatch and power the stairs to ground level. When they were secured, he climbed up.

The pilot exited the flight cabin as Tilly boarded. "This aircraft is now the property of the United States Government," he announced, showing his credentials to the pilot, and speaking loudly enough for Dakota, the team, the medics, and the oil execs to hear. "This jet has been confiscated in conjunction with the seizure of Blackfox assets, physical, digital, and financial. A Federal pilot with the ATF will take control of the jet.

"Jerry Moran, Bill Vincent, and their medical team will continue on to John Wayne Airport in the Venezuelan jet, accompanied by a member of the Venezuelan Diplomatic Corps, along with a member of the State Department. A press conference will commence upon your arrival. Your families will be there to celebrate your freedom, and the humanitarian medical release aided in large part by our friends in the Venezuelan government." Message served, he walked back down the stairs.

———

Dakota and the team deplaned, their rucksacks in hand. Dakota walked up to Ed Tilly. "What about us?"

"The hangar has a back door. I'm sure you can find your own way home. You're free to take your personal belongings, but the ATF will want any and all firearms, equipment, and explosives stowed on board that are part of the Blackfox arsenal."

"Check the hold," Dakota said.

"Thank you. And as far as I'm concerned, you men don't exist. Take off, the clock is ticking."

Dakota and the men walked out the back door and double-timed it heading for the coffee shop at the far end of the airport where they would be out of sight of the Feds, and could make arrangement for an Uber driver to ferry them to Orange County.

The men were uniformly dressed in Camo pants, and clean T-shirts, carrying rucksacks with their personal belongings, and their pistols.

"It's damn hot," Janko bitched.

"But it's a dry heat," said Avila, always the arbitrator.

"If I don't see another rainforest for the rest of my life, I'll be okay with that," Janko said, shifting his rucksack to the other shoulder and wiping the sweat from his broad forehead with the back of his hand. "Wentworth better have wired our money before he got arrested or we'll have issues."

James chimed in, "Did we just risk our necks for bullshit?"

"No, we saved two lives," Dakota said. "This is all subterfuge. Face-saving for Venezuela, who probably got paid mega millions to play along. Money talks."

No argument from the crew.

———

As the Venezuelan Gulfstream jet taxied off the runway, heading toward the Blackfox hangar space at John Wayne, a crowd of reporters, two ambulances, television vans, and on-camera talent waited to document the joyful return of the Rentex Petroleum executives. Their families had been alerted and were there with a crowd of children, and wives, and Rentex personnel.

It was a blur of action after the cabin doors swung open. The two patients were carried down on gurneys and wheeled past their crying families, who watched their husbands and fathers being loaded into the emergency vehicles. Jerry Moran was slotted in the lead EMT vehicle. His wife held his hand until his gurney was secured into the rear, and jumped in behind him. The driver slammed the door, and with sirens wailing, powered away.

Nothing but smiles from the rest of the families who shared personal stories with reporters about the constant fear they lived with for the past two months. And the anguish that had been put to rest by the hard work of the Rentex Company. They will be forever grateful for Senator Bradley's support in securing their husband's release.

———

It was quiet at the airport as Dakota and the men jumped out of the van that ferried them from Barstow to John Wayne. Their cars were parked in the rear lot of Blackfox's hangar. The sound of jets landing and taking off, the soundtrack of their adios. Dakota shook the hand of each man on his team.

"We started out rough and ended tougher for it," Janko said. "I'll follow you into battle anytime, anyplace."

"Feelings mutual, Janko. I'll make sure your money's secure, no matter what's going on politically at home."

"Good to hear. Later, boss." And the big guy fist-bumped the team, jumped into his Hummer, and motored away.

Dakota reached out to Avila. "Your work was impeccable. The timing of the charges detonating kept the guards and the soldiers busy while we grabbed our guys and escaped with our lives. Nothing but praise is going into your folder."

"Let's do it again."

"Count on it," Dakota said as Avila jumped into his pickup and drove off.

Dakota and James stood watching their two comrades disappear into the night. James broke the silence. He turned and stood face to face with Dakota. James's eyes were clear. No attitude, no recrimination, no defensiveness.

"I don't know how we got to this point, Dakota. I was there in a support position every step of the mission. I've been your biggest ally on the team. I gave you two thumbs up when Wentworth asked for my opinion on hiring you. I testified on your behalf at the court-martial. One of the only men on the planet who stood up for you, at great personal cost. I don't want to get all sensitive on you, but this hurts to the core, man."

Dakota let him make his case.

"There is no way on God's earth I was going to kill you. It makes no sense. None. I dodged a bullet, recovered, and took out the shooter. Our angles might have been off, but we were taking incoming. Standing too close. I corrected my stance and fired. The man went down. I might've saved your life."

Dakota didn't speak for a moment and let the noise of a jet taking off subside. "Okay, James. If I misspoke, sussed the moment wrong, I apologize. I can't make sense out of what happened either. I just called it as I saw it."

James gave off the vibe he understood the pressure Dakota had been operating under in the heat of battle. His face creased into a smile. "I'm willing to put it behind us," he said. "You were great out there, Dakota. As always. If it weren't for you, none of us, including the oil execs, would have made it out of the jungle in one piece."

"Okay, James. Thank you. You were strong under fire and never let up. The suppressing rounds you laid down with Avila, while Janko and I loaded the hostages onto the bird, didn't go unnoticed." And then as if he was coming to a decision, he nodded his head and said, "We're good to go." Dakota left it at that and walked to his car.

"Thank you," James shouted over another plane taking off.

"You need a lift?" Dakota asked.

"I texted a friend. He's on the way."

If James was a liar, he was a damn good one, Dakota thought. But he didn't buy the act. Dakota traded his 9mm for his phone in the steel lockbox behind the rear seat of his Bronco, jumped behind the wheel, and headed for Redondo Beach.

———

Dakota checked his private phone. There were three calls from Agent Steele. The first came in around the time the arrests at Blackfox were being carried out, and Dakota was fighting for his life and the lives of the American hostages in Venezuela. It was short on details, but high on emotion. "Call me as soon as you get this. It's a 911!" He listened to the next two calls. Both 911, both without content. She was hiding specifics in case Dakota was dead, or alive, or under arrest, and they confiscated his burner.

Dakota pulled off the highway and texted Steele in case she was in a meeting. His cell dinged before he placed it down on his center console.

"Jesus Christ, Dakota. You scared the everlasting life out of me. I've been calling for two days. As soon as I got word they were planning to raid Blackfox."

"I couldn't bring the phone."

"I understand, but I panicked."

"I'm home, I'm fine."

"I just saw the press conference. You weren't there, and the hostages got off a Venezuelan jet. What the hell?"

"I'll explain everything when I see you. It looks like the ATF were the principals in the raid. They were waiting for us in Barstow and took control of the jet with support from the DOJ. Someone leaked details of our incursion. Any ideas?"

"I'm trying to get to the bottom of it. Agent Chase shared the information with me at great personal risk. His career was on the line."

"Forgive me if I'm not impressed. Six American citizens could have been killed in the jungle yesterday. And I was one of them."

"I know. It was already in process before Chase brought me into the loop. Someone with a heavy hand at the ATF shared their intel with the DOJ. They pulled strings at the White House and the powers that be agreed to the arrest warrants. I couldn't do anything to stop it. The only way I could've reached you was through Blackfox and that would've been a death sentence. I'm so sorry, Dakota, I was worried. I started praying again. I made promises, promises if you made it out alive, promises I only hope I can keep." Steele's voice broke and

Dakota wished they were together. "I need you to know I was doing everything possible to protect you?"

"You did all that you could. There's no blame in your direction."

"You're sure?"

"Damn sure. But I've got to learn who provided the intel to the ATF."

"We're working on it. Chase is in Washington; I'm expecting a call later in the day."

"What's the word on Blackfox?"

"Wentworth and Ant were arrested and have had their assets frozen. The bail hearing is scheduled for tomorrow. The rumor is, the bond will be hefty. The government's worried about flight risks, and the judge handling the case is a hardliner. The District Attorney gave Kathy Nalvin a flyer. Called her a worker bee without any knowledge about the legality of the raid.

"Thomas Wentworth should be out in about a week, give or take. It's not easy raising twenty-mil with your assets frozen. His lawyers are getting the paperwork ready to post bond. The DA is inclined to allow home confinement, wearing an ankle bracelet. It's good to have friends in high places. Ant, not so lucky."

"I've got to get home, Jean, talk to Billie, take a shower."

"I'm really glad you're in one piece, Dakota." And Jean, overwhelmed with emotion, clicked off.

Dakota sat for a few minutes, stilled his beating heart, turned the key, and headed back to the 405. He was home in twenty minutes, splashed water on his face in the kitchen, and grabbed his personal cellphone he'd left on the table. It was good to be home.

He picked up messages, and was surprised to hear Sarah's voice. She was just checking up on him, hoped he was doing well with his new lease on life, and apologized for any discomfort she might have caused. She only had good intentions at heart. Excited he was out of prison. Not her best move, she said, but true. Hearing her soft voice stirred distant memories. They were only good. Dakota saved the message, and made a mental note to return the call when he caught his breath.

The next message was from Billie. "911. Call ASAP!" Dakota almost laughed, retrieving the second 911 call of the day. He punched in Billie's number.

"You're alive," Billie said, sounding relieved. "You scared me to death. No way to call you, no way to warn you."

"How did you know?" Dakota said, cutting her off.

"Know what?"

"About the raid at Blackfox. We were left high and dry fighting our asses off in the rainforest. Our support cut off."

"You've got to be kidding."

"Well...not kidding. I'll fill you in later. What were you calling about? Warn me from what?"

"I followed Mullrooney to the beach in your mother's car where he met up with Doug Darby. The douchebag whose car I trashed."

"Okay?" he said, wanting her to get on with it.

"He was driving a new car. Made sense after what I did to his ride. I grabbed the plate with my phone and sent it to an old friend on the force. She did some digging and told me the car was registered to James Marshal."

Silence.

"You there?" Billie asked.

"I'm here. I need a few minutes to process that. If you're not busy, why don't you meet me at the house, and we'll get caught up. Let yourself in. I need a shower and a drink. We gotta talk."

"Done," Billie said.

Dakota listened to clips of the press conference being replayed on KNX 1070 talk radio, as the State Department official was introducing the joyful families of the men who had been held hostage for two painful months.

It was a smart move on Wentworth's part to get ahead of the publicity. An obvious sea change had taken place in the government's stand on the incursion. Wentworth probably had no idea he'd already be behind bars when the press conference was in full swing.

CHAPTER 29

Dakota walked out of the bedroom, towel drying his hair with such ferocity, it kept Billie silent. She understood her nephew and waited for the man's anger to subside. Knowing he'd talk when he caught his breath.

Dakota hand-combed his hair off his forehead and let loose. "James has a relationship with Doug. There's a good shot he was the initial leak. A couple of drinks, how was your day sort of bullshit, kept Doug up to speed on our training, and the specifics of our travel itinerary, and the planned timing of the attack."

"Does Doug have enough juice to generate a call to action from the ATF. This isn't small potatoes," Billie said.

"No. And up pops Captain Mullrooney. He's got connections in high places. Doug shares the intelligence with Mullrooney, who calls an old friend at the ATF.

"We were locked down with a barrage of incoming, and when I called for air support, the arrests at Blackfox were playing out in real time over our radios. We were left hanging."

"Jesus, son."

"And here's the kicker. I believe James was going to kill me on the battlefield. He could've blamed it on friendly fire. But then, without

Kathy able to fire her missile, there were only four of us standing against eight heavily armed soldiers. The armored truck was inching closer to our position, and if anything happened to our hostages, there would have been no payday.

"I think James changed course, stepped up, put himself in my line of vision, and clicked into Ranger mode. He denies it, but Billie, he was about to cut me in half with one squeeze of his M4."

"I'd go with your gut, Dakota. It's primal. A man, a woman, knows when they're about to be killed. The fear response is hard-wired in our DNA."

Dakota nodded and tossed the towel onto the back of a kitchen chair, and continued his train of thought. "And on the plane traveling back, after I'd confronted him, and he lied like a rug, I took some time and replayed our relationship. From Afghanistan, to the courtroom, to Blackfox.

"That's where James confessed – in our first meet after my interview with Wentworth – to feeling guilty about not visiting me in prison. Took it on the chin, but the emotion was strained. He'd lost a hard-earned promotion in the service because he supported me at the court-martial and knew his possibility of moving up the ranks was nil. The Army didn't take kindly to him testifying against the captain, who was a military rock star. So, he mustered out.

"I walked through my moves at the senator's fundraiser. After I ordered him to call in the chopper and headed up the hill, things started to settle down. He got me on the cell, complimented me for saving the senator's life. Said something like, I hadn't lost any moves in prison. I still had it. But the vibe was strange. I chalked it up to a little green envy. First day on the job, and playing the hero while he did cleanup again.

"I flashed on something I hadn't given much thought to as it played out. When we were crossing the senator's lawn before the attack, heading toward the tennis courts, James checked his watch and then sent me forward alone for the meet-and-greet. I thought he was being selfless, giving me the lead, being a loyal friend."

"But he may have been leading you to slaughter," Billie said, finishing Dakota's train of thought. "The senator's bullet was meant for you, compliments of Captain Mullrooney." Billie spun as Dakota's story played out in her head.

"I'm feeling it," Dakota said. "Can't prove it. I think so. We know Doug was a sniper serving under Mullrooney in his last command before he mustered out. And we know Doug was trying to get his hands on Sarah to set me up and take me out."

"How do we move forward?" Billie asked.

"You jammed up Doug's SUV pretty bad from what I could see on the video Sarah texted me. An expensive car usually takes some time to be appraised by insurance. Might still be sitting at a body shop somewhere. My guess, somewhere close to where his condo is situated. Let's comb the area, pull up all the body shops within a two-mile radius, and give it a try. See if the wreck has any secrets to share."

"Sounds like a plan. I'll head home, get on my laptop, and pull up a list."

"Let's toss one back first." Dakota poured the aged scotch into two glasses, and handed one off. They clinked. "To being alive," Dakota toasted.

"And to keeping it that way," Billie added.

They sipped the scotch and savored the moment. Then Billie added, "For cheating death, once again." They tossed back their drink. "You must be dead on your feet," Billie said as she placed her glass on the counter and headed for the back door.

"Too much adrenaline. I'll pick you up around nine?"

"Works for me."

Dakota heard the Vette's eight cylinders rumble alive and head down the road.

———

Dakota nursed a second glass of scotch as he sat on the front porch, pushing the old rocker back and forth, pleased to be home. He was a free man, but life was so complicated he questioned if he was up for the challenges that lay ahead. It took all of his resolve not to call Steele and invite himself over. He knew she had feelings for him, he also knew she wouldn't sacrifice her career for their relationship. And he wouldn't want her to. So, he'd keep his powder dry and push forward. He wondered where the neighborhood tabby cat was when he needed him. The tension of the day was starting to dissipate when he heard a car driving slowly up the block. Dakota reflexively reached for his 9mm that was secured in the Bronco's lockbox.

A white Honda pulled tentatively to the curb in front of his house and turned off the lights. Sarah stepped out, and smiled shyly over the roof of her car before walking up the driveway. Walking wasn't the proper word, Dakota thought, she almost glided, light on her feet. She was dressed casually, jeans, light green t-shirt, ballet flats, designer hoody and looked like a million bucks. She could wear anything, Dakota remembered, and all eyes would focus on Sarah when she entered a room. He never really understood what she saw in him, but she made him a better man.

"You pouring?" she asked, smiling as she stood in front of the porch. Sarah was always comfortable in her own skin, but Dakota understood it couldn't have been easy for her to show up unannounced.

"What are you drinking?"

"Anything crushed from grapes."

"Have a seat," he said, inviting her up. Dakota remembered what Sarah enjoyed on their date nights and opened a bottle of chardonnay and poured a glass.

They sat side by side on the rocker, the way they had on so many nights, making plans for their wedding, for their future together, before he deployed for the last time and his life blew up.

They had no trouble sitting in comfortable silence, and Dakota waited for Sarah to open up. She took a sip of wine and started: "I want you to know that I won't ask you any questions you're not ready, or willing, or able to answer. It's not because I don't care. I know it's what you need."

Dakota gave that some thought and sipped his scotch.

"Me." She looked at him over the rim of the wine glass and her face split into an easy smile. "I don't need anything. I'm self-sufficient. I don't need to be saved. I don't need someone to take care of me. It took me a while to accept Billie's wise counsel, but it finally penetrated my thick skull and hit home."

"What did?"

"That I was angry, and broken. I tried to replace you. It didn't work. You see, the problem was you were always alive in my heart. And I couldn't let go of that. You're still there. After all these years, can you believe it? You were the only man who could move me, touch me in that way. I'm sorry for complicating your life. But there it is."

Sarah took a big sip, handed Dakota her glass, and kissed him lightly on the lips. She stared into his eyes, and his stomach did a flip. She smiled at his reaction, turned, and walked down the driveway, got into her car, and drove away from the house. Sarah took the shortcut home, Dakota noticed. The route down the hill that only a woman who had spent many years with her lover knew how to navigate.

Dakota wasn't a metaphysical kind of LA man, but he sure felt the universe was working in mysterious ways that night. But just in case, he walked into the garage, took his Glock out of the lock box in the back of the Bronco, and walked into the house.

CHAPTER 30

Dakota and Billie's first day in their search of body shops, looking for Doug's trashed Mercedes, came up with nothing but dead ends. They decided to pack it in, and start again in the a.m. This time they'd widen the perimeter of their investigation, and add any shop that had German repair somewhere in the name.

Second day on the job, when they walked out of the third shop with nothing but bad attitudes, they got cranky.

"Maybe it was a stupid idea?" Dakota said.

"Might be, but it's the only one we've got."

"You were supposed to say there are no stupid ideas."

"Nah, there are plenty of stupid ideas."

They hit gold on the fourth.

A repair shop that specialized in Mercedes. Run by an irritable German who stonewalled them, refusing to allow them to inspect the interior of the vehicle. But after Billie flashed her badge, and Dakota slipped him a C-note, Hans gave up some information, admonished them not to damage the wrecked car, and disappeared into his office.

———

Dakota was sitting in his Bronco with Billie, drinking coffee and eating ham and cheese croissants keeping an eye on the matte gray Mercedes, parked in the rear of the body shop. He texted Steele, and was waiting on a return call.

Dakota answered on the first chirp of his burner. "I can't be involved in this, but we have a strong lead into the attempted murder of Senator Bradley. You have to get a team over to Hans German Body Works ASAP. It was like pulling German teeth, but Hans, who owns the shop, let it slip the USAA insurance appraiser is scheduled to check out the car later this afternoon. And we don't want a potential crime scene to be toyed with."

"I'll get on it. What do you have?"

"I took a few pictures of the sniper's shooting nest when I first discovered the location the day of the fundraiser. And I got a clean photo of a boot print left at the scene.

"I explained the strong connection between James and Doug to you this morning. We found Doug's car, wore gloves, and tore the Mercedes SUV apart. Under the brake pedal are two or three clumps of dried mud that, from my eye, seems to match the boot treads in the photograph. There's also dry grass or weeds, in the corner of the driver's side mat, with the same color mud staining them. I texted you the new photos, and the car's location. We've got eyes on the vehicle, but we're playing beat the clock.

"And here's another thought. I never heard if you retrieved a clean bullet from the grass, the night of the fundraiser. It was the first round fired, and it kicked up turf, but I don't think it hit anything solid.

"It's possible you'll find a match to one of Doug's weapons if he stores them at his condo. You have his address. There was nothing in the rear of the car, but the rear compartment was pretty torn up from an accident."

"Great work, Dakota. As soon as our team arrives, take off. I agree you should have no involvement. If the investigation gets tied to you, the target on your back gets bigger."

"Copy that." Dakota clicked off and turned to Billie. "Let's see how fast the Feds can get their act in gear." Billie was grinning and trying not to laugh.

"What?"

"Pretty torn up from an accident," she said, quoting him. "Good one."

"Damn Billie, you are still one hell of a detective."

"Eh, yeah…thanks," she said, deflecting the compliment. "I think this Starbuck's crap is better hot."

"Everyone's a critic."

———

The two hours that passed felt like ten. Dakota was still jet-lagged, and his surprise visit from Sarah went a long way to helping his psyche, but little to reset his time clock.

"Shit," Billie said as a car with a USAA logo plastered on the side of the car pulled to the curb. A middle-aged insurance adjuster stepped out and stretched.

"Lemme handle this." Billie slid out of the Bronco and approached the man. She flashed her retired badge and a serious smile and explained the situation.

To Dakota's amusement, the man responded to her female wiles, checked his watch, nodded his head, mounted up, and drove down the road.

Billie jumped back into the car, "I've still got it. He was happy to help out an officer of the law. I sent him to Starbucks."

And then, as if with perfect coordinated timing, two gray Government Issue Sedans and an ERT, Evidence Response Team truck, pulled into the repair bay and surrounded the Mercedes.

They watched as Hans ran out of the office, and was stopped in his tracks as he read the search warrant the lead FBI agent handed him, and relaxed some. Not pleased, but not about to mess with the Feds. Smart man.

Dakota started the Bronco and pulled away from the curb. "It's good having important people in high places."

"Great work, Dakota."

"Back at you. This should get our scumbag's attention. I'm going to need backup the next few days."

"I'll drive the Beemer, and stay on your tail."

"I expect to hear from Wentworth, or his lawyer, sometime today or tomorrow. It'll be interesting to hear what he has to say. I'll give you the car keys when we get to the house."

———

Captain Mullrooney was seated in the power chair in his spacious living room being waited on by Doug and James, who looked ragged after his life-altering warfare in Venezuela.

Doug replenished the captain's whiskey glass, who nodded imperiously when the pour was sufficient, and then topped off James's glass, and then his own. They'd pulled up two folding chairs used for their weekly card games and sat around the wide screen watching the Padres getting tromped by the Dodgers.

"Who did you share the intel with about my trip south of the border?" James's shocking accusation came out of left field and silenced the room.

The captain's eyes narrowed, blinked, and recovered. He looked amused, took a healthy sip, set down his drink, and evaded, "Gotta drain the snake, gentlemen." He stood, stretched his good arm, and took a step toward the bathroom.

James drew a six-inch expandable baton from his back pocket, ejected the length of the steel rod to sixteen inches, and whipped it against the back of the captain's head, hoping he hadn't killed the man. Not yet.

Mullrooney's legs turned to rubber, and Doug caught him before he hit the deck and muscled him onto one of the folding chairs.

James was there in an instant, having pulled two bungee cords from his leather backpack and secured the captain's upper body to the chair. He grabbed plastic ties, bound the man's legs and his one good arm to the side of the chair.

"I feel better already," James said, his eyes blazing with hate. He walked over, drained his glass, waiting for the captain to regain consciousness.

Doug walked into the bathroom and found a pistol buried beneath a stack of neatly folded white towels. He smirked as he walked out and tossed it onto the couch. "Gotta give him credit. The old man wasn't going to go down without a fight."

"Fuck him."

The captain's eyes blinked open, and assessed his dire situation. "Judge and Jury?" he asked his allies turned tormentors.

"You've got one chance to answer our questions," James said, cold as winter.

"It wasn't me who called in the Feds," he barked with the attitude that made his soldiers stand at attention, and salute. "I might have spoken out of turn to Terrance Gorman. He owns the house I'm living in, for Christ's sake. Never crossed my mind he'd use the information for his own political gain. And James, I thought we had a deal. You didn't deliver. He didn't deliver, Doug. What can I say?" His gaze shifted back to James. "I don't know why I trusted you," he said, his glare so sharp, it could cut glass.

James nodded and stepped close to the captain so he could bear witness to what was about to take place. "Last chance. More than you've given most of your victims. Who did you share my intel with?"

"Shoot him!" Mullrooney ordered Doug, who flinched, but stood firm.

The captain didn't see the baton whipping through the air, but felt the pain in his good arm and understood the message being sent. His howl was drowned out by the surround sound of screams on the television, emanating from the rabid baseball fans as one of the Padres hit a home run.

The captain sucked in the wave of nausea that threatened to overtake him. "You're a weak man, James. Always taking orders, never in command. Did you think a few kind words from Doug would cleanse the mortal sin of testifying against me? If Dakota had been left on the battlefield, as planned, this wouldn't be happening."

"And I wouldn't have made it out of Venezuela alive. You set me up, my team, and the hostages." And then it all fell into place for James. "The senator would've been in deep shit if we were all dead. Your friend, Terrance Gorman, who envies his seat in the Senate, would have been thrilled with that turn of events. Give him a chance to move up the political ladder."

"You're delusional."

"What did it take to turn your back on an American squad? He offer you a platform for a big mea-culpa, and redemption of your sins?"

The captain's eyes seared into Doug's, "There's only one way to make it out of here whole. Untie me...and kill your weak sister. All will be forgiven. Shoot him now!!!"

Doug's silenced Sig Sauer made a spitting sound as the bullet blasted through the captain's mouth and scattered brain matter across the living room rug.

Doug and James slipped on latex gloves. The two men worked in silence with military precision. James took the gun from Doug, wiped it clean, and snipped the plastic tie off the captain's good arm. He placed the 9mm in his left hand and squeezed his dead fingers around the weapon. He fired a second round that penetrated the overstuffed couch and disappeared in the folds of the thick black leather, but left powder burns on Captain Mullrooney's hand.

Doug went to work on the captain's legs, snipped off the plastic ties, unhooked the bungee cords, and tilted the chair sideways until the captain's lifeless body tumbled to the rugged floor.

After James unscrewed the silencer, he tossed the pistol a few feet away from the captain's outstretched hand, and stowed the silencer in his leather bag.

Doug ripped a few strands of bloody hair from the back of the dead man's hair and swiped them on the sharp edge of the chair back, trying to paint a picture of suicide. He grabbed the captain's 9mm off the couch and slipped it into James's backpack.

The men bagged the glasses they drank from, wiped down the bottle of booze, and any other objects they may have touched that afternoon. After making sure the front door was locked, they pulled the security tape out of the machine in Mullrooney's den, inserted a blank, shut the machine off, and exited the rear door, locking it behind them.

Doug jumped behind the wheel of the rental car he had signed for with a fake ID, and planned on returning after picking up James's Audi. All-and-all, not a bad day's work.

"Did we kill the right man?" James asked, having second thoughts. His voice tentative.

"Terrance Gorman doesn't have the connections to pull off the raid on Blackfox. It was Mullrooney who had ties to Washington. Mullrooney, who was headed for the Pentagon if he hadn't been a killer, taken down by Dakota. But you're right about one thing. I believed the captain when he said he talked out of school to Terrance. They were thick as thieves. We didn't know Terrance owned the damn house he was living in. When the captain's body turns up, he's the first call the cops will make. And Terrance will give up our names as potential suspects. Terrance has to go." The death sentence was meted out with intellectual coolness.

Not what James wanted to hear. He didn't like the growing body count but understood the necessity to clean house. He stared out the window, eyes blind to the passing landscape, and said:

"When we take out Dakota, we'll be home free."

CHAPTER 31

Four government cars pulled to the curb outside Doug Darby's condo at 369 Pine Street. FBI agents Steele and Chase spilled out of their vehicles, and strode up to the security door. The HOA president of the twenty-unit complex had been notified, met them at the glass door, unlocked, and pointed the agents in the direction of Darby's unit on the fourth floor. Chase, rightfully gave Steele the lead on the raid because it was her baby and she had delivered the goods.

Steele knocked and announced their identity in an attempt to raise the occupants and received no reply. She stepped aside, and an agent using a tactical battering ram smashed the door open.

Steele and Chase led with their weapons as they stormed through the splintered doorframe and flipped on the lights. The expansive condo was two thousand square feet of modern living. The agents cleared the unit, did a cursory check to get a feel for the place, and met back in the living room.

"There are two bedrooms," Steele said. "Two toothbrushes, two razors, two full closets, and only one bed," she said with raised eyebrows. "Didn't the HOA guy say that Doug and James had been roommates for the past five years?"

"Affirmative."

"Hmmm. I'm in the wrong line of work. This place is gorgeous. We should clear the cars from the front of the building in case they come home while we're searching the place. Hate to have them on the run. They're driving a black Audi SUV."

"Read my mind." And Agent Chase gave the orders while Steele started searching in earnest.

The second bedroom was outfitted with a personal gym. Free weights, abdominal machine, multi-use strength apparatus, and rowing machine. Nothing seemed excessive or out of the ordinary until she stepped into the walk-in closet. There were multiple pairs of running shoes, a few loafers, and two pairs of military grade boots. She checked the first pair, and it looked like they hadn't seen any hard work. The second pair was worn in the heel, the leather scarred, and the right boot had a few clots of mud in the deep tread. Steele's heart started pounding. She'd wait for the tech crew to let her know if she'd hit a home run.

Both men were ex-military, and James had just returned from a sortie in Venezuela. She didn't know any men still in the business in one fashion or another who didn't carry. There was no sign of firearms in the condo. None. Didn't make sense. If nothing was found on site, she'd keep an eye out for keys to a storage facility. Wouldn't be the first time men hid their cache of weapons away from home base.

Chase walked back into the room. Steele pointed out the boot. "Looks like a potential match." She took a photo of the tread, and left the boot where it lay.

"Did the manager mention individual storage units for each owner?"

"Negative on that. He mentioned something about insurance and fire hazard."

"It looks like one of our men stashed his clothes in the main bedroom, the other in here." She pulled a handful of clothes off the rail and tossed them on the treadmill. She walked back into the closet and started tapping the wall. Her first thought, it was a well-built condo. Better than hers. The construction felt solid. She moved toward the rear, thinking she would kill for this much storage space, and continued tapping with her knuckles. Solid, solid, and then, thunk. The sound turned hollow. "Hey," and Chase popped his head in. "Check this out." She repeated her pounding.

"Sounds like a hidi-hole."

Steele glanced at her boss. "You're good," she said dry.

"Tell that to my wife."

Steele lit her mini-LED flashlight and ran it around the perimeter. She could see a faint seam in the plasterboard wall. "You have a blade?" she asked, excitement coloring her voice.

Chase got caught up in her energy and traded the pocketknife he was never without for her flashlight. She pulled out the long blade and wedged it into the seam. A four-by-six panel pulled away from the wall, and slid down into her hands. Steele's heart rate ticked up a notch. "Holy crap! Weapons storage," she said and propped the panel against the back wall.

"Lemme in."

Steele changed places with Chase, and they could both see a cache of automatic weapons: M4 assault rifles, M9 Beretta, and assorted handguns of every make and measure. An MK12 sniper rifle looked like it has seen combat. Steele made a mental note to have it checked for recent activity. Metal crates were filled with hundreds of rounds of ammunition, full banana clips, and firearm cleaning kits.

"Son of a bitch," Agent Chase said. "There were two empty suitcases in the front closet, and a rucksack in the bedroom that's partially unpacked, it's gotta belong to James. It smells like deployment. Funky. The boys are definitely still in town. I'll make sure the front and the back of the complex are covered."

Steele said, "Let's get a car at the turnoff on PCH and another at the far end of Pine, in case they come in the back way."

"You and I can sit tight," Chase said, "while the tech crew does their job. If the man loves his weapons and thinks he's gotten away with attempted murder, the sniper's weapon might still be here in his closet."

"If we get lucky," Steele said, "and can match the rifling on the round we pulled from the senator's house to one of his guns, he's ours."

"I'll set men in the fire exits on both sides of the building," Chase said, his energy through the roof. "Let's kill any lights that can be seen from the street."

———

James and Doug traded in the rental sedan and drove James's SUV across Rosecrans. He made a left onto Pacific Coast Highway. They were both toasted from the booze and adrenaline. James was about to make the left onto Pine, and:

"What the hell?" Doug shouted.

James startled and put the turn signal on.

"Keep driving! Don't stop!"

James jerked the wheel, and continued down PCH.

"There was a light on in our unit," Doug said, his voice sharp. "It snapped off when I glanced up. Gotta be cops."

"Are you sure? What the fuck?"

"Keep driving! It can't be about the captain, but someone was in our condo. They've got something on us."

"What?"

"How the hell would I know!"

They drove in paranoid silence. "What do we do?" James asked, his voice unsteady. On the edge. Not enough sleep. In over his head.

Doug had seen his partner unravel before. "We stay cool, James. We hit the bank first thing in the morning. Grab what we need in our storage unit, and hit the road until we know where we stand. My sister's on the East Coast, we can crash at her place in Big Bear. You just returned from a deployment and deserve a little downtime. We gut it out."

"Is there anything at the condo we could get nailed for?"

"My MK12 is still in our stash."

"I told you…"

"Shut the fuck up. It hasn't seen action since Afghanistan; it's my baby. Got history. If I'd used it, we wouldn't be up to our ankles in horse shit. And no lectures for Christ's sake, we're no good if we're not a unit."

"You're right. Okay, sorry." James sucked in a long hard breath. His mind spinning. "Sounds like a plan…we gotta take out Dakota before he talks. He doesn't really have shit on me."

Doug was all in.

"Dakota's gotta go."

CHAPTER 32

Dakota was sipping coffee in his de facto office at Peluso, Costa, and Litto, waiting on Agent Steele. She'd been up most of the night and was wired to the gills. Her adrenaline filled the room, and she started talking before she took a seat. Dakota poured her a cup.

"The ERT team will do ballistic testing on the sniper's rifle found at their condo. They're backed up, crying budgetary constraints, but promised to try and push our case to the top of the list. The FBI does have the first round fired at the senator's fundraiser. It was pancaked some, but the rifling marks are clean enough to provide evidence at trial if they match the spiral grooves inside the rifle's barrel. And damn it, Dakota, we're on our way."

Dakota looked at Steele over his coffee cup, his eyes creased into a grin, enjoying her enthusiasm.

"The mud clots you discovered appear to match the treads in Doug's boots, also found at the Pine Street condo. Speaking of which, did you know James and Doug are an item. They've been living together for five years, and there's only one bed in the unit?"

"I did not," Dakota said, raising his eyebrows. "News to me."

"The evidence response team is trying to match the grass and soil and whatnot they collected from the sniper's nest above the senator's house, to the samples you found in Doug's SUV. We should get verified results of the chemical composition test of the mineral and plant debris sometime tomorrow, or Thursday at the latest. They're crossing the T's and all that, but it's looking good for a solid arrest.

"The men never showed last night. They could be partying; they might have taken some spur-of-the-moment vacation time. We've got men on the ground in case they turn up. We'll take 'em in for questioning, but not drop the hammer until we know for certain the samples are a slam-dunk. We don't want to scare them away.

"Their backs will be against the wall," Dakota said. "If they were dangerous before, they'll turn into rabid dogs now."

"Agent Chase is elated. Made a crack about hiring you and Billie."

"All good news. I'm headed for the RockPile to shoot the shit with Ralph who reached out, which is unlike him."

"He must need something. Stay safe, and watch your back."

"Will do." And Dakota headed for the elevator.

———

Dakota was shooting the breeze with Ralph. They had the bar to themselves; the late afternoon crowd was non-existent. Two men could be heard talking trash at the pool table, the sound of pool balls clacking rose with the number of empty long necks drunk. Trish was turning the pages of a *People Magazine*. Checking out the pictures and bypassing the stories. "A picture is worth a thousand words," she once explained to Dakota, who nodded politely. He needed all the allies he could muster with this group.

Ralph was silent, lost in thought, and then, "What's the story with Ant?" Ralph didn't like to probe, he hated when people questioned him about most anything.

"He's in deep shit."

Ralph's lined face couldn't hide his concern. "Then so are we."

"How so?"

"Our quarterly news pamphlet was due last week. We knew Ant had a lot on his plate, but we don't. We don't fire out the pages, our bottom-line suffers. And we run a tight ship."

This was news to Dakota, who acted like he was up to speed on the action. "What was the substance of this month's issue?"

"Senator Bradley's socialist opponent is nipping at his heels. This issue was supposed to spread enough leftist bullshit to make QAnon recoil. A shitstorm of truth and near truth that our readers suck up. Ant is a genius at writing simple ideas that can be repeated, shared online, and rile our soldiers who are angry to begin with. We got trolls out there snorting crank and spreading our word twenty-four seven. Gives them a reason to exist."

"Good subscription list?"

"Six thousand and growing. Keeps me off the streets. We hit militia groups all over the country, toss in the prisons, and we do okay. Our people share our posts, and we build our list, raise funds, and rake in the cash. It's what keeps us afloat. Kid has a gift. Knows how to make a woman like Stacey Abrams sound like the whore she is. Christian-right eats up that kinda bullshit."

"Fuels the flames," Dakota said.

"And then we alert the troops when our enemies file for a permit to march."

"How do you stay on top of that?"

"Wolf Pack and our network of underground militias have loyal members on the inside in almost thirty states. Cops, service men, white-collar workers, whatever, they give us a heads-up, so we always have a presence. Our guys show an hour before curfew in volatile situations, agitate, and turn the already pissed off Black Lives Matter crowds violent. Turns a peaceful protest into a riot. And we have the twenty-four-hour news cycle on the left and the right to thank for punching up the coverage."

"Fuckin' smart."

"You're telling me. We put out a call to arms we get results. Antifa gets blamed in social media, on Fox News, Newsmax, and our radio DJs, who do the heavy lifting. We're a well-oiled machine, but Ant is our man. You gotta get him out. Kid like that, don't know how he'll deal with lockup. And we can't survive without him."

"All he needs is computer privileges inside, and he should be good to go."

"Not if the dude's someone's bitch."

"Shit." Dakota nodded in agreement.

Dakota caught Trish's eye, and she poured another round of drinks. He clinked Ralph's glass, and they tossed back the liquor.

"So, was this your brainchild? It's a smart move."

"It started as a side hustle for Blackfox. Ant made the offer, and I built the brand. Win, win. We have our thumbs on the hatred. Entire fuckin' families who hate the government more than we do. Most of us served in one form or another and now we're suckin' hind tit."

"Where does Terrance fit in? He seems to be a little out of his league."

"Douche is riding the conservative wave. If Senator Bradley stumbles in the midterms, he'll run for office. Total asshole, but might be good for the movement."

"I saw him making moves on the donors at Bradley's fundraiser."

Ralph nodded. "Rich keep gettin'richer..."

"Money talks," Dakota said.

"You said it, brother. So don't forget your friends as you move up through the ranks. But get our little guy out of the slammer or we're in deep shit. We have just enough dough to send out this month's issue, but without content, we're dead in the water."

"I'll do what I can."

Nick banged the front door open and made his entrance, heading for the bar. He didn't walk with his usual strut, and Dakota thought he might unload on him. He cut the man off at the pass with, "Buy you a drink?"

The nod was instantaneous.

Dakota turned to Trish, who was already in motion. Dakota winked, and she pulled out a glass for Nick and one for herself.

Ralph gave his bud a glare. "You have something to say?"

Nick's eyes narrowed slightly. "Sorry I gave you a hard time last week, bro. Terrance had his head up his ass. Bad on me, brother."

"No worries, Nick. We can never be too careful in our line of work. Let's toast to my team and the hostages coming home alive." Dakota made a mental note to thank Steele for saving his bacon again. He knew how he'd like to thank her, but that wasn't in the cards right now.

Four glasses came together, and the bourbon disappeared.

CHAPTER 33

Dakota was driving the Bronco, a smile on his face. Steele had saved his life again. He was surprised at the intensity of his feelings for this powerful woman, but instead of worrying about the complex nature of their relationship, decided to let it ride.

And then there was Sarah. The honesty and strength it took to open up after her life had been seriously jeopardized because of their past, was impressive and confusing. His attraction to Sarah was hard-wired into his psyche. It was never casual, and never dishonest. And the target on his back, could bleed into her life if he shared his truth.

His cell phone rang, and he answered on the Bluetooth.

"Sorry for calling so late, Dakota, but Thomas is heading home, security bracelet on his ankle, and hunting for bear."

"Senator Bradley?"

"Yes, my apologies. The ego's a terrible thing to waste, and I'm guilty as hell. But Thomas isn't. It's complicated, but Thomas sent his heartfelt apologies and asked you to meet us at his house in about an hour. He has to shower and rinse off the stink of the holding cell. Apologies again. I'm a dunderhead sometimes. This whole affair has me off my game. I'll text you Thomas's address, and hopefully see you."

"I'll be there. Thank you, senator."

"Please, call me Jack."

"A pleasure, sir."

"Jack," he said with a smile in his voice.

Dakota made an illegal U-turn on PCH and headed in the opposite direction.

———

Thomas Wentworth's estate was a modern architectural masterpiece set in the hills of Orange County with a dramatic view of the Irvine Business Center skyline in the distance. A blanket of lights spread out below, rippling with the evening heat escaping the valley floor. Four Blackfox security guards stood at the perimeters of the property, nine millimeters holstered at their sides. Keeping a protective eye on the three men locked in serious conversation on the massive patio.

Wentworth looked like he'd gone six rounds with a heavyweight. Unshaven, hair flying in all directions, and a level of anger no one at the meeting had ever witnessed before. He hitched up his pant leg and showed Senator Bradley and Dakota his newest accessory. An ankle bracelet. A gift from the United States government to monitor his movements. It was the legal concession his team made that allowed him the honor of suffering house arrest after handing over his passport and a twenty-million-dollar bond. "When I find out who shared our intelligence with the ATF, I'll skin them alive."

The men sat in silence as Wentworth's assistant, Bob, an elegant, silver-haired man who ran the estate, delivered three glasses of scotch, a leather-bound bucket of ice, and the bottle on a silver tray. He expertly set it down on the inch-thick glass table that fronted the pool and the killer view below.

The men picked up their glasses. "To better days," the senator said. They tapped and drank.

"I was taught never to apologize," Wentworth said tight. "That it intimated guilt. A sign of weakness. But, Dakota," he said and he sucked in a deep breath. "I offer you my sincere apology. Your life was threatened, and that of your comrades, and the Rentex hostages. I can promise you this. You and your team will be well compensated for the added danger you fought your way out of. Your heroics did not go unappreciated. Ant and I watched your mission in real time, and it was epic."

Dakota didn't know how to respond. "Thank you," was all he could come up with. "How's Ant doing? Did he make bond?"

"Doesn't look that way. And my discretionary funds were tapped dry getting myself out. I'll do what I can, but they've frozen all assets associated with Blackfox until their forensic specialists' comb through my books. Sons of bitches. Could drag on for months.

"For some reason, they hit Ant with the same number I suffered. Now Ant has money, but not that kind of cash. The DA made the case to the judge; he'd be a major flight risk. He might not be wrong. My lawyer said he was really shaken up."

Senator Bradley remained stoic. Not mentioning he had been with the FBI when they sold out Ant to Ted Northrup, the DOJ lawyer, at their Washington breakfast meeting, in an attempt to stop the raid on Blackfox. They failed, the wheels of justice were already turning, and it was too late for Wentworth's wunderkind.

"And Kathy Nalvin?"

Wentworth answered, "Of course, you know Kathy was arrested. And then, after four hours of interrogation, released. They decided a drone operator was a hired hand, and not privy to the inner workings of my company. You and your team fell into the same designation. The only aspect they got right."

"What now?" Dakota asked.

Senator Bradley said, "It's why we're here. Trying to figure that out. Hoping you might help."

Dakota waited for Wentworth to answer the million-dollar question. The boss took a thoughtful sip of his scotch and then knocked the rest back. He tilted the bottle, topped off his glass, and poured for the other two.

"I'm just working out the particulars. The reality is, I'm going to come out on top of this, but the trial...who knows how long that's going to drag on? It's going to take months to negotiate the details. If I appear to be out of step, show weakness of any kind, there are four contenders ready to fill my shoes, claw over my back, and take what's mine. Fifteen years of hard work. I'm never going to let that happen.

"I'm looking for someone to step in and become the face of Black-fox. Someone I'd trust with my life. Someone with the backbone to negotiate with authoritarian strong men, egotistical heads of state, and homegrown militia units. I'm looking for an Executive Consultant with the bonafides to *still* wagging lips, and learn the ropes on the job." Wentworth glanced at the senator, took a sip of scotch, and let that percolate. He knew Dakota was smart enough to have some idea where the conversation was headed. But this was a hell of a lot to assimilate in one sitting.

"I came up with a short list of men and women who could fulfill my special needs. I would still be running the show. I'd be there every step of the way, to counsel, explain the missions, how to fulfill the contracts, and keep Blackfox afloat. The senator would be available to help with any political ramifications that might occur, and trust me, they will be never-ending."

Dakota's eyes moved from Wentworth to Bradley's, whose eyes narrowed in anticipation.

"In the end," Wentworth continued, "the answer was clear. There was only one name that remained at the top of my list.

"It was you, Dakota."

CHAPTER 34

Dakota was cruising home, Diana Krall was singing "Walk On By" on the radio. His ears were ringing after spending the afternoon with Ralph at the RockPile and the heavy rock that played nonstop on the jukebox, at mind-numbing decibels. Steele picked up the phone on the second ring.

Dakota started talking before saying hello, fueled by expensive booze.

"Wentworth offered me Blackfox. Or, at least to become the face of Blackfox while he's fighting criminal charges."

"Damn."

"He'll be the puppet master working behind the curtain, and I'll be the front man. Senator Bradley will be there to help with any political obstacles, and I'll get on-the-job training."

That bit of information silenced Steele, but her brain was processing at the speed of light. "The press will dig into your past."

"Wentworth believes in redemption. Says I'm a brilliant tactician, I've paid my dues to society. I'm battle-proven, and braver than he is. He might take some heat from his investors, he said, but nothing he can't handle. Blackfox is still a privately held company, and if the board of directors raises a fuss, they'll be replaced. The DOJ already helped the cause with Washington's press release, and the press conference that put a happy face on our illegal incursion."

"This is big, Dakota. It's what we've wanted from the beginning."

"To infiltrate Blackfox."

"To have you rise to a position where you'd be privy to their internal workings. No one, and I mean no one but me, thought this would become a reality. You made it happen."

Dakota processed that and waited for her to go on. He knew there would be more, there always was.

"What did you say?" she asked.

"That I was flattered. I'd need some time to meditate on what would be a life-altering move. That I was seriously grateful to be given the opportunity. After six-plus years behind bars, it was a dream come true. I just needed to do some soul searching to make sure if I accepted the challenge, I could dig deep enough to fulfill Wentworth's expectations."

"That was good. How did he respond?"

"He agreed with me. Didn't expect an immediate answer. But wanted me to know, he wouldn't have made the offer if he weren't sure of himself, and my gifts. His words."

"How does it make you feel?"

"Jean, in all honesty, it's an out-of-body experience. I really do need to give it some serious thought. First, I knew I wouldn't make a move without your input. It's a tough call."

"You're telling me."

"If I say yes, I won't blink an eye. I'll find a way to shut them down, and watch their careers topple like dominos. Getting out of there alive is another matter."

"If you say no?"

"My guess is…I'm out the door and will have squandered a once-in-a-lifetime opportunity. A man like Wentworth doesn't gamble on his business, his lifeblood, and lose. He'd hold a grudge, for sure."

"Just remember one thing, Dakota. You are a free man. If you decide to accept, it has to be the absolute, correct move for you. Don't do it for anyone else. Don't pull me into that equation. You've already more than proven yourself in my eyes, and up the ladder of the FBI. You earned your freedom. I want you to be able to enjoy it."

"Life's full of surprises."

"Thankfully. Or we wouldn't be working together."

———

Terrance Gorman stormed out of his house, phone plastered to his ear. He held the phone away from his mouth and shouted, "Answer your phone, captain. Call me back, and save me the drive over. Son of a bitch," he spit as he clicked off, strode down his brick path, jumped into his Bentley, powered down his convertible top, and made a tire squealing exit onto the quiet road.

The sun was shining, the Southern California cumulus clouds were thick and sculptural, but Terrance's mood was dark. He pulled up to a light, and the Bentley's start-stop system shut the car's engine off. He tapped Mullrooney's number into the car's info system and wasn't aware of the Audi SUV pulling to a stop next to him at the light. He didn't see the rear window roll down. Or hear the silenced .22 fire a bullet that pierced his ear, rattled around in his skull, tearing up brain matter until Terrance Gorman was dead. His head dropped and his chin came to rest on his chest.

The back window of the Audi rolled silently up as the light turned green and the SUV drove away.

With his head tilted forward, Terrance looked like he was asleep or stoned. He blocked a lane of traffic behind him. Cars stacked up, horns blared, and drivers flipped-off the dead man as they drove past, no one the wiser.

———

Dakota had the news on low in the living room, while he hand-washed his lunch dishes, and contemplated his life. His mother had installed a dishwasher, but Dakota's time behind bars left him with a need to be hands on. Anything he could control.

Something on the TV pulled him out of his thoughts, not sure what he'd just heard. He ran into the living room, hit rewind, and replayed the news segment. A young male on-the-air reporter stood on the sidewalk, talking in hushed tones. A Bentley convertible was parked in the south lane, and police tape cordoned off the entire street, along with cones and flares. Cars driving in the opposite direction slowed to check out the action. The car in question looked like Terrence Gorman's ride, he thought.

The reporter said, "At eleven thirty this morning, a man, whose name is being withheld until his family is notified, was found dead sitting in his luxury vehicle waiting for the light to change. The car sat idle, creating a logjam of traffic. An irate commuter jumped out of his car and started shouting for the driver to move. He soon realized he was yelling at a dead man. He called 911, and the first responders arrived in a black-and-white vehicle. The uniformed police shut down the road and waited for the EMT.

"They pronounced the man dead at the scene, and are now waiting for the forensic techs to arrive and try and discern exactly what occurred, before removing the body. Was this a random act of violence, or a methodically planned murder?"

Three more police vehicles pulled to a stop, and the first responders brought them up to speed.

There was video of the EMTs pushing the gurney away from the Bentley. A black body bag, carrying the victim, rolled past, and the camera caught a quick shot of the vanity license plate on the rear of the car. T-Gorman. The dead man on the stretcher appeared to be Terrance Gorman.

Dakota lowered the volume, pulled out his private line, and texted Steele. As soon as he got his hands soapy wet in the kitchen, the phone rang. He grabbed a dishtowel and moved back into the living room to see if there was anything else being reported as he answered the call.

"Have you been listening to the local news?"

"Up to my elbows in work."

"A man was discovered sitting in his car around 11:30 today. Drunk, stoned, whatever, blocking traffic. People were pissed, thought he was high, turned out he was dead. The man died sitting in his Bentley, waiting for the light to change. They withheld his ID but the vanity plate is Terrance's."

"Hmmmm," she said.

"Indeed. Have you picked up James and Doug yet?"

"Negative."

"I were you, I'd put an immediate call to Captain Mullrooney. If he doesn't answer I'd send an armed team to his place."

"What are you thinking?"

"I'm thinkin' Billie tied Terrance to Mullrooney...Mullrooney to Doug. And on the same day, Doug to James, for Christ's sakes. What a barrel of snakes. Terrance and Mullrooney both had something to gain from taking down Blackfox.

"James knows with the raid at Blackfox's, he could have been killed on the battlefield. I'm picking up a strong whiff of payback. Possible retribution for setting up our team in Venezuela. It's all conjecture, but I know one thing for certain, these guys have to get pulled off the street."

"I'm on it," Steele said, and then, "we got bad news on the slug they pulled out of the senator's lawn. The rifling doesn't match the sniper rifle we picked up at the condo."

"Damn."

"But." Steele's voice rose with excitement. "The mud clots found in the Mercedes and Doug's boot treads were a perfect match with the soil above Bradley's estate. Looks like Doug was the shooter. We're doing a full-court press. Gotta run." Steele hung up before Dakota could respond. He was confident Steele would follow up on the captain.

His next call was to Billie, who listened and responded, "I'm on my way over. Stay in the rear of the house where you can't get picked off at long range. If they're doing cleanup, you, Dakota, are on the top of their list."

Agent Steele strode back into the conference room at FBI Headquarters that was alive with activity. Eight agents sat around the table, phones out, tablets, and yellow pads to notate. A large screen was set up in the front of the room. Photographs of James and Doug topped off the pyramid, with pictures of Terrance Gorman and Captain Mullrooney below, on either side.

Steele walked up to the screen and penned a red slash across Gorman's glossy headshot. "Terrance Gorman was shot at a light on PCH this morning. Turn on the local station, and we'll be brought up to speed. Mitchel, dial Captain Mullrooney's number. If he answers, hang up.

"Finish filling out the family tree of the boys on our board, and all contact information of family and friends as the list grows. Start at direct relations and work your way out. Someone knows where James and Doug are. Keep it friendly, you just need to contact them. You've been calling and haven't heard back, you're concerned…you know the drill."

The group at the table turned to Agent Mitchel, who sat with a pen poised, and his cell phone to his ear. After a few seconds, his head popped up, "It went directly to voicemail."

And then to Agent Chase, Steele's eyes bright, "Let's hit the road with armed backup. I have a feeling Gorman was just the beginning. Our boys might be cleaning."

Chase gave the nod to Mitchel and Stevens, who jumped up from their seats. "Suit up, vest, MP5, and 12-gauge. We'll meet downstairs in five."

The television set was now showing a bystander's cell phone video of Terrance Gorman, sitting in his Bentley convertible, his lifeless head propped on his chest, as the four FBI agents rushed out of the conference room.

CHAPTER 35

"Weapons for protection and destruction, if need be, and you're wondering if I was excessive?" Doug Darby said almost to himself with all the emotion a gun-nut could muster. He unzipped his rucksack and unloaded his weapons of choice, picked from the extensive cache warehoused in their storage facility. And talking loudly, over the TV volume in the other room: "It physically hurt to toss the rifle that could be tied to Senator Bradley's shindig into the ocean. It wasn't my favorite, but the sniper rifle with the most notches on the stock is probably in police custody as we speak. They will both be missed."

"But why?" James shouted back. "What could they have on us?" James sat slouched on the threadbare living room couch, with his stocking feet up off the worn rug, trying to figure out how to use the two burner phones they picked up at a liquor store on the way up the hill. The flat screen television hanging on the pine tongue-and-groove wall above the river rock fireplace was set to a local news channel. Other than the modern television, the room, in fact, the entire cabin, looked like it was built and decorated in the '50s. Warm, homey, but tired. James kept his design critique to himself.

"Maybe they got a line on something from the senator's fundraiser. Who knows?"

Doug's volume didn't match the television's, so James stopped listening and tuned him out.

Doug persisted when he got no response. "It's why I tossed the fuckin' rifle into the Pacific, along with our two iPhones. There's about eight grand down the toilet. Then there's the .22," Doug shouted over the sound of the TV. "A well-balanced pistol that served its purpose. The timing was almost poetic, don't you think?" he said, not expecting a response, he got caught up in his own reverie.

Doug laid each weapon gingerly on his sister's kitchen table in the forest of Big Bear. The nearest house was a quarter mile down the rutted dirt road that fronted the property. The only sound, besides the television, was mind-numbing silence.

"C'mere!" James thundered. Doug ran in. And there it was on the eleven o'clock news. "Someone shot footage with their cellphone. Got Terrance with his head down."

"No shit, looks like he's asleep. Damn that was a good shot. No blood, looks natural."

The video changed to the local news coverage, moving Terrance, secured in a body bag, into the EMT van and driving off, inter-cut with shots of the police walking shoulder-to-shoulder, covering every inch of asphalt, looking for the .22 shell that had been tossed into the Pacific along with the murder weapon. "Only an amateur would leave a shell casing behind," Doug said, smug.

"I think we've got everything covered for the next few days. I don't know how the hell they could find us here. But they'll get one hell of a surprise if they do. Let's kick back, raid my sister's liquor cabinet, and get down." The grin on his face dropped as he watched the next news story. "Holy shit."

"Goddamnit!" James said through clenched teeth.

"Well, had to happen," James said, his mood darkening.

A female reporter was standing on the road in front of Captain Mullrooney's house. The wind was whipping off the coast, and she had to hand-comb the unruly hair that threatened to block her perfect face. A phalanx of police cars, mixed with a few Federal vehicles, a Tech truck, and an EMT truck, were all parked surrounding the California Ranch the captain had called home. All the lights were on at the house and the surrounding property. The captain's corpse had been secured in a black bag and was being wheeled down the driveway and then stowed in the body of the EMT vehicle, ready for transport to the county morgue.

"You gotta figure the man looks like shit," Doug said. "Walking in on that, the smell, four days in, no air-conditioning."

"Could you give it a fucking rest? Just listen. Stop talking."

Doug tamped down his immediate response and took his partner's advice. He was proud of his anger control, because he wanted to slap the shit out of James. But, if he did that, his bed would be lonely and cold that night.

———

The day after the captain's body was discovered, Dakota was paid a visit from the Homicide Detail of the Orange County Sheriff's Department.

Dakota was sitting on his metal rocker with his pal, the neighbor's tabby, rubbing his scruff and sipping a cup of coffee when a clearly unmarked vehicle pulled onto his driveway.

A tired, middle-aged investigator nodded to Dakota and approached. Dakota wasn't surprised to see the detective. He being the one who alerted Steele to the possibility the captain was already dead. Oh, and his history with the deceased. But hell would freeze over before he'd be tied to the case in any other way.

"My name is Deputy Sheriff Joel Royce of the OCSD," he said, flashing his gold badge. "Gotta a couple of minutes?"

"A couple," Dakota said without attitude but laying down the parameters of the interview.

"Good. Do you know a Captain Mullrooney?"

"You can read Wikipedia. Good for you."

"Okay, it's been a long night and I don't want the day to turn to shit. I know you're aware of Captain Mullrooney. You served under him. Spent a good piece of your life behind bars because of him. What I need to know is when was the last time you saw him?"

"Six years, pushing seven."

"Where were you on the ninth, around two o'clock in the afternoon?"

"Hanging with my aunt. Watching the game."

"And after that? Where did you spend the night?"

"None of your business. Why are you here, and what case are you trying to tie me to?"

"Why would you go there?"

"Because it's eight o'clock in the morning, and you're spending your breakfast time talking to me. What am I being accused of?"

"You didn't watch the news last night?"

"My sleep is erratic, after six and a half years in lockup. I don't watch the evening news because it depresses me. You know who I am, I know your type, spare us a lot of posturing and get to the point."

"Captain Mullrooney is dead," Royce said nonchalant but maintaining eye contact, looking for a tell.

The officer was disappointed. Dakota's face was a blank slate.

"Turn on the *Today Show*, and I'm sure the case will be front and center. It was only reasonable that I would start here. Enjoy your coffee, we'll talk again."

The cat emitted a guttural hiss as Royce walked away. The deputy heard the cat, turned, and grinned. It was a hard grin before getting into his car and driving off.

Wentworth was back to his manicured, well-mannered self. They were seated on the patio when Bob delivered a tray of Canadian lox, cream cheese, bagels, onions, tomatoes, lemon, and capers.

"Pleasure to see you again, Dakota," the silver-haired man said.

"Pleasure's all mine, Bob."

"Yup, nothing but a love fest here," Wentworth added droll. "How is your day going?"

"Been better, sir. Had a visit from a Deputy Sheriff who showed up on my front porch this morning. An old officer of mine, Captain Mullrooney, died a few days ago. They discovered his body yesterday. I was his first call today."

"You could read the innuendo between the lines in the reporting. They weren't buying the suicide," he said, letting Dakota know he was aware of the case.

"That's their issue, sir. I just want you to know, if you were having second thoughts, I wouldn't blame you. I stand by you, and whatever your needs are. I don't want to muddy an already difficult time."

"If you hadn't mentioned Mullrooney's death, whatever the particulars are, Bob would have escorted you off the premises. He's a black belt in taekwondo and carries a loaded Sig Sauer."

"Good to know. As long as he's polite in his attempt, I won't hold it against him."

Wentworth said, "There's no way on God's earth a man like you, given a second chance at life, would jeopardize a new beginning by even entertaining payback against a lesser opponent."

"You're correct on that score."

"That, on top of Terrance Gorman's murder in as many days, is very concerning."

"I think they're both connected, sir."

"Go on."

"I'm sure you're aware there were multiple attempts on my life during my incarceration."

"I was."

"I never got to the bottom of who was paying the tab on the hit men. The captain was at the top of my list. Seemed reasonable. My aunt, who's an ex-cop, knew about the target on my back and started doing recon on my behalf, after my release. Long story short, she was able to tie Captain Mullrooney to Terrance Gorman."

"I was sorry to hear about Gorman's murder, but was never a fan. The man wanted the senator's job and didn't hide his ambitions."

"Keep that in mind, sir. My aunt also tied the Captain to Doug

Darby. Darby was a ranger-sniper who served under the captain. That same day, my aunt was able to tie Darby to James."

"Our James?" he said, hoping he was wrong but starting to put together the connective tissue.

"Yes, sir. James Marshal is Doug Darby's roommate. I believe someone in that mix notified the ATF, almost got us killed in Venezuela, and was responsible for your arrest."

"That's a lot to digest. I see four different scenarios playing out, and they're all treacherous. Kudos to your aunt."

"She's a keeper all right."

"Give me your gut feeling on how you think this played out."

Dakota took a sip of coffee and gave Wentworth a carefully amended version of the events that led to the murder of the captain and Terrance.

"I think Doug was the shooter at the fundraiser, doing Terrance Gorman's bidding. I'm pretty sure James leaked our mission to Doug. And Doug leaked to the captain, who seems to be the only man in the group who had the juice to call in the ATF. James knows he could've lost his life with the rest of us in Venezuela. Retribution? Maybe. James had plenty of motive. All conjecture."

"I've got some calls to make. Wasn't there something else you wanted to tell me?"

"Sir, I am all the way in, if you're still on board."

"I am. If things ever get too hot to handle, we'll revisit this conversation. Until then, let's you and I move forward."

"Then, thank you for the opportunity."

"Good to hear, Dakota. I look forward to the adventure." And then, "Keep your phone charged, and your aunt at your side. I fear the target on your back just doubled in size."

Dakota lifted his coffee cup to his boss, took in a deep breath, and enjoyed the moment. Let the chips fall, he thought. What a trip. He stood to take his leave, and Wentworth was already making his call, his brow creased in anger.

CHAPTER 36

South Coast Plaza is famous for its luxury shopping and the highest concentration of designer fashion retailers in the country. It's the main reason Sarah loved her job as a top buyer of women's fashions at Bloomingdale's. High-end clientele, decent pay, medical insurance and travel benefits on her buying jaunts to Paris, Milan, and New York. It had been a day of multiple meetings, phone calls, and sales reports. She skipped lunch, was a bit light-headed, and dead on her feet. So, she decided to feed her face when she got home. Put on her sweats, pour a glass of wine, and dine on the pepperoni pizza waiting for her in the freezer.

The sky was still light, the blue darkening slightly. A blanket of orange spread over the sun as it dropped below the sea of buildings in the distance. Sarah was walking with a cell phone to her ear, she laughed at something her friend said while she stopped near her white Honda and rummaged in her gray Celine bag looking for her key fob.

"Need help?" a man behind her said with a smile in his voice.

Sarah turned toward the voice.

Doug slammed the Taser against her chest. Her body shook, her phone dropped to the pavement. Doug took her in his arms as if saying good night to an old friend.

A shopper walked by, hands filled with bags, paying them no mind.

James pulled the car into the empty space next to her Honda.

Doug guided Sarah's body onto the rear seat of the Lincoln Continental and gently closed the door. He picked up Sarah's cell phone and could hear a voice asking if she was okay.

Doug clicked off the call, pocketed the phone, walked around the car, eyes scanning the parking lot. All clear, he jumped into the car next to her prone body, while James pulled out of the lot, traveling west toward Newport Beach.

Doug grabbed a roll of tape and wrapped it around Sarah's mouth. He taped her wrists together, in front of her, so she could be moved without inflicting too much pain, and bound her ankles.

Doug pushed back against the leather seats and caught his breath.

Sarah moaned, and her eyes blinked open, fighting to focus, and then fighting to talk, and fighting to breathe, as panic overtook her entire body. She realized she'd been bound and gagged and was in the back seat of her abductor's car. She was going to puke, but realized she might choke to death before the man staring at her had time to release her bonds.

She fought to slow her breathing like she'd learned in Yoga class, but couldn't stop the steady flow of tears leaking from her blue eyes, which momentarily blinded her.

———

Dakota threw a flank steak on a gas grill he had delivered that afternoon and was giving it a test run. He had a couple of ears of corn, wrapped in foil, and heavy on butter, salt-and-pepper, the way his mother liked it, and a few red peppers, he cored, and tossed on the grill the way he liked them.

Billie joined him in the backyard with two glasses of red.

Dakota was reaching for the wine when his cell rang. When he saw the caller ID, he realized his life was now set to Blackfox time.

"Mister Wentworth," Dakota said, his mood good.

"Let's stop with the formalities, Dakota. Thomas isn't too much to ask."

"Thomas," he said.

"That's better. Spoke to my friends at the DOJ, and it was Captain Mullrooney who tipped the ATF to our incursion. Dates, times, destination, mission, weaponry, drones, and explosives."

"Good to know, Thomas. The captain won't be missed."

"For good reason. Now, Terrance is obviously out of play, and James and Doug might be on the run. We have Derik Traina, the senator's head of security on the case. He's well connected and learned the FBI was already looking at James and Doug. The more, the merrier in a situation like this. And Traina saw the autopsy report on Captain Mullrooney. Trajectory of the bullet, and non-existent powder burns around his mouth precluded suicide. It appears the men are cleaning house. So, stay alert, my friend."

"Thanks for the heads-up. My aunt's sitting here, and we're both armed for bear."

"I expect no less from you. On another note, I received a disturbing call from my lawyer. Ant had a meltdown in his cell. You are now on record as one of my lawyer's associates, and I think you're the only man who could have a meaningful conversation about how to handle himself in lockup."

"Happy to do it," he said.

"Okay. Appreciated. Let me know how it goes. My lawyer is Montrose Steiner, and his assistant will contact you first thing in the morning and give you the particulars. And please let Ant know, I'm doing everything in my power to cut him loose. It appears the District Attorney's Office has dug in its heels, and is unwilling to deal at this point. I'll do what I can from my end. Ant has to keep the faith, stay strong, and know we're on his case."

"Done and done, Thomas."

The men signed off, and Dakota picked up his glass of wine and took a long sip, taking in the news Wentworth had shared.

Billie sat patiently, waiting for Dakota to talk. They both enjoyed the summer night, the sound of the birds, and the complexity of the cabernet. They were joined in the backyard by the tabby, who imperiously flopped down at Billie's feet and head bumped her ankle until Billie rubbed his scruff.

"Wentworth connected with his resources in Washington," Dakota started. "He was told in no uncertain terms Captain Mullrooney sold out our team. He was also copied on Mullrooney's autopsy report. The scumbag was murdered. Wentworth wasn't aware of it, but he also corroborated my gut instinct James wanted to kill me in Venezuela. If the pair is cleaning, I'm next on the list."

"How do we proceed?" Billie asked.

"We let the steak rest for a couple of minutes, pour another glass of wine, and enjoy dinner. And then tomorrow, we'll hunt down Doug and James and take them out, before they have a chance to finish the job."

———

The Lincoln Continental snaked silently down the macadam while Doug copied Sarah's phone numbers into his burner. He checked texts and found Dakota's number along with the video Sarah sent him.

Doug hit play, and his jaw tensed. It was a cell phone video of his wrecked Mercedes, and a crazy man, who was him, throwing the driver's side door – that had been smashed off its hinges by a gardener's truck – into the rear of the SUV along with the rear bumper, before driving off.

He leaned over and slapped Sarah's head. Hard. She grunted, her eyes opened wide with pain and surprise. "You little shit," he said. They drove along a short block with a pizza joint, liquor store, dry cleaner, and a deli. "Pull over up here. I'll be right back."

James pulled to the side of the road and parked on the wooded street beyond. Doug jumped out and hoofed it back to the retail block. He pulled a baseball cap down, obscuring his face, in case security cameras were in play, and deftly slid Sarah's phone, decorated with a pink leather phone case, on top of the knee-high wall separating the pizza joint and the liquor store.

He turned without running into anybody, and this time sat in the front seat. "I give it three minutes before it's picked up, and long-distance calls are being made to Zimbabwe."

"Good move."

"Any worries from our guest?"

"The perfect hostage."

Sarah wasn't sure what the men wanted with her. Sex, rape, murder? And then as the shock of the blow to her head wore off, she realized she was going to be bait to lure Dakota to his death. She fought the bile that again threatened her throat. She would keep her wits about her and make a move the first chance she got. She couldn't talk, scream, or run with her mouth, hands, and legs bound. She would sit tight, not anger her kidnappers, and hopefully be spared any more physical violence.

———

Dakota called and brought Steele up to speed on his conversation with Wentworth.

"I received a copy of Mullrooney's autopsy," Steele said coyly. Wanting to drag out the reveal of her intel.

"I'll bet there were no powder burns around the captain's mouth," Dakota said, playing her. "If that was true, I think it proves the gun was too far away to be self-inflicted. Had to be murder,"

"How did you know that?" No attitude, but Dakota knew her mind was spinning a mile a minute.

"Wentworth."

"You're pretty cocky, aren't you?"

"Eh."

"But did you know, smart man, that the coroner discovered an angry black and blue welt across the captain's good arm. Also, not self-inflicted. Interesting though." There was a smile in Steele's voice.

"Am I a suspect?"

"I'm going to have to give that question some serious thought and interrogate you until I get the truth."

"I wish you would."

"What?"

"Interrogate me."

The innuendo made her heart pound.

Dakota talked over the silence. "I have to visit Ant tomorrow, I'll call you when I'm done. Gotta go, Jean." And he clicked off, before he took the conversation where his libido was guiding him.

CHAPTER 37

Dakota felt his blood pressure rise as he stepped through the metal detector and heard the steel door slam shut behind him at the Orange County Central Men's Jail that houses both sentenced and pre-sentenced maximum-security inmates. How or why Ant was being housed here was a mystery, but it didn't bode well for the young man.

And then it made perfect sense to Dakota. If the state wanted to put the fear of God into the young man and flip him, this jail was a good start.

Ant was the poison pill that could destroy Blackfox, and take Wentworth with him, potentially damage the senator's bid for re-election, and shut down the RockPile militia and their white supremacist disinformation network for good.

Dakota wondered if he could facilitate Ant turning on his benefactors to save his own skin. Horse-trading makes the judicial system go round. Definitely something to think about.

Dakota was led to a stark visiting room.

Ant was already seated at the metal table. He looked diminished in size, if that were even possible, and more a teenager than his twenty-three years. His usual exuberance was replaced with white-knuckled fear. As if he were drained of all blood. He had a major dark purple bruise on his forehead, tinged in green.

"What the hell happened to you?"

"I banged my head against the wall a few times trying to break out."

"The guards?"

"Just me."

"Why'd you do that?"

"Frustrated, afraid, angry, claustrophobic, bored, hungry, I could go on."

"Stop doing that. My God, Ant, you've only been in for a fucking week."

"Ten thousand and eighty minutes. Six hundred four thousand, eight hundred seconds."

"Ant, this is a very bad way to start your incarceration."

"I don't expect to be here long enough to care."

"Your lawyer shared the charges against you? The district attorney is licking his chops, building his case, and waiting to get you in a courtroom. My guess, they'll discover more. Am I wrong?"

"Depends how smart they are. I've used encrypted files for most of the dicey missions."

"You're dealing with the Federal Government, Ant. Hell, they broke the code on an encrypted iPhone when that killer shot three students on the Navy base in Pensacola, and Apple refused to help the Feds. The FBI's on your case; the ATF orchestrated your arrest. They're aware of every move you were responsible for in our Venezuelan incursion. Your plans, your guidance, your expertise. You are in some deep shit. But you won't make it out of here alive if you don't relax and take care of yourself."

"When am I making bail?" he asked, jumping to his feet as if Dakota hadn't just painted a grim picture of his new reality.

"Thomas sends his best. He wants you to know that he's doing everything he can on your behalf to help you make bail. He scraped enough together to make it home with an ankle bracelet until his trial date. But his well is bone dry. Everything is frozen until the District

Attorney's accountants do a forensic audit of Blackfox's finances. In all honesty, Ant, that could take months."

"That sounds bad. My lawyer was more optimistic."

"It depends on what they discover, and they'll dig deep and keep digging until they have a slam dunk in the courtroom. It's as bad as it sounds. And how you exist on the inside is totally up to you. Did you eat?" Dakota asked.

"Yes!" he shouted. "Then I puked my guts out."

"Ant, I need you to sit down and focus. You need to get some control over your emotions, or you'll spiral down and not make it through the weekend. I've seen it happen, it's not a pretty sight."

"Thomas isn't taking my calls."

And there it was. Dakota backed off some. "I'm sure you understand the man is under unique stress trying to keep his business alive and his own skin out of prison, where he'll be of no use to anyone."

"I know, I know, but really? Okay. All right. Hmm… I'll sit tight."

Ant grabbed a chair. His foot started tapping uncontrollably. He put a self-conscious hand on his knee, but it didn't stop the tremors. He gave up and stood again.

"What the hell am I going to do?" he asked, manically running his hands through his greasy, unkempt hair. "They won't let me near a computer. Really?! How did you last? Six and a half years. That's insane."

"Take a deep breath," Dakota said, evenly. "We can't have this conversation until you're calm enough to be able to listen and comprehend your new reality. You have to accept what is, and use your massive intelligence to change your reality. Sounds abstract, but it's the only way you'll survive. And I want you to survive, Ant. You're too smart. That's a blessing and a curse, man. Make it a blessing, and we'll find a solution."

"I didn't sleep again. I'm like the walking dead."

"Go back to your cell, eat your lunch, something you can keep down, and we'll talk again when you're back in your own body. You need to sleep. Get some rest, and we'll talk. Believe you're not alone. We'll get you through this."

"I'm not built for this kind of experience." His body started vibrating.

"Nobody is, Ant. Understanding that is a good place to start. But first, you've gotta get your strength up. You've lost too much weight."

"Food's disgusting."

"Eat the protein, and juice, and mac-and-cheese, anything you can belt down. All three meals. Do they have you on suicide watch?"

"They called it, administrative segregation, but I think so, because they came in when I was hurting myself, and told me to fuck off and stop."

"That sounds about right. That's the good news. The last thing we want is for you to be put in general population. Solitary may be lonely, but it's safe. Stay strong, and do everything you can to get stronger. Wentworth is in your corner. I'm in your corner. I'll come back again next week.

"You promise?"

"Absolutely. Now, Wentworth wants a full report. I won't tell him you're a big pussy, if you promise you'll take care of yourself."

"Thank you. Okay. I'll try." Ant's eyes welled with tears. And then he raised his hands in supplication and cried. A chest heaving, shoulder bouncing, cry.

Dakota let him be for a few minutes before lowering his voice and going on. "Crying's fine around me, but keep it to yourself with any guards and inmates you might come in contact with, even passing in the hallway. Never show fear, Ant. Start acting like one of the video heroes you created. You know what I mean?"

"I think so," but he didn't sound convinced.

"Plaster on a tough veneer and wear it like armor. The more you do it, the better you'll feel. Practice in the mirror if you have to."

"There's no mirror in my cell."

"You know what I'm saying."

"I do."

The guard tapped on the metal door.

"Buck up, my friend, I'll be back."

Ant tried for tough, and fell short. Dakota knew the kid would be labeled a *fish*, and wouldn't make it through his first night without getting raped if released into gen pop.

———

The afternoon sun sliced through the thick bows of old growth trees surrounding the cabin in Big Bear like stained glass in a chapel. James and Doug had to be extremely careful now that their Army induction photographs were being shown on every network, in the city, and nationally. Neither man had shaved in the past four days, and didn't look as polished as their ID photos taken when they were shavetails in the army. But the likeness was damning.

The men had taken the gag off Sarah, so she could eat and it gave her a modicum of hope she might be able to escape this horror alive. A thought occurred. She spoke quietly, non-confrontationally.

"You let me see you. That means you won't let me live."

"Shut up and eat," Doug said, his eyes glued to the screen. "Not a bad picture of me."

James nodded as he spooned out cold Chinese takeout he picked up from San Bernardino on the way up the hill.

"You want Dakota," Sarah said, ignoring Doug and directed her speech toward James. "If you don't kill him before you take off, wherever it is you land with the publicity you've already generated, he's going to find you and skin you both alive. I know how he operates. He won't stop until he's run you directly into an early grave."

Doug took a menacing step toward her, his fist pulled back.

"Sit down, Doug!" James ordered. "Let the woman talk."

"Thank you." Sarah let out the breath she'd sucked in, anticipating an attack. She summoned all the strength she used negotiating with Italian designers in Milan on the price of their haute couture fashions and continued.

"And?" James prodded, irritated now, wiping hoisin sauce off his lips with the back of his hand.

"I can deliver Dakota. He'll show up wherever I tell him, to save my life. You pick the time, the location, and a promise to let me live.

The cops know who you are, what you look like, I can help you with that. Change your looks. I'm in the fashion industry, it's what I do.

"And since they've already identified you both, and know your histories, and are already talking to your parents, and friends, there's nothing I can give the police they don't already have. I have no idea where I am, and I don't care. If you play this right, by the time they find me, you'll be long gone.

"Help me and I'll help you."

"She's buying time," Doug snarled.

"So are we," James fired back.

Their attention was pulled back to the television screen as their faces appeared again, with their height, weight, eye and hair color, and a number at the bottom of the screen to contact the FBI. The crawl beneath the headshots read: *Doug Darby and James Marshal are armed and dangerous. If you recognize these men, do not approach, call 911 or the number on your screen.*

———

A single soft-white light glowed in the men's bedroom. It was sweltering hot and the men were stretched out on top of the sheets naked. Sarah was secured in the second bedroom. It was mind-numbingly quiet.

James turned his head toward Doug and whispered, "What did we do?"

"What we were trained to do. Someone comes after us, we take them down. Kill or be killed. No regrets. You really think the captain wouldn't have come after us, one by one, when he heard you made it out of Venezuela alive? Man needed killing."

"A lot of years in. All crashing down around our necks."

"He set you up to kill Dakota. And then what did he do?"

"Sold us out."

"Tried to kill you, James. Un-American dipshit got what he deserved."

"Sarah was right, we've killed ourselves into a dead end."

Doug ignored that. "We finish this, we head up North. I have a list of like-minded people who'll set us up for a while. When things cool, we cross over into Canada and start spending some of our hard-earned cash."

"I was hoping for a warmer climate?"

"And I was hoping to win the lottery."

"It all started when you missed Dakota at the senator's bash."

"Really? Not in Venezuela?"

"I wouldn't have made it out alive. Would that have made you happy?"

"Fuck that. And you know it wouldn't. So shut the fuck up with your second-guessing. And that asshole Terrance would have skewered us. He had to go."

"No doubt." The men sat in silence and let their anger dissipate.

James couldn't sleep. "Whadda ya think about her offer?"

"We need more time."

"Times running out."

"Then yes. Fuck it. Let's listen to her and move forward with our plan. Dakota has the weight of Blackfox behind him. What she said was true. Man's a machine."

"If she can deliver Dakota…"

"Says she can."

"I believe her."

"Woman's trying to save her own skin."

"I believe her."

Doug could hear a drip coming from the kitchen sink, and it pissed him off. "We gotta change how we look. I have no idea what the wrong move was. I didn't think we'd be on the run for the rest of our lives."

"We still don't know what they have on us."

"They tied us to two murders. Not sure if they can prove anything."

"I'm gonna ask you a question," James's tone was soft, "and I don't want you to flip out."

"Just fucking ask. I hate when you set up a statement like that."

James pushed on, "Are you thinking of turning yourself in?"

"Fuck no," he said, and the room chilled. "Are you thinking of turning me in?"

"Don't be ridiculous."

"Why would you ask that? Because I'm the only one who pulled the trigger?"

"If it makes you feel any better, I'm a double accessory to murder. We are both culpable. And if we don't stay sharp, we'll both go down."

It didn't make him feel any better. "Turn out the light."

And the house went pitch black.

After a few moments James spoke softly, "First time I moved from the city to basic training, I couldn't sleep. Like this. Too quiet."

"Listen to the fucking drip of the sink, it'll put you to sleep." Doug was doing a slow burn.

Both men lay in total darkness, eyes wide open.

Doug sighed.

James asked, "Do we let her live?"

"I've gotta think on that."

"She made a good case."

"I can't commit one way or the other. Let's exploit her talent, see what she comes up with."

"I can't sleep."

"C'mere."

CHAPTER 38

Thomas Wentworth paced in the massive office at his estate. His personal tax attorney, his litigation attorney, and their forensic accountant were seated around a modern ebony wood table, scouring both sets of the Blackfox books, trying to stay one step ahead of where the strong arm of justice would land.

"Dakota, I'm glad I caught you," he said into his cellphone as he walked out onto the back patio and closed the door behind him. "Check your bank statement when you have a moment. It should put a smile on your face. Two hundred thousand was wired into your account. A hundred and fifty to Janko, Avila, and Kathy. Please call and alert them to the good news. Sadly, there wasn't enough to bail out Ant. How is the young man doing?"

"In all honesty, sir, he's a mess. He's having a rough time of it. It doesn't bode well for his future if he loses his court case."

"Help him through the process, Dakota. Do what you can. The man is an incredible asset to us. He must believe we have his back."

"I was planning to. He'll have more questions than there are answers, but I'll do what I can and share what I know."

"In the meantime, go out and celebrate tonight. Dinner's on me.

You'll get a Blackfox credit card when the freeze thaws. We're working on that now."

"Thank you, Thomas. I'm happily surprised, I thought you were tapped, sir."

"Were you worried?"

"I don't do worry."

"Good to hear. Rentex owes you and your team big-time. They're funneling your salaries through the Super PAC that supports Senator Bradley's re-election campaign. Dark money at its finest. The corporation is in your debt and ready to back your promotion with the Blackfox board of directors."

"Appreciated, Thomas." And the men signed off.

Interesting conversation, Dakota thought. He was fairly sure money generated in a Super PAC could only be legally spent for events surrounding an election. Not siphoned off as dark money to pay for armed incursions. Even if it was organized and supported by the candidate.

And his reaction to Ant's imprisonment was odd. Wentworth said, "He must believe we have his back." It sounds like he might be afraid of Ant flipping.

And that, Dakota thought, was the tell he'd been waiting for.

He dialed Steele's number.

———

Dakota and Billie were in the Bronco, doing a drive-by of James and Doug's condo. It was locked down tight. There was one FBI vehicle parked in front. Billie got the agent to spill, the men were still no-shows. Dakota did a second drive down Pacific Coast Highway, and pointed out the men's condo as they passed.

They continued driving and visited the location where the drive-by of Terrance took place. They stopped at the same traffic light where Terrance had been shot. There were still stains on the street from the flares the cops left behind, blocking off the scene from incoming traffic.

"A twenty-two round through the ear. That's some damn sharp-shooting. Sounds like Doug to me," Dakota said.

"Two murders in two days. The men are already freaked. And then, as bad turned to worse, they're driving on PCH, before the FBI shut off the lights in their condo, and as you proved, they could've seen the back bedroom from their SUV. Discovered their condo was being searched. What would you do?" Billie asked.

"Keep driving."

"James's car would be easy to trace. Hell, the Feebs could get the number from the DMV in a five-minute search. Next move?"

Dakota: "Dump the car ASAP."

"Where, and how?"

Dakota gave that some thought. "Fastest way out here, John Wayne Airport. Jump on a flight. As far as they knew, if it was the cops who were in their condo, and they weren't being robbed, they had no reason to put out an APB."

"Or...," Billie said, "drop off the car, pick up a rental, and take a road trip until they discovered who was in their unit. If it was the cops, what the hell were they looking for?"

"Two good options," Dakota said. "Let's start at John Wayne."

Dakota headed for Airport Way in Santa Ana, while Billie brought up the airport on Google and got a line on Long Term parking. "They have three parking structures across from Thomas Riley Terminal. Check the signs for Alaska Airlines and United. Directly across is B2. Path of least resistance."

"I'm taking your lead," Dakota said and hit the gas.

———

An hour and a half later, Dakota pulled the Bronco to a stop, blocking the egress of a black Audi SUV. License plate number 37065A. Dakota grabbed his private cell and sent a text. They sat drinking lukewarm coffee they'd picked up on the road, and in a few minutes, Steele called back.

"Hey," Dakota said instead of hello.

"You've got that funny tone of voice. You have something else, don't you?"

Dakota grinned and cut to the chase, "Billie worked her detective magic, and James Marshal's SUV appeared. We are in parking structure B2 at John Wayne, across from Alaskan Air, on the second floor, the far end. It would make sense to send your tech team. We haven't touched the vehicle, but we might get lucky. If it's the car they used for the drive-by, there may be gunshot residue left behind. Worth a shot. The printed ticket on the dashboard gives the time and date of the SUV's drop-off. It looks good that one of our guys killed Terrance."

"I'm heading over, I'll call in the team on the way. As soon as I show, you pull out."

"We were going to check the rental car companies, if they didn't fly out. But we'll hit the road after you show, and clear the field for you."

"We'll talk later tonight. Tell Billie she's the bomb."

Dakota hung up and smiled at Billie. "She said you were the bomb."

"I'll take it."

"You, my friend, are putting the FBI and the OCSD to shame. Now we just have to find James and Doug, and shoot them dead, before they kill me."

———

Homicide Investigator Joel Royce pulled to a stop at the curb in front of Dakota's bungalow. He got out of the unmarked ride, stretched, and walked up the path to the porch where Dakota was sitting, nursing a glass of wine.

"What can I do for you?"

"What were you doing at six-forty-five Wednesday night?"

"Why?" Dakota asked.

"Answer the damn question or I'm taking you in."

"Home with my aunt. Ease up, officer."

"I'm a fucking Deputy Sheriff, and you're an ex-con. Give me the name and number of your aunt, and sit tight. As in, if you move from this seat, you'll spend the night behind bars."

Royce walked down the driveway, got Billie on the line, talked for a few moments, turned, and flashed angry eyes at Dakota. He got off the phone and started talking as he made his way toward the porch. "We got a call on a missing person. A Sarah Moore."

Royce saw Dakota wince hearing the name.

"Her car was left in the Bloomingdale's parking lot overnight, and when she didn't show up for work the following day, her manager got concerned, and I took the call. The manager tried her cell, and a man who said he never heard of a Sarah Moore hung up on him."

"Did you track the call?" Dakota asked, urgency in his voice.

"You're the felon. I'm the investigator. I ask the questions." Royce gave him a tight, frustrated look. "Phone turned up in Sunset Beach. The man using the phone found it outside a liquor store. We followed up, and he had an airtight alibi."

"Sarah's never without her phone. It's a second appendage."

"Why is your name front and center in two different cases that came across my desk in as many days?"

Dakota thought long and hard before answering. "Because it may be the same case." Dakota was trying to still his breathing.

"I was hoping you wouldn't say that."

Dakota pulled out his phone and showed Royce the video Sarah texted him after Doug was rear-ended in front of her condo. "The man in the video is Doug Darby. We think he was trying to abduct Sarah the day she shot the video. Darby and James Marshal are the two men with an APB regarding the murders of Mullrooney and Gorman. They may have grabbed Sarah to try and get to me."

"And why would they want to get you?"

"Because they were thick as thieves with both the captain, and Gorman. And the captain, for reasons I'm sure you understand, wanted me dead."

"Have they tried to contact you?"

"Not a word. This is the first I'm hearing about Sarah being missing. I'll do anything I can to help the investigation. Anything. Have you looked at the tapes from the Bloomingdale's parking lot?"

Royce struggled for a moment, then said, "It's the same man." He pulled out his cell. "This is my number. Text me the video." And then, "I need you at the station to file a report. I'm inclined to let you come down in your own vehicle. Don't make me regret the offer."

"I'll follow you there."

———

Steele was sitting at the desk in her condo, working on her laptop. Papers were strewn about, a worried expression played across her face. "We were just copied on the Bloomingdale's tape, Dakota. Chase has been alerted. He wants you to know we're on the case and the FBI will do everything in its power to help. I'll keep you up to speed on the investigation."

"Royce wants to be the first call I make if there's any contact," Dakota said from his home office.

"What are your thoughts?"

"James and Doug are trained killers. I'm not sure the investigator is up to the task. He's got a different skill set."

"You have to be ready to move on a minute's notice. Chase is sending over a team to put a trace on your cell and your landline at the house."

"Okay." Dakota didn't know what else to say. He felt certain they abducted Sarah to use as bait to kill him. If he offered himself up, he couldn't guarantee she'd make it out alive. He wasn't ready to gamble on the outcome. If summoned, he'd arrive ready for warfare. Kill or be killed.

"The tech team should be there in an hour," Steele said, filling the silence. And then, going on, "We have Doug Darby for attempted murder on the sniper attack at the senator's fundraiser, and now murder-one for the drive-by shooting of Terrance Gorman."

"Huh, that's something."

"He left fingerprints on the rear car door, and the guys ran a gunshot residue analysis. The sill of the rear passenger side door tested positive. It could've been transferred from Doug's hands to the windowsill, or directly from the barrel of the gun.

"And our guys canvassed the rental car companies at the airport, and got a hit before the Audi was towed out of John Wayne. Someone who looked like Doug used a credit card under a false name. So, they may have passports that correspond with the name change.

"I had to get tough before the night manager showed us the security tape. It was Doug all right. And he drove off the lot in a new Lincoln Continental. So, we don't think they're in the air. We'll put the description of the vehicle and the license plate number into the system. There aren't that many of them on the road. Maybe get a hit and grab them before things go from bad to worse. We'll do everything in our power."

"So will I."

"Try and get some rest, you need to stay sharp."

"If I hear from them, you'll be the first call I make," Dakota said, and clicked off. He grabbed his father's police issue Glock 22 from the side table next to his bed, checked the 15-round mag, grabbed a box of cartridges out of the catch-all drawer, and sat back down. He called Billie, who promised to pack a bag, a few weapons, and her blow-up mattress. She would set up camp in the office until this was settled. Dakota didn't object.

CHAPTER 39

After six rocky hours of sleep, Dakota leaned back in his chair across the metal table from Ant in the visitor's room in Orange County Central Men's Jail, and tried to be present. Struggling to focus on what Ant was spewing, and waiting on his phone to ring with information about Sarah. Praying she was still alive, and frustrated that the next step was in James and Doug's hands.

Billie was car-sitting in the parking lot, in case Dakota heard from the killers, and they had to run. Steele was ready to call in the troops for support if Dakota thought it necessary, or the proper move. The offer of support, but giving him free rein to handle the kidnapping, was appreciated.

Ant appeared to be in better shape than their last visit. Maybe it was the Xanax he'd been prescribed since his last meltdown, the only thing Montrose Steiner had been able to deliver to his young inmate. Or maybe Ant was acclimating to his surroundings and getting a little sleep himself.

Whatever it was, he was leaning forward listening to Dakota speak about his time on the inside, with rapt attention.

"Look at me," Dakota said, comfortably.

Ant knew he was talking about his physique. Hell, Dakota was built like one of his video heroes. Ant's face scrunched up in anticipation of what was coming.

"And now, look at yourself."

Ant understood. He'd spent many hours staring at himself in the mirror growing up. Praying to God to let him break five feet. He did… just. The problem was, he stopped growing in the tenth grade. Ant had never reconciled himself with God, but he was a praying man now.

Dakota continued, "I could handle another couple of years behind bars, piece of cake."

"And me?"

"You won't last an hour in the general population. When the Black crew learns about your racist rants, the ones you shared with the Wolf Pack and posted on social media, you'll be giving blowjobs until you can't swallow."

"What?"

"Blowjobs, Ant. Then they'll shove stinking socks down your throat to stifle your screams while they dry fuck your ass until you can't take a shit without filling the bowl with blood. And that's just the honeymoon. Until they break you in."

Ant sat still, mouth breathing, no words coming out.

"If you're lucky, you'll become one man's property. And he'll beat you until you submit to his freaky sex. Because, what the hell else is there to do behind bars? Nothing.

"You'll be forced to prostitute yourself for protection from the rest of the inmates. Your man might make you tattoo his name on your body to prove ownership.

"Or, they'll tattoo Ant on your skinny arm to brand you as a sex slave. A fish. Fresh meat. It's no way for a civilized man to live."

"You exaggerate some, right?"

"Not at all," he said, never breaking eye contact.

"How did you do it, Dakota? I'm already losing my mind."

"Don't take this the wrong way, Ant, but I don't think my way would serve you."

"Why?"

Dakota took a deep breath. "Prison is a human jungle twenty-four seven. Mental strength can only take you so far. Physical strength wins the day. You've got plenty of the first, and none of the last."

"What do I do?"

Dakota let him dangle, waiting for an answer. "I make it part of my creed, never to advise a man when he's facing life-altering decisions. But there is one nugget I can share. You are the man behind bars. Not your super-lawyer, whose only concern, your words, was figuring out when he was going to get paid."

"He's a douche."

"You know how politics works. When heads roll, it usually doesn't take down the leaders. The powers-that-be toss the second, or third, man out the window. You're number two."

"Are you fucking kidding me?"

"I don't kid," he shot back.

"I'm fucked...totally."

Dakota didn't dissuade him. "Think long and hard. I'm confident you'll come up with a plan you can live with." Dakota knocked on the door and left the young man with his thoughts.

————

Dakota phoned Steele's number on the burner while he and Billie drove back to the house. He always felt a need to shower after visiting Ant in lockup.

Steele texted: I'll call in twenty.

Dakota turned on KJazz, and Billie Holiday's voice filled the cab of the Bronco. She was singing "Solitude," a '30s Duke Ellington song about loneliness and loss. Emotions he hadn't felt in a while. Well, ever since he met Steele, he realized.

She phoned as he and Billie were pulling into his driveway. Billie stepped out of the car and headed toward the house to give Dakota some privacy.

Dakota turned down the music, picked up the cell. "It's time for Chase to reach out to Agent Stryker. Have a discussion about a plea deal."

"First, how're you holding up?" Steele asked.

"I'm holding."

"Okay," she said, knowing it was all she was going to get from Dakota. "So, bring me up to speed."

"Unless Ant has a nervous breakdown, I think he's ready to talk."

"He's going to dump Steiner?"

"He's leaning in that direction."

"I'd love to be a fly on the wall when Steiner delivers that news to Wentworth."

"You've got a dark streak, Steele. I like it. I've got Ant primed. You step in, take Ant to school, and flip him."

"If Agent Stryker can trade Ant for Wentworth, it should be a no-brainer for the DOJ to approve witness protection for the kid. I'll get Chase on it as soon as I hang up. Not bad, Dakota."

"You're welcome."

"Is that Billie Holiday I hear in the background?"

"It is."

"Huh. No word from James and Doug?"

"Nothing, not a thing. Keep a good thought and knock 'em dead, tomorrow. Do what you do best. Ant's not gonna know what hit him."

"Get some rest, Dakota."

"Will do." Dakota clicked off his cell and dismounted. The tabby was sitting on his metal rocker on the front porch. He walked over to take care of business, knowing he wouldn't find sleep anytime soon.

––––––––

The sun had just set over the Potomac River. FBI Agent Stryker was walking next to Ted Northrop, the lawyer at the DOJ he and Senator Bradley shared breakfast with the morning Blackfox was raided. The two men strolled along the National Mall. The long pool reflected the darkening blue sky while the sculpted image of Abraham Lincoln looked down on the proceedings.

"Looks like bad-to-worse for Thomas Wentworth if all proceeds according to plan," Northrop said without judgment.

"Agent Steele and Dakota Judd have never disappointed. They deserve full credit. They're making me look good. They're making the

FBI look good. We need all the positive press we can muster. We're thinking payback is in order. Bringing Chase to Washington, and moving Steele to Orange County Agent in Charge."

"That should rattle the old dinosaurs."

"Steele's the best I've ever worked with. We need her talent. She deserves the promotion."

"What can I do for you?" Northrop said, getting down to it.

"It looks like Steele is going to flip the Blackfox brain trust. Ant is the young man's name. I offered him up at our breakfast meeting. He's the brains behind the Venezuelan hostage extraction and every other meaningful incursion Blackfox has been involved in the past three years. We need an offer to cement the deal. We're thinking a Witness Protection situation. Of course, he'd have to give up Wentworth.

"Dakota spent some time with the young man scaring the guy straight, give Steele a half hour with the kid, and she'll close the deal."

"Wentworth has made more than his share of enemies at the DOJ. You deliver Wentworth, and I'll deliver the Witness Protection."

"Good to hear," Stryker said.

"Let me get back, I'll get clearance and send Sherry Motlin from the State Department. She loves dropping hammers, and never turns down a trip to Southern California. Tough as nails."

"Much appreciated. I'll let the team know."

The men picked up their pace and split off at the steps of the Lincoln Memorial.

CHAPTER 40

Agent Steele sat across the metal conference table from Ant in the stark room at Central Jail. Ant was visibly uncomfortable sitting across from a powerful African American woman, who towered over him and held his fate in her black hands.

Steele initiated the conversation and set the parameters of their meeting. "I've looked over your files, Ant, and if we decide to work together, I have to be totally honest with you, if the truth is too painful for you to deal with, and you're not going to be forthcoming with the intel I already have in my possession, we should stop now and save us both a ton of misery."

"Can I talk to a white agent?"

"No."

Ant sucked it in. "I'm good to go," he said, putting on a tight, forced, smile. "I'm ready to do everything I can but flip. I can't flip, I couldn't live with myself."

Steele: "Fair enough. The reality, as I see it, Ant, and you tell us if the DA has it wrong, because he's bringing the charges against you as eight men died in Venezuela, and you're culpable for the incursion. The Feds have you on tape planning the raid, supporting the ground team, down to choosing the explosive charges used to extricate two

Rentex hostages from a prison in the jungles of Venezuela. The best-case scenario," she said, hammering *best*, "is 25-to-life as an accessory to eight counts of murder, committed outside our borders, in an illegal action not sanctioned by the United States Government." She gave him a moment to consider that. "If I'm off base, Ant, please let me know?"

"No, ma'am. I don't know how you received the information, but no. And I realize now how big a mistake it was to leave a video fingerprint."

Steele nodded her head knowingly. "It's not a fingerprint, Ant, it's a Yeti Bigfoot. The how, is the FBI has been following you for months because of your relationship with the Wolf Pack, operating in the basement of the RockPile. The Feds have all of your trolls and racist screeds you delivered to Nick and Ralph for distribution and publication across the country. They have all your communications with the Wolf Pack related to a drive-by shooting of a local gangster, where you provided the specifics for the murder. Accessory before and after the fact. Road maps, locations where the bangers hung out, the time, and even an algorithm of the possible outcome of the murder, and the violent retribution from rival gangs that might grow out of the cold-blooded killing."

Ant was stunned by the new revelation. Blackfox was such an insular work environment; it seemed to be beyond the law. Wentworth was plugged into his right-wing cabal in the Senate and seemed to be untouchable. The slight man felt lost in the moment, and was having trouble breathing. He blurted out, "Nick and Ralph came to me. It was their deal. Their idea."

That was two confessions in the first five minutes of the interview. Agent Steele kept her game face on and continued, "Not what your text messages inferred. It reads more like another case of you master-minding violence and being a party to the death of another human being. All in the service of fomenting a white-supremacist revolution on American soil."

Ant was speechless. His head was swimming.

"You have a brilliant mind," Steele said. "No way around it. I'm confident I can help you. What I'm trying to do here is save your life. That's not hyperbole. I believe your only real shot at staying alive, after the court trial, is showing all of your cards. The DOJ has got to believe you can provide enough intel to make you an invaluable asset."

"What if I agree to accessory in those crimes?"

"Not good enough."

"Really?" he said, sounding childish. His mouth turned to cotton. He licked his lips and took a sip of the can of Coke Steele brought in with her.

"Ant, don't take this the wrong way," she said, her strength overpowering him. "At this point, your life isn't worth squat to the AUSA. They've got you dead to rights on the nine counts of murder described in the court documents, and the FBI has already cracked the code on your encrypted files."

"Impossible."

"Done deal."

"What the fuck do you want?" his voice raised to soprano.

"Thomas Wentworth," she said. "You're going away for a lifetime unless you can convince the prosecution you can deliver the gold standard. The man the DOJ has been eyeballing for years," Steele said. "You're a cog in the wheel, and they want the engine. Deliver Thomas Wentworth, and I can save your life."

"I'm fucking dead."

"Only if you don't take action," Steele said, the voice of reason. "You understand that in your heart. It doesn't make your decision any easier. Wentworth elevated you to a position of power most men only dream about. The ultimate power over life and death. You conceived the action and watched it play out in real time. Not on a video game. Flesh and blood. That's a heady experience for a 23-year-old.

"Now you've got sixty years in front of you to worry about if you go down on all the charges that will be filed against you. That's not including new information they'll unearth as they go through your encrypted files. Montrose Steiner will bury you to save Thomas Wentworth's life. You know that for a fact."

Steele softened her stance now and continued, "If I can sell you to the Feds, I can guarantee you a life worth living. A new beginning, Ant. Where you can reinvent yourself. I'll work to unfreeze assets obtained before your employment at Blackfox, where the games you played cost human beings their lives, and could put you behind bars for life. Harsh…maybe. Life-altering…definitely."

"I need some time to think."

"Times up, Ant. Sherry Motlin, from the State Department, is outside that door with a one-time offer. She flew in from DC and has a contract in hand that can lift the thousand-pound elephant off your shoulders. You've got one shot at freedom. It's a no-brainer." Steele's eyes bore down on him. "Should I call Ms. Motlin in, or do you want me to send her home?"

Ant's face hardened, and his mile-a-minute brain played out the pros and cons. He knew it was a fool's game. His choice was clear as ice. He wasn't wired to sacrifice his life for anybody else on the planet. Let alone Thomas Wentworth.

"Send her in."

————

Sherry Motlin was a thin African American who exuded intellect. She wore a modern pair of Gucci horn-rimmed glasses, which only amplified the size of her eyes and her power. No hellos, no ingratiating smiles, straight down to business.

"Let me hear you say it, Ant."

Ant took another hit off his can of Coke and cleared his throat. "Thomas Wentworth paid me to do his bidding. He manipulated me, and paid me crazy amounts of money to fulfill his dreams. I was only the man's scribe. But, in my position, I do know where all the bodies are buried. I helped put them there, and I will share that information with you."

Motlin handed a copy of the contract across the metal table for Ant to check the fine print. After an uncomfortable hour of waiting and another can of soda, Ant signed and initialed on the highlighted lines.

Sherry Motlin spoke to the room, "The United States Attorney's Office for the District of Colombia will sponsor Anthony Bernacki, better known as Ant, for acceptance into the Witness Protection Program of the United States Department of Justice. As long as he fulfills his contractual obligation.

"We'll be in touch," she said, and rapped on the metal door, already texting her superiors in DC as she walked out the door.

Ant rested his forehead on the cool surface of the metal table and couldn't remember a time in his life when he really felt safe. He began to weep.

Steele wasn't sure if it was tears of pain or joy. She really didn't give a damn. The kid was a killer and had just made the best deal of his life.

CHAPTER 41

BI Headquarters was alive and humming. James's and Doug's family trees filled the board set up in the front of the conference room. Included under the family member's names and designations was their contact information.

Mitchel was tracking down Doug's sister, Denise. She wasn't answering her phone or returning messages. He pushed back his chair, frustrated, and then leaned forward and punched in the number again. He got a hit.

Mitchel raised his hand to quiet the crew and smiled as he had a brief conversation with Denise before hanging up. He turned to the room and said, "Denise Darby, who is visiting friends on Long Island, says she's estranged from her brother. Doesn't have a clue where he might be, and hung up on me." Mitchel shook his head grinning. "She's lying."

Agent Steele was riding a major high having turned Ant. Knowing it could be the answer to her prayers, and lead to the successful completion of her mission to take down Blackfox with Dakota's help.

Her total focus was now on finding Sarah Moore, her kidnapped victim. She pointed toward Stevens, who was on the phone with the manager of the local Recorders Office. He explained his rank in the

FBI, the dire need for the information requested, laid the schmooze on thick, and it was well received. He was rewarded with intel he jotted down on his pad.

Stevens looked up pleased with himself. "Sister's got two properties. One of the houses is a three-bedroom in El Segundo, the second is a vacation home in Big Bear." The agents pulled up Google Maps, and pushed in on both properties.

"El Segundo is a dense middle-class suburb," Steele said to the room. "Plenty of kids, no real privacy. Stuck between an elementary school and a high school. Doesn't have the right feel.

"The second property is in the San Bernardino Mountains surrounding Big Bear, about a half-mile beyond the lake. It appears to be a cabin, might be on a dirt road. It's forest land in the middle of nowhere." Steele looked at Agent Chase, who nodded his head. "Let's take a road trip," she said.

Steele and Chase enlisted Mitchel and Stevens. The team was having great success and wanted the chance to close another case. They sent a second group of agents to El Segundo in case their intuition was wrong. If it was a dead end, they'd continue to Big Bear and provide backup.

"Let's suit up, vests, weapons, radios, and stay safe," Agent Chase said to the mobile teams. And then to the men and women left behind, "I want everyone on the team to stay put. Order food in. And be ready to deploy if we get lucky. Call your loved ones and let them know this could be a long night."

Steele called for a chopper to be fueled and ready to fly if needed. It would take an hour and forty-two to reach their destination, 89 miles from Orange County by car; the chopper could make the trip in fifteen minutes.

———

Sarah was hard at work in the cabin's kitchen in Big Bear. She applied a tinted foundation to Doug Darby's face, darker than his natural skin tone. And now, with a black cap, sunglasses, jeans, and running shoes, he could pass for a mixed-race Hispanic. They sat around the kitchen table and penned a list of things to buy to disguise both men, a change of clothes, and food to take on the road after they killed Dakota.

"I just want you both to hear this." Sarah's tone was sharp. "Dakota left me. He broke my heart, and I never heard from him again. For over six years, not word one. And now he's home, and I get embroiled in this. Fuck him. If you need help taking him down, I will happily be there. I'm just saying."

"Something to think about," James said as Doug turned a cold shoulder and got ready to leave. "How do I look?"

"Like a hot Hispanic."

Doug gave his partner a hard grin Sarah pretended not to see.

The men hadn't heard or seen their neighbor, who lived a quarter mile up the dirt road, but were still taking no chances at being recognized.

Doug backed the Lincoln out of the tight garage and headed down the hill, leaving James alone with Sarah in the kitchen as she washed the breakfast dishes.

They agreed to let Sarah shower and raid Doug's sister's closet. She felt better in a clean pair of panties, jeans, and a plaid shirt, but had to work at tamping down her fear. The more she could ingratiate herself to her captors, the more likely she could make it out alive.

James looked like he hadn't slept. Red eyes, bedroom hair, and wound so tight she was afraid he'd explode. She gave him some time to unwind, let the food digest, before laying the pipe for what was to come.

"I've got to go to the john," he said. "Can I trust you not to run? It wouldn't go well for you."

"No worries," she said. She was aware that both James and Doug were trained Rangers and understood how rigorous the path to earning that status was. She wouldn't last five minutes in the forest if she ran, and she'd be dead the minute her value delivering Dakota was accomplished. She heard the toilet flush and was wiping down the last plate when James walked back into the kitchen. His hair was hand-combed, and he looked a bit brighter.

Sarah sucked in a deep breath and said, "Don't kill me, James."

The frank plea startled him. He didn't answer and evaded her stare.

"I think you still have a heart beating in your chest. I know you love your man. You don't need another murder to haunt your dreams. Please don't kill me, and I'll help you. No matter how this plays out. I will help you, James. I have no allegiance to Dakota."

James nodded his head, walked into the living room, and turned on the television.

CHAPTER 42

Dakota and Billie were on the move. The electricity flowing through their car was palpable. Billie had made a breakthrough in the kidnapping case and they were armed, dangerous, and headed east, driving up Rosecrans Avenue at breakneck speed into El Segundo.

Dakota: "Why haven't you married again?"

"Where the hell did that come from?" she asked, not pleased.

"You spend five minutes on the phone and get men to open their computers and files, and share them with you. You could probably use the same skill set and get a man to open his heart, and move in with you."

"Nah, I'm like one of those bald eagles."

"You're not bald."

"No, but those birds mate for life. And I thought it was a better image than a goose. Never much had the will to pursue it after Harry passed."

"You still have the gift."

"Who the hell are you to ask me about my personal life? I don't see you going out on the town. You've got two beautiful women attracted to you, and you're not a priest, Dakota."

Dakota wished he'd kept his big mouth shut. "One of them works for the FBI and will lose her life's work if we're caught in a social situation. And Sarah, we've already discussed. Look what she's involved in now."

"I'm sorry, Dakota, but this isn't on you. This is on Doug and James. The bad guys. The killers. I want you clear on that."

They drove in silence for a while. "Well, you did good," Dakota said, changing the subject back to the business at hand.

"The list of potential locations was cut in half when I discovered James Marshal's folks lived in Chicago. If they're headed there by car, we leave it to the Chicago cops, or the FBI to keep an eye out."

"If they turn up in Chicago, I'm on the first flight."

Dakota skidded the Bronco to the curb on Lomita Street in the suburbs of El Segundo. The middle-class neighborhood had a family vibe. That, and the bikes and toys strewn haphazardly on a series of modest green lawns. The smell of oil from the huge Chevron refinery operating on the edge of town hung heavily in the air.

Dakota got out of the Bronco. His Glock in a shoulder rig. Billie followed, her 9mm in her hand, secreted in her loose jacket pocket, ready to provide backup if needed. Dakota started up the front path,

"I'll save you the effort," a young mother said from across the street.

Dakota turned on the sound. Billie kept her eyes trained on the house, looking for signs of life.

"Denise is visiting family on Long Island. She's been gone a few weeks and not expected back anytime soon. May I help you with something?"

"That pretty much sums it up," Dakota said, smiling. "Have you seen her brother, Doug, by any chance?"

"I was just waiting for someone to come by and ask. Been on the lookout. No. He's all over the news. The whole neighborhood's talking about it. Personally, I don't think Doug could've done it, but, what do I know."

"Thank you. You've saved me some time. But, if you see him, call 911. The Doug you know might be full of surprises, none of them good."

Dakota slid back into the Bronco. Billie followed, stowed her weapon, and showed him the Google map of Denise Darby's second property located in Big Bear. "This has more of the cabin feel," she said like a real estate broker. "Has the look of a place I might hang out in if I were on the lam."

"I agree." Dakota started the car, executed a squealing U-turn, and waved at the neighbor as he drove off. "But on the lam? What are you, a hundred years old?"

"Fuck you, Dakota," Billie said, eliciting a laugh. "At least I knew *the bomb* was a good thing."

"Yeah, back in the '70s. Let's pick up some lunch and hit the road. We should be there in less than two hours if the traffic's light."

"I could do a double quarter pounder with cheese, fries, and a Coke."

"I can't believe you're still alive."

Dakota set his iPhone's GPS for the cabin in Big Bear and hit the gas. He knew they'd pass a Mickey D's on the way.

———

James was sitting in a kitchen chair, a towel over his shoulders as Sarah clipped off the last long locks of his hair. She had a pan filled with warm water, applied shaving cream over half his scalp, and started shaving the uneven short hairs the dull scissors left behind.

The television was on low in the living room, and the growing heat of summer in the mountains was almost unbearable for the uninitiated used to central air.

"You already look different," Sarah said, taking a step back and admiring her handiwork.

"Feels strange, but what the hell."

"So would handcuffs."

James stiffened in his seat, and Sarah wondered if she'd gone too far.

She spread more shaving cream on the second half of his scalp and kept talking. "You're going to have to watch out for sunburn," she said, changing the subject, but keeping it personal.

"You're right about that. When Doug gets back and we pack up, we'll have you make the call to Dakota. I've written a message. This is very important, Sarah, you read what's written, and don't change a word, or you'll never see tomorrow. If Doug smells you're anything but compliant, I won't be able to control him."

Sarah continued to shave; her stomach flipped, afraid she might lose her breakfast. She finished her work, wiped down James's scalp with a wet kitchen towel, and stepped back. "Even without sunglasses, if you weren't with Doug, no one would recognize you from the headshot they're using."

"Not sure I understand."

"They're looking for two men, James. You and Doug. You have to be careful when you're on the road. One man drives, the other rests out of sight in the backseat. That way you can make good time, and put as much distance between yourself and California as possible."

"Smart. Very good. Okay."

And then the news flash on the television crushed the good feelings.

"We have breaking news in the manhunt underway for James Marshal and Doug Darby," a serious reporter shared. A new photo replaced the men's headshots. It showed a grainy Lincoln, with a man who was clearly Doug, sitting behind the wheel. The reporter went on, "It appears the men are traveling in a 2021 black Lincoln Continental, with the California license number 3555 P 278."

They heard the Lincoln driving up to the cabin, and waited in silence as Doug pulled into the garage, and yelled for James to help unload the car.

James stuck his head out the door and said, "You better come in first."

Doug didn't like his tone of voice and walked in as the reporter wrapped up his segment. "So again, if you see these men driving in a black Lincoln Continental, do not engage. They are armed and dangerous. Dial 911, and let the police get these killers off the street."

The news report sucked all the oxygen out of the room. "Help me unload the car," Doug said, his face stony. His eyes nervous slits. "What the hell did you do to your hair?"

"Changed my look," James said. "You're good to go, I needed some work."

"Okay,"

Three loud raps on the door froze the conversation. Doug drew his weapon, grabbed Sarah, putting his lips near her ear. "Get rid of whoever's out there. Don't make a mistake or I'll kill you."

James had his 9mm drawn, and positioned himself in the kitchen ready to come out firing if necessary. Doug dashed into the bedroom.

Another knock on the door. Sarah sucked in a breath and opened it, forcing a tight smile, knowing her response meant the difference between life and death. "Hello," she said, relaxing some when she saw it was an elderly man in his late eighties.

"Well, hello, young lady. Aren't you a breath of fresh air? I heard some coming and going from my place down the road a piece, and I thought I'd say howdy to Denise. Is she in?"

"No… I am so sorry, my name is Jessie. A dear friend of Denise. She's letting me unwind here for a few days. Work can be so hectic."

The man smiled and said, "Well good for you. It's mighty quiet up here. It should suit your needs perfectly. If there's anything I can help you with, my name's Clarence Greely, and I live right down the lane. Feel free to knock on my door if you need anything."

"That is so nice. We'll see how it goes, Clarence. Thank you very much for stopping by."

"You take care now." As Clarence turned to walk home, he glanced into the garage Doug had left open, and saw the Lincoln at the same time Doug witnessed the recognition and concern in the old guy's face. Clarence shot a look of fear back at the cabin and didn't see Doug drop the bedroom blinds seconds after seeing the old man's change in demeanor.

He waited for Clarence to pass the elbow in the road and stepped into the living room, checking the load in his pistol.

Sarah was about to stop him, but James jerked his head no. They watched as Doug ran out the door and cut through the tree line, trying to beat the old gentleman to his house.

CHAPTER 43

oug Darby's heart was pounding, and then it slowed as he loped across the pine needle path that ran parallel to the dirt road. The smell of the forest, the sounds of wildlife, and the rush of the hunt filled him with a strange feeling of omnipotence. A hunter in control of his destiny.

He wasn't aware of passing the old man, but got his answer when he entered the empty house that had been left unlocked. That made sense to Doug… Who the hell was going to break into this old shack?

He did a quick walk around the living room. A fireplace, an old television with rabbit ears to aid reception. Doug realized that everything in the room was an antique. It probably wasn't when Clarence purchased the furnishings, but it was with time in. That always meant something to Doug. You earned respect in the Army with time in.

He lingered, viewing photos on the mantle over the blackened fireplace. Clarence, in the Korean War. A young buck heading for battle. And a picture of his marriage to a homely little thing, Doug thought, but he looked happy.

And then Clarence walked through the front door.

Doug spun and shot Clarence once in the chest with a jacketed hollow point. It was a kill shot, but Clarence refused to go down. He almost smiled before pushing a medical alert button on a fob that hung from a lanyard draped around his neck. He stood tall even after his heart stopped beating, and Doug put a bullet through the proud man's forehead. Clarence toppled backward onto the thin carpet he and his wife had purchased fifty years earlier.

Doug checked out the man's garage and brightened when he discovered a 1972 green Plymouth Fury. It had a few rust spots around the wheel wells, but Doug decided the old guy had balls as a young man. A cool ride.

He walked back into the living room, stepping over Clarence's body, in search of the keys. They weren't in the man's pockets. Doug tore apart the living room, drawers, the kitchen, the bedroom, and he was starting to freak out. The old guy had pushed an alarm button, and he didn't know how long he had before he'd hear sirens, and an ambulance would arrive. He was about to scream out loud, and there, right next to the front door, on a carved wooden key holder, hung the keys to the Fury.

And then the phone rang.

Doug ran out, closing the front door behind him, and jumped behind the wheel of the car and inserted the key. The motor struggled mightily to turn over but there just wasn't enough juice to satisfy the eight cylinders under the hood. If he could find jumper cables, he might be able to use the Lincoln to spark the Plymouth.

———

The landline started ringing in Denise's cabin. Sarah and James stared at the phone for a moment, and then James said, "Answer it. Be cool."

Sarah picked up the handset off the cordless phone. "Hello."

"Hello, is this Denise Darby?"

"Why, yes, it is. Who am I speaking with?"

"I'm Jeanine over at Security Health. We received an alert from Clarence Greely, lives down the road from you."

"Is Clarence okay?"

"You are on his list of emergency phone numbers. Would you

please be so kind to walk over to his place and see if I should send a team? It's a long way if he just fell down."

"You bet. I'll just run over and check on Clarence right now."

"And please call back and let me know. It's company policy to send a truck unless we receive a verbal report that our client is in good health."

"Will do," Sarah said. And the woman from Security Health clicked off.

Sarah continued talking. "I'll call right back if we need assistance. He falls more than he'd like to admit," Sarah said, and hung up.

"I've got to say. You were great. Let's see what Doug says when he…"

Doug banged through the front door into the house. "We need a cable to jump-start the car the guy's got in his garage."

"Okay, relax, we're okay."

"Watch your tone."

"Sarah handled it," James said tight. "Denise's name was on the old guy's emergency list, call numbers. She told the operator she'd check on the man and call back if he needed assistance. From the look on your face, I'm guessing he doesn't."

Doug banged out the door, grabbed the twelve-pack of Budweiser he bought on his shopping spree, walked back in, and disappeared into the kitchen. James and Sarah glanced at each other and heard the hiss of a pull top being pried open on the beer.

Doug stepped back into the living room and downed the twelve ounces in one long pull off the can.

"Let's roll."

CHAPTER 44

Dakota pulled into the parking lot at McDonald's and they both ordered double quarter pounders with cheese meals. Billie was already chowing down on the fries while Dakota texted Steele an FYI that he and Billie were headed to Big Bear to check out a cabin Doug Darby's sister owned.

———

Steele turned to Chase, who was behind the wheel. "Son of a bitch is ahead of us again. Dakota and Billie are already en route to Big Bear."

"How the hell did they get the jump on us? Tell him to turn around. We don't need the help or the liability."

"You're kidding, right?"

"Just do it, Steele. Call the man. At least we're on record trying."

Steele dialed Dakota's number. "Dakota, Chase wants you to turn around and let us handle it." No response. "Dakota?"

"Heard you loud and clear, Steele, you stay safe now." And he hung up.

"We were warned off by the FBI," Dakota told Billie.

"What're we gonna do?"

Dakota pulled out of the McDonald's lot, paused a moment, and made a right turn, heading for the San Bernardino Mountains.

"Good man."

———

Doug finished off a second beer, crushed the aluminum can with his fist, and tossed it into the garbage bin in the kitchen. "We need those cables. The old man has a Plymouth. Full tank of gas, no juice in the battery. Other than that, it looks solid. Let's get a move on. James, check the workbench in the garage. My sister's a stickler for emergency equipment."

James walked out the door and left the two of them in the living room. "Pack a few bags with the food I brought back in case we get hungry on the road," Doug said to Sarah.

"Where are we headed?"

"No questions. Did James give you the text for your phone call with Dakota?"

"He mentioned it, but I haven't seen it yet. I'm not concerned. Give it to me, I'll sell it," she said hard.

Doug's eye probed Sarah. "Good." He went into the bedroom and started packing clothes, and carefully filled his rucksack with his weapons.

"Got it," James shouted as he walked back into the cabin with jumper cables dangling from his hand like snakes.

"Great, let's do it," Doug said as he slapped a fresh clip of .38's into his Sig and slid it into his leather shoulder holster. As he muscled the heavy rucksack over his shoulder, he said, "James, we need to push the Plymouth out of the garage. It's as tight as ours. We can jump it on the road, hide the Lincoln in his garage, and get some control back on our side. They want a fight, we'll give 'em a fight. All right, let's go. You too, Sarah."

They locked the door behind them, jumped into the Lincoln, and raised dust as they drove down the dirt road toward Clarence's cabin.

———

Dakota and Billie were making good time on CA-333. They sped through Running Springs, Deer Lick, and the Big Bear Dam was in their sights. After they crossed the bridge, the road became CA-18. "We're heading about five miles past the lake," Billie said, looking at the GPS map on her cell phone.

"You and Harry ever spend time up here?" Dakota asked.

"Couple times. Harry thought it was a little too red-necky."

"I came up a few times to go fishing. Stayed over in Fawnskin. Spent the day over near the dam in a party boat, and got skunked. Never been back. Nice though. Smell of pine, all that. You ever see the wild burros?"

"Oh yeah..." Billie let out a light, feminine burp and grinned.

"Warned you about the double quarter pounder."

"I think it was the cheese that's fighting me."

"Yeah, Billie. It was the cheese," he said, chuckling.

"Just drive," Billie said, tight and checked the load on her Colt.

CHAPTER 45

The Lincoln Continental and the Plymouth Fury were sitting side by side, both hoods up, blocking the dirt road in both directions. Doug was behind the wheel of the Fury, Sarah sat in the back seat of the Lincoln, while James tried to get the jumper cables to work their magic. The Lincoln idled as he clamped the positive cable to the dead battery's positive clamp. "Okay," he said. Then he pulled the other cable from the Plymouth to the good battery and tapped it against what he hoped was the negative terminal. Sparks flew.

"Shit."

"Switch 'em around, and tell me when," he snapped.

James followed orders: "Give it a try."

Doug turned the key, and the son of a bitch sparked to life. "Yes!"

James: "All right, keep giving it gas so it doesn't stall. We've gotta build up some juice."

"Keep the cables with us just in case," Doug said.

James pulled off the cables and closed the hood. "What the hell is that?" he said, straining to hear over the sound of two engines idling.

"What?"

"It's a fuckin' siren," James shouted.

"Pop the trunk!" Doug jumped out of the Fury and transferred the bags from the rear of the Lincoln into their new ride. He pulled an AK out of the rucksack, and slammed in a banana clip.

The wail of the siren was growing in volume.

"Everybody be cool. Sarah, I want you to stand in front of the Plymouth and tell whoever arrives the old man is A-Okay and we're just giving his car a boost. And James, crank one in the chamber and hope we don't need it. I'll have you covered from the far side of the house."

Sarah did as ordered. She slid out of the Lincoln and moved trance-like to the Plymouth that was idling and giving off noxious fumes. She was caught in a nightmare and saw no way out.

James followed orders and steeled himself, ready for anything that came his way. He was too far-gone to question the proper move in a dire situation like this. He clicked into combat mode and stood tall.

"Here it comes," James shouted, alerting Doug, who pushed the safety lever down on his AK, ready to fire. "Why the fuck is an EMT truck coming up the road, you bitch?"

"I was only supposed to call if he needed help, Goddamn it. He didn't need help because he was dead!" her voice frenzied.

A large red EMT truck lurched, hitting potholes as it powered down the dirt road, leaving a wide contrail of brown dust behind it. The siren was blaring as it pulled to an air-brake squealing stop.

Something was wrong with the picture. The two men in the cab of the truck appeared to be surveying the scene. The man in the passenger seat stared at the Lincoln and picked up the radio handset.

His finger was about to depress the call button when Doug stepped from the side of the cabin, and sent an arcing shower of high velocity rounds across the EMT truck's windshield, shattering glass, and killing the driver and his partner in an instant.

Sarah screamed hysterically, while James stood silent. Surveying the carnage.

"Let's go!" Doug barked with military bearing.

CHAPTER 46

"What the hell did I just hear?" Dakota said knowing damn well they were driving into a worst-case scenario.

"First left up ahead," Billie said and cocked her pistol. And then grabbed her shotgun off the back seat, and checked the load. Satisfied, she put on her game face.

Dakota pulled onto the dirt road and followed the tracks the EMT truck left behind in the loose dirt. He eased up to the bend in the road, and parked his Bronco across the one-lane road, blocking all egress.

He jumped out of the vehicle, grabbed his Glock, pulled out his cell, and called Steele. He looked around the corner. His heart stopped as he saw Sarah getting pushed into the back of an old green car, and Doug and James jumping in.

He saw the damage to the EMT truck and knew the medics were dead.

"Call in the troops, Steele. It's bad up here. Looks like two medics are down, and the boys are heading our way, with the hostage."

"We're five minutes out, I'm calling backup and a chopper."

"Out," Dakota said.

He waved Billie off to the side, into thick cover, as they waited for the Plymouth Fury to discover the Bronco, blocking their path, the only way off the mountain.

The Plymouth eased down the road, not sure what was around the bend. It pulled to a stop ten yards away from the Bronco.

Doug said, "Son of a…"

Dakota stepped from behind a tree and rapid fired three times.

The windshield shattered and fell in on itself.

Doug's face was destroyed; the side of his skull torn off, blood spattered the window and the seat.

James opened the passenger door, slid out of the car, and sprinted for his life.

Dakota tracked James's route while running to the Plymouth and yanking open the rear door. Sarah was on her back. Her eyes glazed, but wide open. She looked up at Dakota, and tears streamed down her face, her body shook uncontrollably. He took her by the hands, and gently pulled her out of the car. "You're okay now, Sarah. You're okay. Billie's here and she'll take care of you. I've still got work to do."

Billie appeared and walked Sarah away from the carnage.

Dakota took off running, following in James's wake.

CHAPTER 47

hase and Steele pulled onto the dirt road, drove to Dakota's Bronco, and jumped out of their car.

Billie brought the Feds up to speed. Gave them an estimated body count, explained that Clarence lived in the cabin beyond the Plymouth, but Sarah was fairly sure the old man was killed by Doug Darby, who was dead, and bleeding out on the driver's seat of the Fury.

"Darby also killed two EMT first responders still in their truck," she said. "Dakota's tracking James Marshal, who rabbited after Doug was shot. James headed down the slope, directly across from the Fury. Dakota asked for you not to shoot *him* if you join the hunt, and to share that intel with whoever shows up after the fact."

Agent Steele checked on Sarah, who was sitting in the Bronco, clearly going into shock. She called for an ambulance and explained the situation. She also alerted the local cops. The helicopter was en route, and armed with a thermal imagery system. It could pick up the heat signature of a suspect in dense cover and facilitate Dakota's hunt.

Agent Mitchel and Steven's car skidded to a stop. The men jumped out and caught up to Agent Steele as she headed down the hill to provide armed backup for Dakota, with a strict warning not to shoot the man.

———

Agent Chase strode toward Clarence's cabin. He stopped at the first EMT truck, his face an angry mask, as he observed the two young men brutally executed in cold blood.

He continued to the cabin, knocked on the door. No answer. He raised his gun, tried turning the doorknob with the tail of his shirt. The door swung open providing a clear view of Clarence's dead body, splayed on his back, blocking the entryway. Chase led with his weapon, carefully stepping over Clarence to make sure James wasn't hiding somewhere in the residence.

It was all clear, and Chase exited the cabin. The dirt road beyond the Bronco was filling with medical responders, local police, his backup FBI teams, and the helicopter that now circled overhead.

Chase was furious at the senseless murders.

CHAPTER 48

Dakota started his search where James disappeared over the edge of the hillside. He slid sideways down the incline and landed on a footpath that ran parallel to the cabins and dirt road above. He jogged a ways in the direction of Clarence's cabin, looking for fresh tracks, but came up empty. Then realized James had nothing in his hands when he darted out of the Plymouth. He must've been armed, but without food or gear, there was no way he could hide himself in the forest until he came up with a better plan.

Dakota turned and sprinted back past his entry point and pounded the loose dirt of the path heading for the only way out, CA-18. There were only two options for the killer. Travel up and over the mountain the back way or down past Big Bear and land in the valley below.

———

James executed a careful slide a few hundred yards down from the dirt path and was headed for the main road. If luck were on his side, he'd car-jack a vehicle, drive it over the mountain, and disappear. His mind was spinning scenarios, but with the body count he was a party to, they all ended with him strapped to a table, and a lethal injection. He felt a weight on his chest and thought he might be having a heart attack. He was in so far over his head he considered eating his own gun.

He kicked himself in the ass for not shooting Dakota as he stumbled out of the Plymouth, but the moment was a total blur. All that was on his mind was getting out of the car and saving his skin.

———

Dakota continued across the trail, and when he picked up the sound of traffic on CA-18 he started down the mountainside. The thick pine forest muted the sound of rotors beating above the treetops. He stood still and listened for any sign of movement. And then he waited some more. His eyes trying to recognize outcroppings, or fallen tree trunks James might be holed up in, waiting for darkness, or waiting to pounce.

He dropped another twenty feet and stopped behind an old-growth pine. He heard the echoed voices of agents in the distance, and then the chopper circling overhead.

Dakota received a text from Steele. "The bird picked up a body fifty yards below your location. Wait for backup."

Dakota continued down the hill. Paused again and waited. Nothing. He was ready to continue when he thought he heard the faint snap of a branch. And then silence. Dakota remained still. Slowed the beating of his heart, and listened.

There. Again. Very slight, moving away from his position. He did a silent five count, stepped past the tree trunk, and followed.

James was approaching the road and stopped short. It was a fucking parking lot. Filled with lookie-loos trying to shoot videos of what was occurring on the dirt road where all the action was taking place. Police cars sped up the gravel shoulder of the road, lights flashed, sirens wailed, as they passed cars blocked in traffic in both directions.

The helicopter circled, and irate tourists honked, drowning out all other sound.

Dakota inched behind James, his Glock raised.

"It's over, James."

James startled. His head spun toward the voice. He missed a step on the steep incline, his arms flailed as he tried to right himself. His Colt dropped out of his hand as he fell to one knee.

James was breathing hard. He glanced from his pistol, just out of reach, to Dakota's Glock pointed at his kill zone.

"You know it's over, James," Dakota said, evenly. Staring down the man who wanted nothing more than to bury him. The killer who kidnapped Sarah and left a trail of bodies to that end.

"There's no way out," Dakota said, his jaw tight. "Nowhere to run. No way to stop us from hunting you down and shooting you like a dog if by some fucking miracle you managed to get away."

"I should've killed you in Venezuela."

"We wouldn't be having this conversation. We'd both be dead."

James couldn't argue the point.

And then, like a Jesuit Priest, Dakota asked, "How do you see this ending, James?"

James's eyes glanced at his pistol that was half buried in pine needles. "I don't think life in prison's in my cards."

"What's the remedy?"

"I could kill you."

"You could try," Dakota said, shaking his head.

"You always were a cocky fucking prick."

James glanced at his Colt again, fell back in the pine needles, letting the incline move him slightly down the slope as if losing his balance, and drew a .38 from behind his back.

Dakota fired.

The bullet carved a clean hole through James's thigh. His scream was primal, and his .38 slid from his hand.

Dakota hoped it hurt plenty.

———

Agent Steele, Mitchel, and Stevens slid down the hill to the men's location and surveyed the situation.

Dakota walked over to James, who was writhing in pain. He looked at Steele and then down at the guns.

Steele shot photos where the pistols lay with her cell phone, bagged them, and handed them off to Stevens. And then she took a few more of James, who was keening. Steele let out the breath she'd been holding. James was in custody, and Dakota and Sarah were alive.

James let out a labored howl.

Dakota said, "Someone should call the medics. Tell them to send an EMT truck and get here ASAP before the man bleeds out." Mitchel already had his cell in his fist, tapping in the orders.

Steele followed Dakota a few steps away from her men: "You are a real heart stopper, Dakota."

"You would've done the same. We just got here first." His eye crinkled into a hard smile. "Thanks for the heads-up with the chopper. It helped. James was cornered, knew it was over. I think he wanted to die. I wasn't going to let that happen. Man deserves all the hard time he's earned."

"How do you feel?"

"Angry. Frustrated. Disgusted. Really angry."

"Time to finish the job we started?" she asked.

"Let's do it."

Steele's eyes shined as she watched Dakota head toward the main road, and up to the crime scene to deal with the blizzard of paperwork and interviews he'd be inundated with.

CHAPTER 49

The first person who got in Dakota's face as he walked down the dirt road and into the melee was Joel Royce of the Orange County Sheriff's Department.

"I must've missed your call," Royce said, his voice dry as dirt.

"You were on my list. Had a few things to take care of first."

"I don't mind somebody getting a jump on the scumbags. As long as the good guys come out on top."

"It was a fifty-fifty proposition here. Killers were animals."

"You're right," Royce said, showing some heart. "I've already been told the FBI has first dibs on you. Then there're the local cops, and then I'll need a statement. We'll do abbreviated on scene, and finish it off in town, next few days. Your call."

"Appreciated."

Dakota stepped under the police tape and entered the war zone. Tall bright lights on tri-pods hooked up to buzzing generators were next to three red EMT trucks. Red, white, and blue lights strobed on top of police cars, and black body bags were moved on gurneys toward the meat trucks. Tech teams streamed in and out of both cabins and scoured the dirt road for ejected bullet casings. Police photographers snapped photos of the Plymouth and Doug's lifeless body, his head still leaning against the blood-spattered driver's side window where Dakota's bullets left him.

Dakota walked over to one of the EMT trucks where Sarah was being attended. She lay on a gurney in the back of the truck, a saline drip in her arm to help with the shock that overwhelmed her.

"How're you feeling?"

"Sick. Happy to be alive. Relieved to see your face." Her eyes filled again as the paramedic came around back, looked at his patient, and said, "We're ready to roll, Sarah." And then to Dakota, "She's doing fine, we're being cautious. She's been through a lot. We gave her something to calm her nerves, and we'll be delivering her to St. John's. Keep her overnight for observation, and cut her loose sometime in the afternoon."

Dakota touched Sarah's cheek with the back of his hand. "I think they're going to need me here for quite a while, but I'll stop by the hospital on my way down the mountain and check on you."

"Okay, Dakota. Thank you for showing up."

The doors slammed shut, and as the truck wheeled carefully past the action, Dakota was approached by Agent Chase.

"What a cluster fuck. I just received word you tracked down James Marshal. What can I say, at least the killing spree is over. Great work my friend. We'll talk later," Chase said, and continued back down the road toward Clarence's cabin. The man looked tired and depressed.

Three network helicopters joined the police chopper and the FBI's bird circling the scene overhead. Thousand-watt spots crisscrossed the crime scene like klieg lights at a Hollywood premier.

"They look like vultures," Billie said as she stepped up to Dakota. "Sarah was doing pretty well under the circumstances." As they walked shoulder to shoulder toward the kidnapper's cabin, she said, "Doug killed the old man down the road. Name was Clarence. It was his Plymouth they stole. Good shooting, meanwhile."

"Perfect angle, had to take it."

"You had no choice. You saved Sarah's life." Dakota nodded. "You get James?"

Dakota smiled. "Shot him in the thigh. A clean through-and-through. Should hurt him big-time for a good long while. Plus, the rehab. Give him something to think about in the brig. The prick admitted he should've killed me in Venezuela."

"I knew your intuition was right on."

"Good to hear him say it, though."

"I sure could eat."

"Maybe they left something in Darby's cabin."

"I'd rather starve."

"You are the bomb."

CHAPTER 50

t was five in the afternoon the following day, before Dakota and Billie made it back to Redondo Beach. Dakota spent time with Sarah, who was in a very fragile, emotional state. He spoke with her mother when she arrived at Saint John's with a promise to take care of her daughter for as long as needed. Dakota offered to pay for therapy, knowing from his experience on the battlefield, Sarah would likely suffer PTSD from the extreme trauma she endured. Her mother thanked him, smiled and reminded Dakota her daughter was willful, but hopefully too smart to refuse the kind offer. She promised they'd stay in touch.

It felt good to be home. Almost safe. But Dakota had some business to take care of before he could relax. Billie passed out on her air mattress in the office, while Dakota took a cold shower, shaved, poured two fingers of scotch, and dialed Thomas Wentworth's private number.

Wentworth picked up on the first ring, "I've been waiting on your call," he said, curt, preoccupied. Dakota hadn't slept in thirty-six hours, and didn't take kindly to the attitude, so he hit him with the showstopper. "Thomas, we've got bad news on the Ant front." Dakota gave that a moment to sink in. "I'm not sure what went down or why, but I stopped by the prison to check on Ant on my way down from Big Bear, and I've been blocked from visitation rights."

"That doesn't sound good. Hold on for a moment." Wentworth picked up his landline and called his lawyer. "What the hell's going on, Montrose? Dakota's off the visitors list. He was just turned away at the door."

Dakota could only hear Wentworth's side of the conversation, but could feel the icy vibe. And then he heard, "You there, Dakota?"

"I am, Thomas."

"Good work yesterday," came out like an afterthought. "I want to hear all about it when I clear the decks. I'll talk to Bradley, although if he were in the loop I would've already heard. Steiner was afraid to make the call. I could hear it in his voice. Keep your phone charged, Dakota." And the boss hung up.

———

Senator Jack Bradley sat comfortably on his overstuffed leather sofa in his mahogany-paneled office. His wife, Shirley, with her bright red hair, enhanced skin and smile, sat next to him, her arm draped loosely around his shoulder.

"You've had yourself enough action in the past month to last most mortals a lifetime. If I were you, I'd get out of town for a few weeks. Until the dust settles, and the politics play out. In a week or two, the press will have moved on to the next breaking story."

"That sounds about right. I've had a full schedule."

"That's an understatement, Dakota," Shirley said, taking a sip of iced tea.

"Blackfox will be resurrected in due time," Bradley went on. "We're considering a name change, but the organization it services will always need a second opinion on how the government works, and how to best serve their needs.

"The board of directors remains comfortable with you in your advisory position, if the challenge is still of interest."

Dakota kept his own counsel, not willing to commit yet.

"If that's not to your liking, my man Traina is thinking about retirement. He still feels guilty about the attempt on my life, and I'm concerned having someone working for me who is constantly second-guessing himself. You could take over as head of my security department."

"Two very generous offers, sir."

"Stop being so formal, Dakota," Shirley scolded with a comfortable smile.

"I told him, dear," the senator said. "I think it's ingrained, part of his military training."

"You're right about that, Jack," Dakota said. And then, "I'll work on it, Shirley."

"Now go somewhere you can keep a low profile, drink piña coladas, and get some well-deserved R&R," Shirley said, understanding the purge that was about to take place.

"Give it some thought and get back to me," Bradley said. "You can always get me on my private line." The meeting was over.

Dakota stood. "Thank you, Jack, Shirley. You both have been more than gracious."

"It's how we treat our friends, Dakota. And the man who saved my husband's life."

Dakota walked out of their fine home, holding his secret close to his vest.

EPILOGUE

Dakota and Billie, in the Corvette convertible, headed for LAX toward an Alaska Airlines flight to Costa Rica. A beautiful blue sky, white cumulus clouds, wind whipping their hair on the 405. Life was good. Dakota brought Billie up to speed on every front, and she agreed now was the time to keep a low profile. She promised to do a drive-by of Dakota's place a few times a day, in case there was any blowback from recent events. Dakota had been the cause of so many lives ending up behind bars, or buried, he couldn't totally trust the target he'd carried on his back had disappeared.

As Billie pulled into departures. Dakota looked her in the eye and told her none of the cases that they closed could have happened without her hard work and police instincts. "I'm proud to be your wingman," Dakota said and jumped out of the Vette, grabbed his carry-on and a single suitcase, and headed into the terminal.

———

The sound of throaty Harley Engines reverberated and preceded the arrival of Ralph and Nick as they pulled onto the gravel lot on the side of the RockPile.

Ralph pulled off his German helmet, tossed his wild mane of hair off his face, and scratched his beard. Nick dismounted, strapped his German half helmet to his seat. Five unmarked government cars skidded onto the lot, blocking the bikers in place, and swarmed.

If Ralph had been thinking straight, he would have gone quietly, without a fuss. Instead, he swung from the heels and decked the first FBI agent who blocked his path. The agent went down hard, and Ralph was eating gravel as four agents muscled him to the rocky ground and cuffed him tighter than needed.

Nick froze, went through his mental list of the many ways he'd broken the law. But more importantly, wondered, of the many felonies he was guilty of, what was he being arrested for? He wisely assumed the position and dummied up.

Trish ran out of the bar, screaming at the agents, calling them dark-state, un-American, liberal assholes. And ordered them to get the fuck off her property. The lead FBI agent handed Trish the search warrant, entered the premises, and made a beeline down the stairs to where the computers and their racist paraphernalia was disseminated. He discovered multiple e-mails, written by Ant, which tied the OC Wolf Pack to Blackfox.

———

Thomas Wentworth walked out on his patio with a glass of iced tea, and pondered the miserable turn of events. There was no doubt Ant's betrayal was bad news, corroborated when he glanced over the railing. "Bob," he shouted. "We've got visitors."

His silver-haired assistant ran onto the patio, and looked down as eight Government-issue sedans, pulled to a stop at the front gate, and FBI agents deployed around the lower perimeter of the house. Agent Jean Steel, and Will Chase stood in front of the speaker and announced their presence.

"Buzz them in, Bob. Our afternoon just turned to shit."

"Yes, sir." And Bob ran into the house and hit the buzzer before the Feds had time to damage anything on the property.

Agent Steele handed the search warrant to Wentworth, who thought it was overreach, and watched fifteen men go to work.

The accountants, who had been scouring both sets of Blackfox books, looking for ways to mitigate the possible charges of bank fraud, had taken the hard copies with them. What they left behind was a trail of handwritten notes on yellow pads that ended up in the recycling bin. More than enough evidence to get warrants and search their offices.

The accountants, with the threat of being arrested themselves, made side deals to cooperate with the FBI and immediately handed over the doctored books and the originals. If the state found it difficult to pin murder on Wentworth in the Venezuelan operation or his other incursions, there was more than enough tax fraud to lock him up. Thomas Wentworth was led off his estate in handcuffs. His bail rescinded, he was remanded back to prison to await trial on his original charges, and the new ones he was sure would come to light when Ant started singing.

———

Ten unmarked vehicles descended around the etched glass entranceway of Blackfox. They stormed the complex, collecting anything of value for their case against the organization. Federal cars filled with phones, cameras, electronic gear and computers. White vans arrived to take the overflow of files that documented past engagements. Specifics of the illegal incursions to be provided by Ant. When the place was cleaned out, the FBI looped a heavy-duty chain around the front door, and set the lock.

———

Three FBI agents rushed Ant out of Orange County Central Men's Jail in handcuffs. He was hustled out a back door, secured in the rear of an unmarked car, and driven to a safe house where he'd await trial.

It was an okay condo, Ant thought. No view, no electronic equipment, but a passable flat screen and cable. The Feds were treating him well enough, but he wasn't presently in good shape. He'd been forced to give up Wentworth to save his own skin, but even with the knowledge that his boss had turned his back on him, it still left him feeling like a rat.

He ordered a pizza for lunch, and when the Feds approved his order felt things were looking up. After the second slice of very good pie, he accepted his new reality and decided it was better to be a live rat than a dead one.

———

Dakota stepped off the plane in Costa Rica, and the rush he felt from the soft buffeting of the trade winds put an instant smile on his face. He made his way through the terminal, where a driver waited to take him to the Airbnb he rented for two weeks. The fine home was situated on a secluded jetty with an ocean view. His phone hadn't rung, and no news was good news.

———

Senator Bradley skated from any culpability related to the Venezuelan incursion. After the oil execs had been returned home, the press release delivered from the DOJ and the White House thanked President Maduro for the compassionate release of the infirmed hostages, with promises of increased aid to Venezuela in their time of need. Bradley made out like a bandit, his influence and support, responsible for saving the men's lives. The incursion only bolstered Senator Bradley's status with his constituency. His fundraising shot through the roof, and he was a shoo-in for the midterm election.

———

Dakota slept for ten hours that night. The sound of the surf was hypnotic. He had a great breakfast, walked down to the infinity pool with the unobstructed view of the ocean. He didn't remember falling asleep again, and was aroused by the trill of his phone.

It broke his trance, and there was a whiff of a scent that hit him before he could tap on the call. Still half asleep, he answered and heard Steele's voice on the other end of the receiver. Dakota glanced past the infinity pool and saw a vision walking toward him over the white sands of the beach, holding a phone to her ear. His face creased into a relaxed smile. Agent Steele, wearing a delicate red two-piece that highlighted all the parts of her body she had saved for him, stepped off the beach and fell into his arms.

ACKNOWLEDGMENTS

Writing books is said to be a lonely profession. But, that's not really my experience. Okay, I come up with an idea and write a book. After many months, I cobble together a first draft. And then some of the real work begins.

I have to thank John Paine for another terrific edit. He has a way of seeing the entire story and then throwing me curveballs. Not easy to take sometimes, but the second draft is always better for his contribution.

I have beta readers who read the work, answer questions, share their time and ideas throughout my process. Diane Lansing is great with story, as is Phil Casnoff. Punctuation…is not my forte. Annie George did an amazing job fixing my mistakes, and Alaini Caruso, a wonderful copy-editor, cleaned up the final manuscript. Thanks to Sue Trowbridge, for her incredible technical expertise that is beyond my skill set, and Karen Phillips, who created this wonderful cover art. And to Vida Spears, the love of my life, who is a crazy talented writer herself, shares her knowledge, support, and gives me generous time, and notes. A big thank you and a warm hug!